" THE PAST COMES LOOKING "
BY
RAY BURTON

' It was happening. The signs were all here, right in front of me, in the skies above. The chaotic patterns and designs, constantly shifting and reforming. The thunderous boom and then the unexplainable entity entering into this world as if ripping through cheap fabric. It could only mean one thing. The world was beginning to shut down...'

THE PAST COMES LOOKING 2025. All rights reserved by Ray Burton

ISBN 979-8-35099-459-9

THE REVIEWS ARE IN!

From over (7) review houses and professional book readers and editors!

"The Past Comes Looking" is mind-blowingly scary!"—Nikki Allison, Nashville Book Editor

"Slick, Raw, Shocking! Horror with a fresh, new urban feel. Unlike anything I have ever read!"—Joe Meyers, Tennessee Review

"The ultimate horror novel! Totally different! A real scary page-turner!"—Thomas Gordan, Literary Agency

"Creepy, chilling. *"The Past Comes Looking"* is a nail-biting, shocking horror ride!"—Chicago's Once-a-month Book Club

"Shocking, Raw, Hardcore, unfiltered, not for the faint-hearted!"—Southern Horror Review

"Slickly-written, mind-blowing"—Northwest Editing *"The Past Comes Looking"* is a gutsy, scary, horror novel on a whole new level!"

"A real page-turner, scary, and brutally shocking! My entire book club was blown away!"—Nashville Urban Readers

"A must-read, must-have book! *"The Past Comes Looking"* is in a 'stand-alone' class by itself!"—South Regional Book Review

"Not for weak-hearted. Unnerving, shocking, scary, brutally raw! It will leave you staring at the walls and checking your doors at night!"—Darryl Covington, New Author Review

"Unbelievable writing! The author puts you right in the middle of things! A true rollercoaster ride through terror!"—Thomas Moore, Thriller House Hub

"Simply put: *"The Past Comes Looking"* is an unforgettable horror novel that will stick with you for years. Truly a rollercoaster ride, filled with dips, turns, chills and thrills!"—Ladies of Vision Book Club

"The Past Comes Looking" is an urban horror Masterpiece!"—Matthew Kale, Thriller/Horror Review

"There is only two words that describes *"The Past Comes Looking"*—mind-blowingly shocking!"—Renee Wilson, Fears and Horror Book Club

THANKS!!!!

As always, a thunderous, humbling, uplifting praise to **GOD** above for allowing me to see and appreciate each and every day that **HE** has given me.

Secondly, to my wife and Chief Editor: **Krystal**, for being my constant ear-piece and advisor during the writing of this, as well as all my books.

To **all** my family and friends who has supported me from the *very* beginning, both near and far: Daughters **Lanae** and **Dana.** Granddaughters: **Nia, Katalina,** and **Aria.** Nephew **Darryl White,** Niece **Pamela Little.** Cousin **Rhonda Dorsey-Prude.** To identical twin brothers: **Alvin** and **Calvin Almond: 'The Godsons'** of Mr. James Brown. To **Will Smith, Andre Dawkins, Fernando** and **Candy Murphy, KL Wilson.** To **all** my Facebook *friends* and *family* who supported me. You know who you are! Thank you!

Special thanks to my daughter **Dana,** who designed the *entire* book, from the front cover to the spine to the back cover. Awesome job, Dane Dane!!!

Also, special, sincere thanks to **Gretchen Brown, Veronica Wiley** and the **Women of Focus Book Club** and to **Valeri Hardy** and the **Sista+Sista Book Club**, for their overwhelming support, and for inviting me to meet with them. Ladies, thank you for the engaging conversations!

THE PAST COMES LOOKING

PART ONE

PROLOGUE

'That Bad Penny'

Death, I understood now, could come in countless forms, in so many ways, at any given moment. For several months I have endured, more like *survived,* a lot to make it this far—doing what was necessary to keep my life as well as my sanity intact.

I had to remain one step ahead.

Always ready.

Always alert.

And yet nothing could prepare me for a fate that was terrifying and unnatural as the one about to befall me.

I knew *it* was coming.

...again...

The signs were all here and accounted for: the mysterious ringing of the bells, the rancid smell—both dampening and clotting the air, seemingly from out of nowhere. Then it was the unusual sights, the unexplainable sensations, the weird vibrations and the unsettling turbulence, and as always: the brutal aftermath that followed.

At times leaving me horribly battered and bruised—wishing I were dead, instead.

I honestly can't say how long I will last, living like this. Locked in permanent survival mode. Constantly afraid, cautious, leery of everything around me. Even my own shadow.

With everything in me, I've tried to fight *it*. Tried to outrun *it*. Lords knows I even tried to outwit *it* by hiding from the damn *thing*. But *it* always seems to find me. And then *it* punishes me. One way or another.

Why? I couldn't begin to tell you...

And now this whole ordeal—*this fuckin' nightmare!*—is beginning to take its toll on me!

I'm wearing down fast...

My body is running on fumes and I can barely keep my eyes open.

I haven't slept in nearly forty-eight hours, and probably won't sleep for another forty-eight. I guess it's time to be real with myself, to finally open my eyes to the saddening, disheartening truth: there's no logical way to beat this *thing*. No final page to this madness. Not even a light at the end of the tunnel.

It will keep coming for me.

Unexpectedly.

Relentlessly.

Over and over.

Again and again...

Like a bad penny, *it* will forever keep showing up. No matter where I am or what I'm doing.

...until it's finally over for me...

As putrid smells throttled my nostrils, as deafening bells blasted, careened, and punished the inside of my head—feeling as if the last threads of sanity as well as my life were about to be snatched away, my instincts kicked in.

I wasn't going out without a fight.

Once again, as always, I readied myself for battle.

With balled fists.

It's all I had on me.

I peered into the darkness, just beyond the realm of my vision. Once more, again as always, I felt my body ready, on full alert. However, *this* time around, I actually felt stronger.

On the inside.

The true test, I reminded myself, was not what was on the inside of me, but rather, what was on the *outside...*

...coming for me...

CHAPTER ONE

'Hustle Game'

On the fringe of a boisterous crowd, engrossed with a televised basketball game, I was sitting alone at a table for two in a secluded corner of the bar, knocking back a shot of Crown Royal, straight, no coke or ice to water it down.

No big surprise.

Alone.

A glass of Crown Royal in my hand.

At this point, the two were practically a way of life for me.

The attitude inside was friendly and warm. It was one of those high-class bars located on the first level of a five-star hotel, in Chicago. A place where people and money gathered and played. Where the money was old but the people were not.

There was a tone here: folks who want to be left alone are left alone. Those who want to chat get chatted with.

I sat there sipping on my Crown. Watching. Observing. I'd been here at least a dozen times. I was almost a fixture here. I knew the crowd. Almost like family. And knew from my previous visits, something involving either women, sports, or money was constantly being discussed.

Especially when it came to the men.

You could tell each by their body language. When it came to a discussion about women, their bodies leaned against the bar, sort of relaxed, or they sat at tables with their elbows perched, heads bent, as they whispered all kinds of vile shit, wearing devious smiles.

When it came to sports the voices were loud and challenging. When it came to money, they melted in their seats with their chests swelled, fingers interlaced, appearing knowledgeable.

The women on their arms were usually dime-pieces, trophy-women, more like hand puppets—smiling, laughing, giggling—at shit they had no clue about. All the while hoping for a decent payday at the end of the night. Or at the end of the date. Or session.

Or whatever.

Makes me no-never-mind.

I didn't start this game nor would I be the one that ended it.

My glass was near empty and just like clockwork, the waitress came over to me, a pretty little blonde thing with a great smile and an even greater ass. I told her to hit me with another shot of Crown Royal. An old school drink. I got it from my dad who had gotten himself killed nearly ten years ago doing something he shouldn't been doing. He was a seasoned drinker and now so was I, with a stiff wrist and an easy swallow to prove it.

Wetting my lips with another sip of Crown, I scanned the crowd around me. Taking in my obscured family. There was no need to put on airs. So I was dressed in a pair of black fitted jeans, a black molded pullover sweater, with black gators on my feet, appearing to be a man just leisurely killing time. But my agenda was different; I was hoping to come across that perfect woman.

A dumb one.

Desperate, eager, lonely, brimming with low self-esteem, one I could easily win over with a warm smile, an understanding nod, some intriguing conversation, a few *soft* lies, a little hand-holding or that occasional rub on the back. And, if need be, I could even supply a shoulder to cry on, tissue and all.

Whatever the moment called for.

But it came with a price: money.

Aside from selling residential and commercial real estate, this was my second job. My side hustle. I guess you could call it a hobby. I was a habitual womanizer. And I was pretty good at it.

At thirty-two, I still had a few good years remaining to exploit my craft. I was told I was a good-looking guy: tall, trim and solid, a bit on the buffed side. Brown skin, brown eyes. I kept my face clean-shaven, and my hair, black and neatly-styled, was cut short. In addition, I had a smile that women couldn't resist—couldn't seem to look away from, and one of those voices you could hear coming, which made women shake, quiver, and melt.

I considered myself the ultimate package. Full and complete in *every* way. The walking billboard for male sexuality, in and out of a suit: masculine, confident, dominate—I oozed that shit through my pores like a lemon being squeezed.

It was the sole reason why I got into this game. This semi-lucrative side hustle. I could use women easily. I had what it takes; I could see it in their eyes. They all looked at me hungrily, circling, like a starving jackal—at times trying to appear unfazed but damn near drooling.

No matter where I was or went—whether it was subtle or blatantly obvious—I saw want, desire, and lust in their expressions, in their gazes and gestures.

But like all good things, Father Time had a clock ticking on me; loudly, and lately all my luck has been bad. A culmination of real lousy months. I didn't have time to bullshit—nor did I have time to be wasting on women with attitudes, or women who just wanted me to blow their backs out, especially the young women who may or may not be just out of their teens.

I needed that *certain* woman.

One who has some serious pocket change stashed away—maybe a decent 401k that she could tap into. A mortgage she could borrow from. Or better yet, one who was married, with a generous husband pulling down a nice income, who was off doing his own 'thang', who had no qualms on who or how his wife spent his money, or her free time.

I'd had a few women like that. Unfortunately, the set up always ended up taking a nosedive: the husband found out, couldn't deal with it and threatened to cut the wife off dry—the financial fallout would be devastating. Or worse still, when things became too personal with the women I was seeing; when the lines of the relationship became *blurred*, the angles of the agreement less defined, the rules indistinct, causing the women to try to *own* me—trying to tell me how to come and go, when and where we should hook up—on *their* schedule, and that wasn't happening.

Not in my lifetime.

Finally, it was the women who became sexually obsessed with me. *Hooked!* for a better choice of words. I understood why but this was *way* too much wasted responsibility for me to handle.

They had sex toys for that shit.

But I always kept my head in the game for new prospects. For the life of me I had no idea why I was like this. I guess it was just something I like to do.

Had to do...

And I was committed to doing it—there was no way I was going to miss out. Which at times, caused me a few sleepless nights.

That was my sacrifice.

My compromise.

For now.

But not forever.

Without warning, a thunderous rise coming from the basketball patrons glued to the television screens, lit up the entire bar. It stayed that way for a while, making it impossible for me to think.

Making me feel all that much more...*alone*...

Once again, I cast a glance around me, taking inventory. Nothing. Not a *damn* thing. I knew it was time to leave. There wasn't a single woman in sight. The only prospects were a cluster of college girls giggling and falling all over each other while taking selfies.

Nothing useful here.

But as I was in the midst of settling my bar tab, I spotted a small, petite, Black woman, appearing to be in her late sixties, maybe early seventies. She was dressed in a powder-blue suit that I wasn't sure, but suspected, was a genuine Chanel. A triple strand of jewels circled her neck. Her hair was bleached white, short and perfectly cut. She looked mixed; her skin was the color of creamed coffee, almost beige.

I could tell she'd had some work done. Her face had that overly *pulled* look that came with too many plastic surgeries. Almost to the point it had been pulled so tightly that it seemed molded to the bones beneath.

The lie didn't stop there; she had enough makeup on to fuck up a good suit jacket, and wore layers of fake lashes and blush. She also had a bright, scarlet mouth with oversized, plumped lips, like she'd just swallowed a live beetle—obviously accompanied with a pair of enhanced tits—several times over. She reminded me of those Hollywood celebrities *way* past their prime trying to look young but instead looking like they could be on an episode of *Botched*.

As dazzling as she *thought* she was, standing dead in front of the bar for everyone to see—especially the single men, no one seemed even remotely interested in this solitary woman.

But I was!

I saw her as easy prey. A mark. Her vainness was mine to exploit. I waited awhile to make sure she was alone. After fifteen minutes or so I came to the conclusion that she was. I drummed my perfectly manicured nails on the table and decided to make my move. I had a game plan. I would introduce myself to this old bag of dog chow—this pig with lipstick—and run my usual line of beautifully-wrapped, hand-delivered, velvety bullshit.

Hey, what can I say? I was at it again. *And? What of it?* We've all done shit to get shit.

Killing the last of my Crown and then popping a mint into my mouth, I rose from the table and strolled casually towards her. Right away she saw me heading in her direction. I could see her eyes and facial expression dancing wildly between desperation and hope. She quickly turned her back to me. I could tell she was trying to play hard to get. That dumb, old school, kid shit.

But this did nothing but make it personal. I tightened my game—strutting proudly, boldly, while fighting the urge to smile.

It wasn't long before I stood directly behind her. I drew a deep breath and wished I hadn't. Though her outfit was classy, the perfume she wore was not, lending a nauseating sweetness to the air that didn't exactly mingle well with the cologne I had on.

Let it go, fool, I quickly reminded myself. *If you blow this one, who knows when the next mark will come along!*

It was at that moment when adrenaline shot through my blood like a sharp snort of cocaine. Which, admittedly, I did from time to time, depending on which one of my buddies, more like which mood, I was running with.

I tapped her lightly on the shoulder. "Well, hello there, gorgeous," I said warmly; my deep voice hung in the air like a mystic cloud. "I couldn't help but notice that you were standing here all by yourself, all by your lonesome."

The woman turned and looked up. At first there came a moment of silence. I saw she was holding her breath, then I caught her eyes widening, and her brows twitched ever so slightly. "Hello," she managed to seep out.

I leaned on the bar and smiled, extending a hand in greeting. "My name is Derrick Archer. It's a pleasure to be talking with you. So, tell me, are you here with someone? Waiting on someone?"

She turned her frail body to fully face me. However, she did not accept my hand. "That's a neither on both," she replied. "And what can I do for you, Mr. Archer?"

One couldn't help but notice her rough, cigarette-coated voice. But I also noticed the stunning gems in their magnificent setting, nestled beautifully around her neck.

Undoubtedly her best feature so far.

Her gravelly voice made me clear my throat, as I stated mildly, "Well, if I may, you can start by giving me your name."

With that, she eyed me up and down curiously, then said, "Tell you what, Mr. Archer, I won't be rude. You can just call me Janet for now. How's that?"

"That'll work." I signaled the bartender and ordered yet another shot of Crown. I had to be careful to limit my alcohol intake in front of this woman; there was no need to reveal that I had a drinking problem.

"Can I get you something to drink, Janet?" I asked politely.

She firmly replied, "A shot of Patron would do very nicely, please, Mr. Archer, if you will."

I nodded and told the bartender to hit us twice with the same order. While waiting for our drinks, we engaged in light conversation, the kind two people covered when just meeting. I learned that she had just celebrated a birthday, and was seventy-one, married twice—to two rich and successful men, now single, and was basically living her best life. I noticed as she talked, she had taken on a veneer of calm professionalism.

Like she was reading from a script...

In addition to being her own woman, I learned she was originally from New Orleans, a Creole woman, and had several condos scattered about, one in Florida; a couple in Hawaii. She appeared to be very well-to-do. She also quietly maintained a two-bedroom suite in this very hotel.

She said it was for the overnight use for her out-of-town business clients, but I suspected that she did some personal entertaining with some 'younger' clients—who were undoubtedly smashing her up *very* well.

Not that it was any of my business.

Approximately thirty minutes passed when she said she had some business to tend to. We exchanged numbers and agreed to get together soon. Before parting ways, I leaned in for a kiss; she offered me a cheek, instead, her right one, and I gave her a nice, sensuous peck. I didn't doubt for a second that she wanted more. Her brown eyes said it all; there was something about them, about the depths, that practically screamed—*take me!*

Before heading out she took a step closer to me, so close I felt crowded. She smiled and ran a hand across my firm chest. As she stared in amazement, I could see the tiny lines around her eyes that surgery failed to erase; I also noticed the deeper ones bracketing her mouth as she licked her lips with a slow tongue, as she hummed while floating a hand over my flat stomach. When she felt the ripples of my abs underneath my sweater, I felt her breath catch.

I saw it, too.

She was hungry.

This I knew.

I started to go for the kill and kiss her passionately—giving her something really nice to think about. To masturbate on. But chose not to do so.

Easy, Derrick, I smiled, thinking better, *play the hand out.*

It was funny; it appeared she'd picked up on that very same vibe. Once more she smiled, giving me a pleasant *'it's been nice'* expression.

"Would you mind walking me to the elevator, please, Mr. Archer?" she asked coolly.

"It would be my pleasure," I smiled. I settled the bar tab then took her by the hand. With a dismissive nod, she stepped away from the bar. I watched as she led the way. Using her confidence as a makeshift battering ram, she managed to wedge through the stream of patrons as she made her way out of the bar and onto the emptying elevator, just ahead of the hordes of people still more or less politely waiting their turn.

It was a sight to see.

As frail and as tiny as she was, the woman exuded power and authority.

And then more power and authority…

She stepped inside the elevator with a few people joining her. She turned to face me; our eyes collided. Like the proverbial elephant in the room, she was impossible to ignore—and since ignoring her was impossible—I smiled and threw a kiss at her. In response, she gave me the smallest of a mocking expression, and then turned her head, looking away.

"Seventeenth floor, please," she said to the man nearest to the button. She could feel my eyes on her. It was at that moment when the elevator doors began to close. For some strange reason, as the doors closed in front of me, my stomach clenched, and I felt a chill.

I scowled.

I frowned.

I thought.

Finally, I smiled.

Then, after a brief glance at my Rolex watch, I peered at the elevator doors, which were all polished to a silvery shine. I could see my reflection, though slightly muted and distorted. I turned and walked away, confident and pleased with my recent encounter with this woman. That things just might turn out to be okay—*rather nice!*

The old girl seemed to have her shit together, and I wanted some of her shit.

I had to devise a game plan. A good one. No, not good—*great!*

Foolproof!

Not just a simple hit-and-run, either. Some serious finesse was needed. The bitch may be old but I'm sure she wasn't dumb. Not by a long shot. I needed to establish some strong roots, set up some long-term parking on this one.

Whatever she wanted me to be, or *appear* to be, I was down for whatever. I had to connect the dots just so…

I thought about this woman, as we left the bar, how she parted the crowd as if she were parting the Red Sea. I knew I had to be careful on this one. I don't know why.

… I just knew …

CHAPTER TWO

'A Family Affair'

It was Thursday morning.

I stood perched over the toilet with my head back and my eyes closed, taking a long piss and hoping my aim was good. It felt like standing on the cusp of another world. I thought about the day ahead of me. My plate was pretty full, starting with me dropping in on my older sister, Melody. Now pushing forty, she was once a real head turner in her hey-dey—all hips and ass—a dime-piece, and a bit on the wild side. All my friends wanted a shot at her, and let me know it constantly.

Hook a brutha up! they used to say to me. *Tell your sister Melody to come hollah at me!*

Of course, Melody never gave them a second look or the time of day. Back then she was into drug dealers, athletes, successful men, and dated her fair share of each. You couldn't tell my sister a damn thing; armed with a killer body, a drop-dead gorgeous face, she was out there living her absolute *best* life.

But all that ended after she got married. That's when the dominoes slowly began to tumble. One after the other: A kid. Another kid. A divorce. Nearly forty extra pounds added to her frame.

With her stock somewhat devalued, she had to 'settle'—claiming she'd met the perfect guy, some fool named Sam, a supervisory exec for a major business chain, which in reality turned out to be true, I guess: he was a second-shift manager at *Burger King*.

He turned out to be a fuckin' bum.

Right from the very start, I never liked the guy. I knew his M.O. Translucent as tracing paper, I could see and smell his shit coming a mile away—always smiling like a Chester cat and slithering like a snake. I knew I could never trust him with Melody.

He knew this too; because of my size and demeanor, he always tried to establish some type of alliance with me, probably on the theory that it was better to be on my good side rather than on my bad.

I never gave him the chance.

His game soon became weak—weaker, actually, and he got fired from his *Burger King* gig. For stealing. What he stole I couldn't begin to tell you. Knowing Sam, it was probably hamburger buns. He was too stupid to steal money. Like a cocky, aging boxer, his gift for gab as well as his body quickly went to flab; there was no hiding the roll of pudge that hung over his belt and spilled from his mouth.

Melody eventually dumped his sorry ass and went back to her ex-husband, Malcolm, off and on. She still loved him, I could tell. She always wanted to 'work things out' but he wasn't trying to hear it. Yet he still took shameless advantage of her affections; he'd sleep with her whenever he wanted to.

That's my Mel, I could hear the son-of-a-bitch saying. I never interfered as I watched from the wings, as long as he didn't lay hands on her. All I could do was shake my head, feeling a bit hypocritical.

Essentially, I was doing the same thing.

Damn my damn conscience…

Finally finishing up a minute-long piss, I washed my hands with vigorous and thorough efficiency. I was sort of germophobic. Even if it was my *own* germs. Add that to my list of multiple flaws. After giving my hands a thorough washing, I showered—*go fuckin' figure!*—and then I went to my closet and selected a pair of loose-fitting jeans and a white pullover sweater. I had a nice, little set up on the South side of Chicago, a two-story townhouse with a small, manicured lawn, in an upscale neighborhood with plenty of mature trees lining the streets.

A few years ago, when my money was hitting on all cylinders, I had it fully renovated to suit my personal taste and needs.

Again, it was that germophobic thing.

After having a light breakfast of scrambled eggs and toast—no ham, no sausage, two strips of turkey bacon—I hopped into my white BMW SUV, the *XM high-powered series,* worth well over a hundred and fifty G's, and headed over to the North side of town to see Melody. I figured I'd kick it with her for an hour or two before taking in a round of golf with some buddies of mine.

I was making good time when thirty yards ahead of me I saw the traffic light changing from green to amber. I accelerated to make sure I wouldn't get trapped if the light changed, and I shot through the amber light.

And that's exactly the way I saw it.

Trapped.

To me, sitting at a traffic light was like having years sucked from your life, like a spider sucking blood from a fly, trapped in its web.

As you can see, I had *yet* another flaw: I was extremely impatient…

When I made it to Melody's house, a small but quaint little ranch-style home with an attached one-car garage, I mentally prepared myself for the bullshit to come. I knew she was going to give me the third degree about my lifestyle, about my hustle game with the ladies.

Derrick, boy, get yourself a nice Godly woman! I could hear her saying. *Nothing good is going to come of what you're doing!*—looking as if she could stab me in the eye with a number-two pencil. I envisioned her looking just like Mama—arms crossed tightly over her chest, feet planted firmly apart, eyes narrowed, a fierce expression on her face.

Or—worse yet, just like Mama—*was Melody giving me a premonition of something bad to come? Mama always told us that our Daddy's days were numbered.*

…and lo, and behold, she was right…

God, I hoped Melody was wrong.

Of course she was! I told myself.

When I rang the doorbell I had to once again, mentally prepare myself. A few seconds later Melody opened the door. She greeted me wearing nothing but a silky, cherry red bathrobe; her face was flushed; her hair was a frazzled mess. To top it off, I smelled traces of weed and her left tit was peeking out from underneath her robe.

Her ex, Malcolm, must have recently been here, I figured. I knew the look: when a woman had just been beat down, probably on top of her very own kitchen table, there was no way to hide it; a futile attempt to bridge the transition from getting sexually-plowed to trying to look dignified.

I was right, as Melody tried to appear poised and composed, smiling weakly, "Hey, lil Bruh, come, come on in…" She took a few steps from the door to let me inside. I grinned at her knowingly, somewhat witty and charming to ease the situation—pleased to know I wasn't about to hear a lecture about *my* lifestyle.

At least not today.

Leading the way through her modestly furnished home, Melody headed for the kitchen where we had some of our 'very intense conversations'. As we passed through the living room I spotted her dog Saber, a two-year old male Golden Retriever—who was lying sprawled on its stomach, looking just like a fur rug, eyes closed, chin resting on the floor, all four limbs and fluffy tail splayed out flat like spokes on a wheel.

Though he knew I was there, Saber never did respond towards me. I guess he could sense I didn't really care for him. And he was right. I didn't. I wouldn't exactly say that I didn't care for him, I just didn't care for the time and energy, and all that other responsibility it took to properly care for a dog. Or a cat. Or anything else that needed cleaning up after.

Bump that!

I had a life to live.

Period.

I took a seat at the kitchen table, praying that Melody and Malcolm hadn't actually screwed on it. After realizing her left tit was semi-exposed, Melody tightened her robe and fixed me a cup of coffee. What I really needed was a shot of Crown; I had a pint in my glove compartment and was almost tempted to step out and take a quick pull, but decided against it. One pull would lead to two, then three, then so on…

The next thing you know I'd be shitfaced drunk, trying to look dignified, like Melody, as I drove my SUV, struggling to stay in between the white lines on the road.

Besides, it was still early in the day and I wanted to be able to play a round of golf with the guys. There was nothing worse than a drunk trying to play golf. I'd seen it firsthand—some real *Three Stooges* shit.

After fixing herself some coffee, Melody took a seat at the table across from me. She swept a hand over her wind-blasted hair, trying to compose herself. She almost had it together but her demeanor was still semi-blown from the aftermath of a hot screwing— still simmering in her mind. The best she could manage was a weak, drawn-out, "So, Bruh, how you been?"

"I'm good," I nodded. "You been okay?"

"I have," she smiled.

"You sure?"

"Yes, why you ask that?"

"Because…" I said, stopping her from opening a fifth packet of Sweet-n-Low sugar for her coffee. She hadn't realized she'd been doing this until then.

"Damn." She emptied the last packet and stirred her coffee with a spoon, still smiling, slightly embarrassed. She knew I knew the deal. She swallowed, feeling as ridiculously uncomfortable as a teenager on a first date. She quickly composed herself and asked, "So, have you visited Mama this month?"

I shifted in my seat. "To be honest, it's been a while since I have."

"Why the hell not, Derrick?" And just like that, in that split second, she was my big sister again.

Outspoken.

And bossy as hell.

She was staring at me, waiting for an answer, which I eventually gave her, "I just forgot, okay? Why does it even matter, anyway? Mama is not with us anymore. She's been dead for nearly five years now."

As expected, Melody's anger brimmed. "Because we said we would, Derrick, that's why. We both agreed we would visit Mama's gravesite at least once a month. This is bullshit, Derrick, and you know it. We promised Mama that we would come see her…even when she left us." She let out a harsh steam of disgust.

I looked into her face; the most striking thing about my sister was how quicky her expression could change. It was like a cantankerous dog that I always knew, at a moment's notice, could lash out and bite. She was clearly pissed; I could feel the heat radiating off her. I wasn't sure if I could come up with a viable excuse. With more shame in my voice than I felt, I said, "I'm sorry, Melody, I'll go see Mama as soon as I leave here, I promise."

In response she shook her head in a tight little arc, almost more of a shiver. "I hope you do, Derrick, because believe or not, in spite of what you may or may not believe, Mama's spirit is still with us."

In that moment, as she looked up, it appeared that she was either deep in prayer or was actually talking with Mama. Either way, I was afraid she was going to ask me to get up and come pray with her. She didn't. Instead, she looked over at me and I quickly turned my head, my eyes raised toward the ceiling—hoping she'd think I was also affected in some sort of spiritual way.

But deep down, I hoped that this little part of the visit would be cut short. As soon as possible would be just fine with me. It hurt me to talk about Mama. It hurt really bad.

Lucky for me, the conversation as well as my visit was coming to an end, as Melody said, "Jayden and Marie will be coming home from school soon.

They had a half-day today. I better get lunch started. My kids know they love them some ham-and-cheese sandwiches with tomato soup. You're welcome to stay but I know you don't care for sandwiches and soup."

"I really don't," I chuckled.

"Then hit the road, Jack," she snapped, "cause I ain't changing the menu just for your ass." Her face and her tone suddenly went soft. "You take care of yourself out there, okay, little brother?"

"Okay, Sis, I will."

"You promise?"

"I promise." I reached out and patted her hand, gripping it. She still had that certain energy about her, like she could attract paper clips if she got too close to them. I found myself lured in by the solemn expression on her face, and oddly, by her hair. She must have recently cut it since my last visit because it was a bit shorter now. The novelty of seeing her long neck and sleek jaw exposed captivated me. She had lost a little weight too. It was as if she was seventeen again. She was indeed, still very pretty.

The spitting image of Mama, I grinned.

Slowly, Melody pulled her hand back and gave me a riveting look. She slit her eyes. "Slow your roll out there in those streets, Mr. Derrick Archer," were her last words, spoken almost in a cop-like manner.

I knew it was time to go.

Standing up and placing my chair back under the kitchen table, I leaned over and kissed my big sister on her forehead and then left. With a little bit of time on my side, I decided to go visit Mama at her gravesite. At South Memorial Cemetery. In no time at all, because of light traffic, I arrived at the cemetery and found Mama's headstone: Sierra Marie Archer.

I peered down at the scraggly grass and took note of Mama's final resting place. *Breast cancer had taken her away much too soon...*

Nobody actually knew how much I missed my Mama. I always downplayed it, but our relationship went *extremely* deep. People always called me a 'Mama's boy'. And I was cool with that because I was. I *loved* my Mama to death. Until her death. We shared a bond that went far further than just 'mother and son'. We had a unique *knowing* of what each of us felt and experienced.

Even if we were miles apart.

I can't explain it.

I just *knew* what it was.

What we shared...

At the moment, as I looked down, I didn't feel I could form the words to say, "I miss you so much, Mama" but I was certain she could *feel* the words, even if I couldn't manage to get them out of my mouth. So, I said nothing.

Instead, I glanced at the headstone to the right of Mama's which was inscribed: "Robert Steward, 1932-2012. Beside him, an identical headstone was simply inscribed: "Wife."

I frowned as my eyes drifted to the endless sea of gravestones surrounding me. The moment seemed haunting, a freeze-frame in time that somehow scared the shit out of me. The life—the bubbling euphoria that had accompanied each and everyone here was long gone.

...as though their lives had never really existed...

I became emotionally overwhelmed by *something*, and then I peered down and fixed my eyes on the headstone of 'Mrs. Robert Steward'.

Wife.

That's all there was. Her life, her entire legacy, summed up in one word: *Wife...*

That is so messed up I thought.

It was time to go.

I said goodbye to Mama and then looked around the cemetery, taking in all the souls that had moved on. I couldn't begin to tell you why but it left me feeling alone.

Terribly alone.

Probably as alone as I'd ever been in my life…

CHAPTER THREE

'There's Still Time'

Nearly two weeks had passed when my phone rang at a quarter to seven that evening. It was Janet. The woman from the bar, and she sounded out-of-breath excited. She was in town with a free schedule and wanted to see me, as soon as possible.

Naturally I was pleased and agreed to meet with her tomorrow night at 8pm, at her place in the Langham Hotel. That settled, I decided to pour myself another shot of Crown Royal. I was in a mellow, relaxed mood as I nestled back on the sofa in my townhouse.

Okay, so I was a bit nervous.

It was crazy, I knew, but I just couldn't help it. Sitting there clothed only in boxers, I stared up into nothingness, my mind still contemplating the thought of seeing this woman again.

Nervousness.

I silently acknowledged this jittery feeling even though part of me wanted to say that it was more; that I was even a bit *scared*. It was evident by my slightly ragged breathing, an upbeat pulse, and the way my glass shook as I raised it to my mouth.

But somehow, after knocking back a few more shots of Crown, I managed to put a brake on my runaway emotions. It was nice to know I still had a handle on things.

If only for that moment…

    The clang of the heavy weights let me know that I still could handle myself well in the gym. I had just finished up my last set of bench presses, calling it a day to my workout. A certified germophobic, I sanitized the equipment as well as my hands and then headed for the locker room.

    I gave my face a final wipe with my towel as I glanced around the gym. That is if you could call this place a gym. Nobody seemed to be working out; it was more of a fashion show. A social gathering in which to observe and be observed—everyone was either self-absorbed or wanted to be noticed. Or super engaged with their cell phones, texting, talking or taking selfies and videos to post on social media—some were actually watching movies!

    If you ask me, it was a waste of gym space and equipment.

    At least the view was good. There were some nice-looking honeys here, coming and going. Tight bodies covered in sheer-fitting leotards which molded to their skin. But some women took it a bit too far; too sharp-edged; too muscular for my taste. I liked my women softer, with curves—natural curves.

    Ain't nothing like a woman with naturally thick curves. Nothing like it in the world.

    I entered the locker room.

    Naturally, I wasn't about to shower here—the thought of *bare* feet and ass—a fuckin' cesspool of germs lying in wait for me—was enough to deter any such thoughts. As it was, the locker room smelled of cheap cologne, rubbing alcohol, and disinfectant. I would just have to deal with my own sweat and stank until I made it home. I grabbed my duffel bag from the locker cubicle and headed for the door.

That's when she walked in...

A beautiful, rare jewel, an Ebony beauty with a gorgeous face and a tight, breathtaking body—swinging her butt provocatively. It was a sculptured butt, big and curvy in a black body suit, and I could hardly tear my eyes from it. Her equally generous tits jiggled like water balloons despite wearing a sports bra. Her waist was so snatched and tiny that I wondered how she could breathe.

She looked to be in her mid-to-late twenties, with honey-caramel skin, light brown, almond-shaped eyes, and a head full of silky, auburn-black waves that was pulled and held back by a pink hair clip.

She literally stole my breath away.

Bump this! Despite me being damp and still sweaty from my workout, I had to say something to her. I'd be a fool for at least not trying!

I made my best play; I didn't have the time for anything else. I stepped up to her, cutting off her path. "Excuse for saying this, but you are one of the most breathtaking women I have ever seen."

Somewhat startled, she looked at me as if I carried some kind of contagious disease. Like I was a grasping leper. Her full lips instantly compressed with obvious displeasure, and her light brown eyes seemed to darken. Whatever I saw in this woman's face must have convinced me that the only way I was getting to know her was if she went kicking and screaming, flung over my shoulder.

But surprisingly, she hit me with a slow, gradual smile. "You're a regular here, aren't you?"

"I am," I said, wiping away any remaining sweat from my forehead. Which might be a good thing. Maybe the sweat-funk combination was the extra edge I needed to win her over.

"I thought so," she said, bobbing her head up and down. Her eyes slid over my face, slyly gliding over my crotch. Slowly, she began rocking back on her heels, folding her arms over her chest, like she was actually considering the possibility of something happening. Finally, she said, "Yea, I've seen you a few times working out. You handle your business well."

"I try." I made an impatient gesture and stepped closer to her. Running her off was the last thing I wanted to do. Although, if she wanted to, she could have easily told me to back the hell off or stepped around me. But she didn't. And that's when I knew I had her. For a moment our eyes clashed, and there was a certain connection hanging in the air.

In just that brief moment I realized that all I wanted—more than anything—was to get to know this woman. To *really* get to know this woman. Never mind what I'd done in the past.

It was just *something* about her, other than that delicious body and gorgeous face.

I went over my approach.

Just keep it short and sweet, I told myself. I did, and when it was all said and done, I had this beautiful woman's name and a number locked in my phone. Smiling at each other, we both went our separate ways. I climbed into my SUV with a smile still on my face.

My flesh pounding her flesh.

But I wanted more.

I hoped there might be some electricity there. Some arc of emotion that suggested a future truly meaningful. Physical attraction wasn't everything, except at first.

And I had to admit, I was not disappointed.

CHAPTER FOUR

'The Tunnel Darkens'

By the time I had shaved, showered, dressed and then left my townhouse, it was nearly 7:15 in the evening. The late October air was crisp, the night sky brilliant and clear, as I headed to Janet's place. It wasn't long before I slid my SUV into the hotel underground parking structure and found a space right off to park. I checked my Rolex watch: 7:50.

My timing was perfect; not too early, definitely not late. Checking my appearance in the vanity mirror, tilting my head back to check for nose hairs, I stepped from my vehicle and brushed the sleeves to my dark blue, form-fitting Armani suit—complete with a white, freshly-starched dress shirt, a smart red tie snuggled at the throat. I locked my SUV and after checking in with the hotel concierge, I took the elevator to the 17th floor.

Minutes later I was staring at the numbers: 1726.

Janet's place.

I took a deep breath and knocked lightly on the door. Seconds later the door was opened, and Janet was standing there before me.

I hate to say it but I was not impressed. Dressed the way she was, she looked like a hooker past her prime. *Waaaay past her prime!* She had on a black skirt that was too short in length and way too tight for her frail body—the soft material hugged nothing but bony hips and thighs. The white blouse she wore was buttoned up to her neck but was still sheer enough to see things that I didn't need to see. Or want to see.

I tried not to stare at her, wanting to tell her that she looked ridiculous. It was hard not to. I couldn't imagine banging this woman even with a gun held to my head but knew I had to play along.

Maybe I wouldn't have to I prayed. *At least not tonight!*

But I knew the possibility was there—when you got down to it, it was a strong possibility—a woman past her prime, dressed like this—it was almost a given. And judging by the demeanor she was exuding she was probably a freak.

A *big* one.

Probably into role-playing.

That stepmom-stepson-'don't tell Daddy' shit.

Or some of that S&M bondage stuff.

I peered into her face, focusing closely on her eyes. There was something peevishly wild in them. I could only hope and pray she wasn't into *toilet games.* Something on that level wasn't going to happen—*could not* happen! I'd be just short of killing *both* of us before that happened.

Giving me a slow nod, Janet invited me inside. The place was laid to the bone, with floor-to-ceiling windows that faced west of the city. The skyline was breathtaking. Like something out of a magazine. As I glanced around, I could only shake my head. Quite a lot of money had been spent to create this look.

All the furnishings, from the furniture to the knick-knacks lining the fireplace mantel, to the tables and lamps as well as the pictures on the walls, appeared professionally designed; handpicked. The floor was made up of some kind of exotic tile with white grouting. The overall effect was calming.

As I stepped further in, I saw there were oak cabinets in the kitchen, with porcelain hardware, white marble counter tops, and high-end appliances at every turn.

Five will get you ten that the two bedrooms were also done up exquisitely and cost a pretty penny in the end. Everywhere you looked you saw and smelled money; the entire place had been designed and furnished by someone who enjoyed the finer things in life and who could afford just that.

The finer things.

The absolute best.

Which brought a new meaning to the phrase: *Well off!*

She must have gotten at least half in both divorce settlements, I thought. *A lump sum. I couldn't see her settling for anything less.* This woman didn't seem the type who would waste her years or her time settling for monthly spousal payments. No doubt she had a topnotch lawyer on her side. It made me question the character of her former husbands.

What did they look like? Did she have something on them? A devious secret, maybe?

I knew my logic of thinking was a bit extreme, and I also knew now was not the time to dwell on it. Right now, I needed to keep my head in the game.

Both, if need be.

"Take a seat on the sofa, please, Mr. Archer," smiled Janet. "I'll get both of us something nice to drink." She cocked a brow. "What'll you have? I have everything here for every taste."

"Surprise me," I said, with a tight grin and a wink of my eye. I took a seat on the sofa and before I could even get comfortable, Janet handed me a glass of white wine. Holding hers steady, she sat beside me on the sofa. She kicked off her heels, drew one leg under her, then gulped her wine down in three long swallows. She then looked at me with eyes that studied, weighed, and judged.

"Do you find me interesting, Mr. Archer?" she asked. She traced my thigh with a long fingernail.

I couldn't say anything else—not a damn thing, but *'yes'*. Which I did, "Yes, I do, Janet, I find you very interesting."

With that, she reached out and played with my tie, loosening it up a bit. "Do you find me sexy?"

"Extremely," I replied.

A slow tongue emerged as she licked her lips, as she scooted closer to me. Her hard brown eyes were like a dissecting probe. "Extreme enough to fuck on the first date?" she asked, clucking her tongue.

Just like that I'd received an expected curve ball early in the game; I delayed answering until I could summon the right words. This was a delicate situation. If I said the wrong thing it could cost me everything.

Literally!

But more than that…there was *something else* about this woman.

In an attempt to calm my nerves, I took a sip of wine, which I knew wouldn't do me any good. I needed liquor. *Strong* liquor. I looked at her but said nothing. I had to play a dual role here—a man who had to appear eager but yet, not *too* eager.

Smiling with her hands to her mouth, on the verge of laughing, she diffused the situation by leaning back against the cushions. She knew she had me at a disadvantage, looking shitfaced and tongue-tied.

She also knew that question wasn't fair, but it was like she *had* to ask it. She reached over and poked me in the ribs with her finger to lighten the mood. Plus, I guess she wanted to hear my voice again.

Instead of waiting for me to reply, she simply said, "No need to answer that question, Mr. Archer. Let me explain myself, if I may. Like anyone else, I have my share of flaws, and I suppose I deal with a few inadequacies that dates way back, sadly to my father's violent death in New Orleans, back in the late seventies. That ordeal was very traumatic. It left me feeling abandoned. Left me with a few deep scars. As a result, because of my father's sudden death, him leaving me, my entire life growing up was clouded and uncertain; I worried about men walking out on me—before *I* was prepared to end the relationship. So, you see, Mr. Archer, because of this, because I am filthy rich, I, alone, decide on how far things go and when it should end. In every aspect of my life."

With those words, seemingly sure of herself, she nestled back and smiled at me. Almost lovingly. As for me, I just sat there dumbfounded, probably looking as if I'd just suffered a mild stroke. I'm thinking maybe I should have said something before hearing all of this. But I was kind of glad I didn't. It was obvious this woman carried secrets that I needed to know about.

Deep secrets.

I wanted to learn more before I, myself, got in too deep. I started to ask her to elaborate a bit more on things, but relented. *No, I told myself. Don't go into any of this. Just enjoy the evening…*

And as the night progressed the both of us actually did have an enjoyable evening. It was pleasant and cordial; we talked, laughed and touched on various topics: politics, food—how the world was quickly changing—the people, our values, the economy, even the climate—how half of the world was being overly-saturated with rain and floods with people working eighty to a hundred hours a week, while the other half of the world was suffering from severe drought with wildfires everywhere, with unemployment at an all-time high.

During our interaction, Janet really appeared relaxed and less mysterious. Sort of playful.

A good sign I thought. *A good, non-sexual sign.*

But it didn't last long.

She caught me off guard. As I was explaining the details about my real estate job, she leaned into me and kissed me. It was not good, not good at all. Actually, horrible. Like my tongue was scraping over sandpaper. But I made the best of it, giving her something of a lesson on how to *really* kiss.

How to really feel like a woman *being* kissed.

I placed my hand gently behind her head, cradling it, and brought her mouth to mine. I pulled her close to me, wrapping her in a captive embrace, keeping her there, as I flicked my moist, firm tongue between her quivering lips, teasing, coaxing, opening them, working my tongue inside her mouth, where it danced sensuously, delicately, and wickedly over hers.

With skilled hands and fingers, with my lips and tongue, I stroked, kissed, probed, and nibbled on her body in all the right places.

In all the *other* places.

Places that *screamed* and *begged* and *needed* to be touched.

The forgotten and overlooked places.

As a result she whimpered as though she were crying, and I could feel her body melting into mine.

Then the moment came.

She wanted me to screw her brains out, and for me to carry her into the bedroom to do this. *Now, please, Mr. Archer, if you will...*

Against my best wishes—despite everything inside me screaming, *NO! Don't do it!*—I did. Needless to say, it took everything in me to keep from going limp, but somehow I placed my mind into another world—another *hemisphere!*—and gave this woman everything I had—tossing and flipping her body like she was a silver dollar—a good three hours' worth.

Nonstop.

No bathroom or water breaks.

Afterwards, with Janet lying next to me in bed, I stared up at the ceiling. I felt hideous, like a used, two-dollar, male whore—who had just been passed around by a dozen cackling women—all naked, with crooked wigs and sagging tits, with cigarettes dangling from their mouths and drinks in their hands.

I wanted to kill myself. To simply die.

In the dimly-lit room, supplied only by candlelight, I looked over at Janet. I wasn't prepared for such a sight—because she was asleep, nearly unconscious with her makeup smeared, and with her face gone slack, it gave her an even more frightening appearance. Like she was damn near lying in state.

It reminded me of a Biblical quote my Mama used to say, *"ashes to ashes, dust to dust."*

I knew I had to get the fuck out of here.

Slowly, I threw a leg over the edge of the bed and eased away. Though I desperately wanted to take a shower, I wouldn't. I needed to place as much distance from this woman as I possibly could. After dressing I stared over at Janet, who was still knocked out. Still looking like something from *The Walking Dead.* Luckily, I knew how to let myself out.

While driving home I felt kind of bad. About Janet. She wasn't such a terrible person. Not at all. Just a lonely old woman with a lot of money.

But I wasn't dumb. I knew somewhere *deep* inside this woman, there was a glitch in the software, and I would need all my wits to spot these 'glitches'.

Until then, I figured I would just enjoy the ride and see where things ended up.

My phone rang just as I was adding some chopped chicken breast and vegetables to the stir-fry. I was feeling good. The first two glasses of Crown Royal relaxed me, and I was considering a third. I picked up the phone, hoping it wasn't Janet but instead, Linda, the woman from the gym. To my delight it *was* Linda, and I couldn't stop smiling as I answered, "Hey, hey, pretty girl, how are you?"

"I'm doing good, Derrick, how are you?"

"Shit, I'm good now." I couldn't help myself, and did a little dance, adding a spin.

"I didn't catch you at a bad time, did I?" she asked.

"Not at all. I was just fixing myself a lil sumthin'-sumthin' to eat. Some stir-fried chicken breast with brown rice, veggies and diced mushrooms."

"Damn, that sounds good."

I lifted the lid on the pan and the fragrance of the stir-fry filled the kitchen. "I got plenty to spare. You hungry?"

"Starved."

"Then why don't you swing by and let me fix you a plate?"

"Sounds like a plan. I can be there in less than an hour. Is that okay?"

"I'll see you then."

"Do I need to bring something?"

"Just bring yourself, baby, that will suit me just fine."

"Well, now, that I can do. See you soon."

Feeling like a giddy high school nerd about to date the prom queen, I hung up the phone and finished out the stir-fry. I turned the burner off from underneath the pan, letting it cook out under the remaining heat. I hurriedly shaved and then jumped in the shower. Afterward I selected some casual clothing from my closet: some loose-fitting jeans and a black wife-beater. Making sure I was properly groomed with freshly brushed teeth, a hint of light cologne in *all* the right places, and the townhouse straightened just right, I told *'Alexa'* to set the mood with some smooth mellow jazz.

I wanted everything to be on point!

Though Linda and I had been on a few dates, we decided to take things slow; nothing sexual just yet. Not in the least. Just some light kissing and hand caressing; everything was tender and respectful, practically innocent—like something out of a *G* rated movie, from the fifties. I was hoping that things might take a turn for the better soon; I was more than ready to demonstrate my skills on her.

And best believe, I had plenty in my arsenal. Not once had I'd been called a lousy lover. I didn't need a roadmap or some fool's 'love-song' manual on how to please a woman. I *knew* my way around a woman's body—

Case Closed!

Forty minutes later I heard my doorbell ring. It was Linda. I opened the door and there she was. Looking absolutely breathtaking; it didn't matter that she didn't have on a stitch of makeup, not even lip gloss. Her warm smile and quirky sense of humor was exactly what I liked the most about her.

She seemed like my destiny...

"Mmmm, smells yummy in there," she said, sniffing the air. "You haven't eaten everything up already, have you?" She began twirling her key fob around her finger as one of her dark brows rose in a question.

Instead of answering, I drew her to me and hugged her. I pecked a kiss on her lips and then stepped back, looking at her. She slowly swept a hand through her hair. "Sorry about my appearance. I didn't have time to change, and besides, you know how I roll, I like to be comfortable."

Dazed by her natural beauty, I hadn't even noticed she was dressed in loose-fitting sweats. I took her by the hand and chuckled, "You look absolutely beautiful, baby, even if you do look like somebody holding up a cardboard sign begging for handouts." I grinned devilishly. "Will you work for food?"

She tilted her head and scrunched her mouth in response. "You know you wrong for that, right?"

"I am." After pecking her lips once more, I took Linda by the hand and led her into the dining room, where I seated her at the table. I went into the kitchen and pulled out two plates from the cabinet, and then I uncorked a bottle of Chardonnay. I knew this was Linda's preferred drink.

With great care, I prepared a plate and placed it in front of her. I poured wine into the glasses and soon after Linda had blessed the food, we both were diving into our meals.

In the three weeks that I've known Linda, I got a grasp on what made her tick; what motivated her. She was an only child with no kids. Like anyone else she carried her own personal baggage.

Some serious baggage.

Her former boyfriend of only three months was abusive, who later committed suicide by leaping off a building, which made Linda hesitant about jumping into another relationship. Her adolescence years were no picnic, either.

Raised by her aunt and uncle after losing both parents in a violent car crash, then losing her uncle a year later in another unexplainable, violent manner, Linda was faced with overwhelming odds. However, despite everything being stacked against her—leaving her more or less punch-drunk, she emerged victorious on her own will to survive—refusing to fail—struggling to work her way through college.

After earning her bachelor's degree, she left New Orleans and moved to Chicago and soon became part of a marketing team for a major advertising firm, putting in nearly sixty-plus hours a week to prove her worth.

But was she really out to prove herself or only denying herself? It was apparent her life was still in limbo, with her personal desires and needs put on hold.

I watched her as she ate, stirring the vegetables aimlessly with a fork before taking another bite. She caught me staring at her.

There was a silence.

I could tell by her expression that she was wondering if she was someone special. *To me.* And would I treat her special. And I looked as though I had a few questions as well. There was a plethora of things transpiring between us; want and desire; hope and promise. Estrogen and Testosterone.

Would this thing work? we seemed to be saying.

Seconds later it appeared that we had come to a decision. We both smiled, almost simultaneously.

That evening, after finishing our meal, Linda and I retired into my bedroom…

Where we made love.

And I must admit, it was the best I had ever experienced. But it was more than just that urgent need for intimacy. That pinned-up rage of raw grinding to see who could finish quicker.

It was different.

By leaps and bounds.

Together, we developed a rhythm that satisfied both of us. We connected in every way, from hands to eyes to lips to pelvis.

Never had I experienced such physical and emotional sex. Nearly spiritual.

That night, Linda showed me something totally new. Something totally different: the true meaning of 'making love'...

CHAPTER FIVE

'Reflections'

As I ran the treadmill for thirty minutes and then rode the stationary bicycle for another twenty, my thoughts lingered on the reason why I suddenly felt renewed. Why my spirit seemed to soar.

I knew what it was. Or better yet, *who* it was.

Linda.

Without a doubt.

Her pleasant, pleasing nature surfaced in my mind, complete with a mental vision of her face. It was all I could do to keep from thinking about her. No other woman had ever matched my wants, needs, and desires—both in and out of the bedroom. She was easy to be with, fun to be around; a regular sweats-and-tee shirt kind of woman, even when she had to hide out in business suits.

She was a proud woman, a trooper, who followed life's driving example—*lemonade out of lemons*, as the cliché went.

I knew she was the one I had to have.

Finishing up my cardio routine, I headed for the locker room. Unfortunately, I would have to shower here. I had some property to show. I had to remind myself that I did have a job as a realtor. I walked in the locker room just in time to see an old white man, no doubt in his seventies, hitching up his trousers over a set of chicken legs, pulling them over the roll of fat that circled his waist. His balding head gleamed in the overhead lights and sweat glistened above his thick brows.

"It's good to get that workout behind us, huh, young man?" he commented, noticing I was dripping with sweat from head to toe.

I smiled back as I slapped the damp towel behind my neck. "Yes, sir, it truly is."

He sucked in a labored breath. "It's also good to sweat out all those unnatural impurities from your body. That's God's way of keeping us righteous and on the right path."

With those words, I hesitated. Absently, I looked over at one of the floor-to-ceiling mirrors to my left. I stared at myself. *Maybe meeting Linda was what I needed* I thought. *I do feel so much better about myself. I haven't felt the need to do anything 'bad' lately, not even craving that shot of Crown to get me through the day. No pun intended, but maybe Linda was the workout that 'I' needed—to rid my body of all those toxic impurities.*

I was sure she was...

I hoped to work on this evaluation tonight, when I met up with her for our Wednesday date-night, at her place. I was really looking forward to it. I thanked the old man before he left with a pat on the back then stripped down and showered, not realizing I wasn't feeling the least bit germophobic. After showering I slid into a snazzy, form-fitting two-piece suit. I checked myself in the mirror and then walked over to the locker cubicle to retrieve my duffel bag.

An hour later, I pulled up to a piece of property I was scheduled to show: a modest brick colonial with an attached two-car garage. It was situated in a decent part of town but not the safest. A closed-down, boarded-up *Church's Chicken* restaurant just up the street let me know that I still needed to watch my back.

I parked in the driveway and then hurried to the front door and retrieved the key from the lockbox. I opened and closed the door quickly and then looked around. The place was very spacious, nice and clean. My clients, a young couple looking to purchase their first home, would be impressed. I didn't expect their arrival for another twenty minutes so I decided to send Linda a nice little text.

As I reached into my inner suit pocket, my phone began to ring. Thinking it was my clients or maybe even Linda, I answered without checking the caller ID.

It was neither.

It was Janet…

My stomach did a little jig and then plummeted straight to the floor. Her face immediately surfaced in my head—clear to see—an over-the-hill woman with permanent, clownish makeup, with a bony body with knobby knees to boot, not to mention a nagging, gravelly voice.

Fuck…

"Hey, Janet," I said, thinking more like: *What in the hell is it!*

"Good afternoon, Mr. Archer," her voice eased out. "And how are you today?"

Frustrated, I answered, "I'm good. About to show some clients a piece of property in a few minutes."

"Shame on you, Mr. Archer, aren't you going to ask me how I'm doing today?"

I gritted my teeth. "I'm so sorry, and how is your day going, Janet?" I rolled my eyes as I leaned against the wall.

"Lovely now."

There was hesitation on her part, so I said while still rolling my eyes, "That's good. So glad I could help."

In response she cleared her throat, then said firmly, "I hope you haven't forgotten about our date tomorrow night. We both agreed to see each other before I depart on my two-week business trip. You do remember when we discussed this just last week, over the phone, don't you, Mr. Archer?"

I stiffened. Shock and surprise registered instantly. How could I have forgotten about this? Had I been so distracted with Linda that I hadn't even *thought* of Janet?

"Eh, no, I mean, yea, I remember when we said this." Though I tried to sound casual my voice shook. *Too much, maybe?*

"Then it's settled. I'll see you tomorrow night, Mr. Archer, seven o'clock, at my place."

Sounding like a fuckin' mechanical robot—just as stiff, I answered, "Okay, it's confirmed: I'll be at your place tomorrow night, at seven. See you then." I hung up the phone and stared blankly at the bare walls in front of me. I then looked down at the phone in my hand. *The twists and turns of life,* I thought. *So unexpected at times.*

I drew a deep breath and anchored my feet to the floor, then glanced back at my phone gripped tightly in my hand. *Deal with it,* I told myself. *No time for wallowing in past mistakes.*

I couldn't.

I wouldn't.

My world was finally on track, and I felt as if I had a bright future ahead of me. I guess I would know in the months to come…

CHAPTER SIX

'Clean Break'

The weatherman said to expect changes soon. For the worst. It was mid-November and in Chicago, that meant things were about to get seriously frigid. I felt a shiver overtake me. But it wasn't from being cold, or thoughts of the upcoming forecast.

It was the thought of riding this elevator to see Janet. But I told myself that this was the last time that I would meet with her. There was no way I could keep playing this game, whether it was innocent or not.

Bottom line is that I felt ashamed, as though I were cheating on Linda, not giving her my all. I knew she was sensitive about my feelings toward her, and I was ready to show that I was serious.

But first I had to jump this hurdle.

The elevator came to a stop on the 17th floor. I stepped off and walked towards Janet's apartment: 1726. I gave the sleeves to my brown overcoat a quick brushing, then I rang the doorbell and soon after, Janet greeted me at the door. She had on a skimpy outfit that was more suited for a woman thirty years her junior. The outfit looked absolutely horrendous on her; one that showed nearly every flaw on her body.

Hanging skin. Wrinkles. Jagged veins that resembled lightning strikes. Lines on a roadmap.

Old, I thought. *An old woman pretending to be young. An old woman who forgot how to dress properly for her age—failing to realize that even money couldn't salvage all the years gone by...*

Without saying a word, only wearing a warm smile, Janet invited me in.

I stepped inside.

She closed and locked the door.

Almost instantly I felt claustrophobic, as if I were already experiencing cabin fever. Janet led me to the sofa and sat me down. She took a seat beside me and threw a bare leg over my lap. There was a hungry look in her eyes.

She was old, all right, but she wasn't dead.

"I want you to take me tonight, Mr. Archer," she said in her usual raspy voice. "I want you to make me feel like a real woman again. Like never before."

I felt a wave of anguish rising in me, and I strained to force it down; I didn't dare give a voice to it, not at this moment. As if reading my mind, Janet stared at me, peering into my eyes. I know she could see deep concern and hesitation in their depths. Slowly, she pulled her leg from my lap and scooted back off me. There was pure silence as we both sat there.

"Something has changed with you, Mr. Archer," she finally said. "You're not the same person that was here before."

I swallowed and then said, "You're right, Janet. I guess I'm not the same person." I lowered my eyes in shame, unable to meet her gaze.

With that, she surprised me and ran her long, supple fingers through my hair, stroking it from front to back. "Tell me what it is, Mr. Archer, I'd like to know. Who knows, perhaps I can even help."

I hesitated, then said, "I met someone."

Stunned, her fingers stopped in mid-motion. She drew a deep breath and I watched as her chest rose and fell. "Is she pretty?" she finally asked.

Once again, I swallowed. "Yes, very much so."

This caused Janet to sigh, deeply. "I see…so, tell me something. Is she…is she young?"

Feeling like shit, I answered, "Yes."

Shutting her eyes tightly, grimacing, she then asked, "How young is she, Mr. Archer?"

It was like sticking a sharp dagger into her chest. "In her late twenties…"

With those words Janet hung her head. It was clear she was hurt. Devastated, most likely. About a minute passed and she raised her head and peered at me. It was like the moment was over. Like it had come and gone. In just that instant she looked like a totally different person. She sat there, a confident Black woman, appearing educated and refined, an aficionado of exquisite things, a lover of exotic artifacts, as warming and as loving as any person I had ever known, capable of a smile that would charm kings and queens.

"I understand, Mr. Archer," she said simply, with a flip of her hand. She sat back on the sofa and crossed her legs. "I'm so glad, no, *happy*…that you found that special person to share your life with."

"No hard feelings?" I said as I placed a hand over hers.

"Not a one, Mr. Archer." She slowly pulled her hand away. "Like I stated before, I understand. I'm a big girl wearing big girl panties. You told me that you found someone better than me and you are very happy. Case closed."

I stood up from the sofa and faced her directly. "It's not like that, Janet," I protested lightly, "It's not like that at all."

"Then how do you explain it, Mr. Archer?" she snapped back in an indignant tone, looking up at me. "You come on to me in a bar, seduce me, lead me on, tease me—*fuck me!*—get your rocks off—mess my head all up, *then*, you have the inflated balls to say, 'you've found someone better'. Now you tell me, Mr. Archer, how could it not be 'not like that', as you say?"

With those seething words she sniffed, trying to maintain control, dabbing at the corners of her eyes with a crooked finger. Her bottom lip trembled as she managed to hold back tears. There soon came a hesitation in her, as if she were mentally shifting gears.

She stared at me.

The look she now gave me shook my very foundation. It was as if she were holding a double-barrel shotgun that looked absurdly large and deadly in the hands of someone who had reached their last straw—who was embracing rage because the only alternative to rage was to kill somebody.

She seemed like the poster child for 'the ultimate woman scorned'. Not just a poster but a real-life symbol. It scared the shit out of me.

My lips were so dry that I had to wet them with a quick tongue. I had the disquieting feeling that I was looking at a woman who was struggling with the grasp of bitter hate and declining patience.

That she'd been fucked over one too many times…

And this was her very last time…

I could only pray that I would leave this place alive. Just like this woman, I was suddenly overwhelmed by a sense of declining patience, far worse than anything I had felt before. I wanted to leap through the window. Part of it was the claustrophobic confinement of this place. The other was from the fact I was a staring at a woman filled with the very essence of something truly and deeply *intimidating.*

She sat there rigid, as still as stone. Her attention remained entirely on me. However, the longer she stared at me, the more her face softened, for no reason I could explain. Slowly, she rose from the sofa and stepped over to me; standing on her toes, her face was about a foot aways from mine. She reached up and slapped my face playfully.

"You stay put, Mr. Archer. I have something to give you," she smiled. "Just a little something for you to remember me by. For your troubles. In spite of how things ended, I did enjoy our brief time together."

I composed myself and said, "Me, too, Janet. It was nice."

She stepped back from me and peered into my eyes. "Then I take it you'll accept my gift of departure, to demonstrate no hard feelings between us?"

I saw nothing but sincereness in her eyes…

"Yes, of course, I will, Janet," I replied.

"Good." She gave me a loving expression and then disappeared into her bedroom. Something told me to turn and leave—*Now!*—to get the fuck out of there! *Maybe this crazy bitch was getting a gun so she could blow my damn brains out!*

But I decided to stay.

About five minutes later Janet returned, her body now fully covered with a black robe, with a warm expression on face. She walked over to me and took me by the hand. She turned my palm, face up, and placed something in it. It was a green silk handkerchief, folded, with something inside. I peeled the handkerchief back.

I immediately frowned.

It was a gem of some kind. Very small. The size of a fingernail.

It was beautiful.

Yet, with a different kind of beauty. Deep blue, nearly black, smooth, broodingly majestic. There was a faint, fiery red speck in the middle that seemed to glow.

No doubt it was worth a small fortune.

"It's beautiful, Janet," I whispered. "I can't begin to thank you."

"There's no need, Mr. Archer, I give it to you as a goodwill gesture. It now belongs to you." Her voice dropped to barely a whisper, sounding breathless. "Take it and go now, Mr. Archer, please, if you will."

I nodded. I folded the handkerchief back over the gem and placed it in the inner pocket of my overcoat. I felt guilty. The fact that I didn't have anything to give back to her bothered me a bit, but how did I know something like this was coming?

It was strange…

Janet seemed to understand my dilemma; however, in response, she just smiled warmly, giving me a pass, as if she had to know this was bound to happen between the two of us—that no matter how good or bad, joyful or painful—it was destined to end, and now she just wanted to get on with her life.

Before leaving I had to ask, "Are you going to be okay?"

"I'm pretty sure I will survive, Mr. Archer," she replied quickly. "No need to worry about me, trust me. Now please leave, don't embarrass me."

I nodded, and took a hard swallow. Much as I would pay twice to know how things were going to turn out for her, I didn't want to take up anymore of her time, or *my* time, for that matter. So, I just said, "Goodbye, Janet, and take care of yourself, please."

"That goes without saying, Mr. Archer," were the last words that were said between her and I. I turned and headed for the door where I let myself out. I soon heard a click behind the door, letting me know that a deadbolt had been set.

I headed for the elevator.

It was over I thought. I felt relieved, like a huge weight had been lifted from my shoulders. But as I got into my SUV and drove away, I could not erase Janet's face from my mind. It was as if I were looking at her now; her eyes were so completely devoid of emotions. She was working hard to hide what she was feeling—therefore she must have been feeling *something...*

It probably was embarrassment, but I preferred to call it resentment. *Deep* resentment. Against me. For allowing me to simply walk away. Letting me off the hook rather easily for breaking her heart.

And I guess in a way, I was getting off easy.

But I wasn't proud of this moment nor myself.

I could only hope that Janet had truly forgiven me, and that she would be okay...

CHAPTER SEVEN

'Strange Visitors'

In my sleep, I moaned softly.

I cried out, "Leave me alone…let me be…please…go away…"

After things died down, I finished out whatever I was dreaming and stared up at the ceiling.

What the hell was that all about…? I wondered.

My head was still foggy from sleep as I went over things. Unfortunately, I couldn't put anything together. I sighed deeply and then pushed back the covers and got out of bed. In the eerie glow of my bedside clock, I could feel sweat coating my entire body, as I still wondered about that clouded dream.

I walked into the bathroom where I lifted the toilet lid and took a well-needed piss. As always, I threw my head back, swaying like I was standing on a roof edge. "Go away," I whispered aimlessly, not knowing who or what I was talking to. "No, you, you keep away. Please, go. Just, just leave me alone…"

It took nearly a minute for me to recover from this strange experience. I finished up in the bathroom and walked into the kitchen where I saw the early morning light bathing the tile floor. I peered out the bay window. The December sky was low, a combination of gray and white.

I turned on the Keurig machine and made myself a cup of coffee then took a seat at the table. I drank the first cup fast, staring out the window. I was trying not to think about the weird dream I'd experienced, just letting my mind fill with thoughts of Linda and I spending the weekend together.

Starting tomorrow.

We planned to drive up to Michigan, to visit Mackinac Island, and take in the winter sights. Linda said her parents used to take her up there when she was a little girl. The best part she said, was the sleigh rides they would often go on. I knew I had to take her there. Plus, with Christmas approaching, the decorations would be beautiful this time of year, with plenty to do. Linda and I had a full agenda scheduled, that would start with a ferry ride to the island and then we planned to visit the many quaint shops and restaurants.

And of course we would definitely do the sleigh ride thing. Drawing from her early days as a child, Linda insisted on this.

The thought brought Linda's face to mind.

I love her, I admitted to myself. *No two ways about it.*

Smiling, I made myself another cup of coffee, loving the *Starbuck's* Veranda blend aroma that permeated the air. *Almost smells better than it tastes,* I thought as I poured the dark brew into my black mug. I sipped my coffee and once again, I thought about Linda. It was still too early in the day to call her. Around this time she'd be in one of her strategy meetings, or on a *zoom* call. I'd wait a couple of hours and then hit her up, if she didn't hit me up first.

Clothed in lounging pajamas, I walked into the living room and peered out the large picture window. Despite the low-lying clouds, it was going to be a nice day. I placed a hand to my hip, feeling genuinely pleased. It seemed as if I'd finally found that unique place that people often talked about, where you surrendered to what is, let go of what was, and had faith in what will be.

It was a place I never wanted to leave…

I sipped my coffee and grinned at a random thought. About how shocked my sister Melody was—nearly beyond belief, when I told her that I was settling down. That I had finally found that special girl, one who meant the world to me. Needless to say, Melody was overjoyed—pleased to see I was at last turning my life around. She became quite emotional; she had to grab a handful of Kleenex tissues to keep her tears at bay, to swab her nose.

Which took me by surprise. It seemed her concern for me was a bit more than just simple worry.

It was more like fear.

I guess she needed to know that her little brother was going to be okay. And I was cool with that. There was nothing like family. *Nothing.* And to tell it, Melody was the only family I really had, at least nearby, which meant I was also concerned about her safety and well-being.

Both as a brother as well as her best friend. Which included every aspect of her life.

Very much so…

—and just like that—in that split second, I found myself like Melody, overtaken by emotions. I fought the urge to shed tears and walked further into the living room, which was a good size. I looked around the room and thought it could use a light dusting. No, a serious dusting. Especially around the windowsills. Something I would jump on the moment I finished this cup of coffee I told myself. Well, maybe after a third cup…*a fourth, hopefully?*

I chuckled, *they had to be putting something in the coffee these days. A sprinkle of crack, for sure!*

I took another sip of coffee and glanced around, trying to figure out where to start my cleaning assault *after* my fourth cup of coffee. Now or later, I knew it had to be done. The place looked pretty bad; you could draw smiley faces on the lamp tables. Deciding there was no time like the present, I took a final sip of coffee and headed to the kitchen to get the cleaning supplies: furniture polish, a bottle of Windex, along with a couple of micro-fiber rags.

Just before I entered the kitchen, there came a slight ringing which seemed to dance and mingle in the air, sort of like fine pixie dust—unlike the dust which coated parts of my living room. The ringing was sort of mystical, almost pleasant, coming in the form of a vibrating sensation.

Something you can *hear, feel*, but could not see.

It reverberated in the air like faint sleigh bells. The ringing soon *whirled* as if it had been caught in a turbulence—bouncing off every wall, floor to ceiling, in every direction—finally gathering into a cluster—as if seeking me out.

It was no longer pleasant.

In a rush, the ringing tightened into a stream and shot like a bullet—funneling into my ears, which knocked me back a few feet. I staggered a bit and soon felt a throbbing which vibrated in my head, but only mildly. I frowned, puzzled. Something weird was going on.

I looked around, hesitating. There was no need to panic I told myself, even though I began to feel lightheaded and staggered a bit more. Slowly, gradually, I found my footing; I started to feel normal.

Somewhat...

I looked down and peered into my coffee mug. *Starbucks new flavor blend: Dark Roasted Crack-Cocaine. Most definitely!* Not giving things a second thought I took another sip. That's when I heard a light *ticking* sound at one of the smaller windows in the living room, to the left of me. I stepped over and peered through the curtains, which had been drawn shut.

Another *tick*.

Coming at the bottom pane of the window.

Sounding like a pebble flicked against the glass.

Pulling the curtains apart, I frowned and peered harder, craning my head and looking to my left and right. Up and down. There was nothing. I shrugged my shoulders, thinking maybe it was just an ice pellet, or something blowing in the wind. I closed the curtains and took another sip of coffee.

Tick.

Seconds later, sounding the same, another.

Tick.

Coming from the large front window.

Tick.

Maybe it was something blowing in the wind, falling from the nearby trees. *Twigs, perhaps?*

I walked back to the front window and peered through the glass, only to see a shiny black crow on the outer ledge, preening its feathers. I smiled. *A crow.* Nothing to worry about. I was relieved to see that it was nothing major.

I took a long sip of coffee followed by a hard swallow.

Tick.

Something coming from the kitchen?

I walked into the kitchen where I saw another black crow perched at the bay window. It was peering in through the glass with cold, dark eyes.

Peering at me.

Knowingly.

Like it knew exactly who I was, wanting me to see exactly what *it* was. I stepped to the window and gazed into the crow's black, glassy eyes. Not once did the lids blink.

I frowned. *Did crows blink?*

"Go away, little birdie," I whispered, shooing at it through the glass. "Don't you have someplace to be?" Feeling playful, I made silly faces at the crow.

That's when it came.

Tick-tick-tick-tick-tick-tick...

Ticks, ticks, and more ticks. There were *ticks* up the ass—coming at me from every direction—from nearly every window—sounding like a multitude of out-of-control typewriters being used. I made a scrambling dash back into the living room.

It was a sight which stole my breath...

There were at least a hundred shiny black crows gathered at the large picture window. One jostling over the other to peer inside. No longer *ticking* but instead, staring.

At me.

I dropped my coffee cup, which smashed into a million pieces. *What the hell is going on?* I asked myself. I stared with my mouth hanging open, disbelievingly. Slowly, I crept to the window. There were crows everywhere. Jumbled everywhere. You could barely see anything else. I made it to the window and leaned in, to get a closer look.

Fuck...

The crows—every last one of them—was staring at me. Their cold, oil-black eyes narrowed to study my face—zeroing in on me—concentrating on my every move, my every action—every flinch or twitch that I made. It was like they were locked in, appearing both hypnotized and possessed.

To make sure this wasn't a figment of my imagination, some kind of dream, I raised my right hand, and the crows tilted their heads curiously, switching their attention from my face to my hand. They watched transfixed at every zigzagging direction I made with my hand.

Up, down; sideways; diagonally.

I couldn't help but notice that one of the crows, perched at the bottom ledge of the window, a much larger one, wasn't interested in my hand, not in the least, but instead, its entire focus was centered on *me*.

...on my face...

I found this odd, considering it was the only one. I bent forward and stared back at it. My gaze caught a faint brilliance in its eyes.

In its unblinking eyes.

A glow of some sort.

There were infinite shades of seemingly all colors, some bright, some dark. Swirling shades melting together like mild chaos.

Set deep in the background...

Like a candle flame flickering in the shadows...

I was captivated, unsure of what I was seeing. The longer I stared, the more confused I became. I tapped lightly on the glass.

"Go fuck off somewhere, little birdie," I said with a seething tone. The crow just stared back at me. Not responding. Not flinching. Not moving an inch.

Neither did I.

Both of us were locked in a tug of war, a pair of dueling eyes.

I leaned in closer and thumped the window with a finger. That's when—without warning—the crow made a split-second lunge of its head and pecked the glass directly in front of me—so hard that the *tap* of its beak startled me and sent me reeling backwards on my ass. I thought the glass had been shattered.

What the f—!

I tried to swallow the sudden lump in my throat and when I finally did, the lump ended up in my stomach. I rose from the floor and stood there waiting for something to happen, when suddenly, as if a connection had been broken, the crows took flight in a crowded mass of fluttering feathers and loud cawing. I watched as they disappeared into the gray skies.

There was a silence that followed, one I couldn't begin to explain.

It was overwhelming.

Eerie.

I shook my head slowly as my heart pounded in my chest. For nearly five minutes I just stood there. I blinked my eyes a few times to clear my head. I wanted to tell myself that what I had just experienced was just a simple fluke of nature. A once-in-a-lifetime event. The kind of shit people posted on *YouTube, TikTok,* or *Facebook,* as some kind of a joke. A hoax.

But it wasn't.

I was there...

I saw it...

A rush of fear and annoyance came over me and, once again, I wanted to tell myself that everything was going to be all right. That it *was* just a hoax. That it was just Mother Nature expressing herself, showing her ass.

But I wasn't convinced.

Somehow, I felt that my fears were valid.

I drew a deep breath and suddenly felt exhausted. Maybe I was still dreaming. Daydreaming, at best. *Go back to bed,* I told myself. *Get a few more hours of sleep. Maybe it's what you need. And lay off that damn crack-cocaine coffee!*

I hesitated, considering my own advice. *I will,* I finally nodded. *I promise, I...I will...*

There was nothing which required my immediate attention today, not now, at least, so I cleaned up the spilled coffee as well as the shattered pieces of my mug. I even dusted the living room furniture. Before jumping back in bed, I went back into the living room.

I took another glance at the living room window, all of them.

I felt an unexplainable chill...

Slowly turning away, I walked into the dining room and peered out through the window, at my outdoor patio. The lock to my patio door was flimsy, engaged by simply turning a silver button. All that was needed to break in was a good kick—one good lunge from a single fuckin' crow—so I grabbed a straight-backed chair from the dining room table, tilted it, then jammed it tightly under the knob.

Don't ever think about coming in here, you little fucker! I grimaced. I drew a deep breath and knew I had to shut my mind down. Focus on rest, sleep, tomorrow, blot out everything else.

I tried.

Dammit, I tried.

Yet, I found myself still shivering as I thought about the multitude of crows perched just outside my living room windows, the kitchen windows. All of the windows.

Watching me silently.

Staring at me...

I fought an urge to scream.

CHAPTER EIGHT

'A Deepening Love Goes Deeper'

Nestled in our spacious hotel suite I embraced Linda, and we kissed. Deep, long and hard. With a tender grip I moved my hands in lazy circles over her shoulders, down to her waist, where I gently massaged her lower back and then the swell of her butt, which was toned and soft.

She felt *so* good. Everything about her did.

Exhausted from travelling and barely settling into our hotel suite, we had not made love since the night we'd left Chicago. As soon as we took in a few sights on Mackinac Island we planned to return to our room to make up for lost time.

I slid my hands down Linda's hips and pulled her against me. Punctuating my whispered words with soft kisses to her throat, cheeks, eyes, the corners of her mouth, I said, "How's about later tonight, when we get back from sight-seeing, after we've had a nice glass of wine with some soft jazz playing in the background, and we're both feeling mellow..."

"...yes?" she said dreamily, "Go on..."

"We..." I continued peppering her lips, her eyes, her cheeks and neck with small kisses, "...we slowly make our way into that beautiful bedroom with that huge, king-size bed..."

"…mmmmm, go on, baby. *Talk* to me…"

"…we strip down naked…"

"…yes, baby," she moaned, "…butt-ass naked…"

"…then we crawl under those cool, thousand-count sheets and covers…"

"…awwww, shit…"

"…then we…"

"…yes, baby, go on…we what?"

"Then we both sleep like there's no tomorrow."

"What the hell?" Linda looked up and smacked me playfully on the cheek. "Oooh, Derrick, you so wrong for that. Sleep? Really?"

"Or we could fuck ourselves silly."

With that, she smiled devilishly and started caressing my crotch. She gripped me firmly. "That sounds so much better, baby. Your little Linda needs some special attention tonight. And you know where and how. And in return, I'll gladly return the favor."

With a slow, wet tongue, she licked her lips and I was instantly hard as a rock; I could have chiseled down a brick wall. I nodded with a sly grin and began a slow grind against her body. "That I can do. In fact, I can do that shit right now."

Linda gradually, yet regrettably, pushed me away. "Slow your roll, big boy. We got the whole weekend before you have me walking bowlegged." She shot a finger into my chest. "So, let's get a move on while there's still some light outside. We got sights to see and some shopping to do. Plus, I still want to have my sleigh ride."

"Okay," I nodded. "Just one more kiss."

Tenderly, I brought Linda's lips to mine, and we explored the sweetness and warmth of each other's mouth and embrace. It was all the convincing that we needed.

We never did leave our suite.

Inside a quaint little restaurant, I motioned for the waitress, indicating that Linda and I were ready to be served because of time constraints. It was nearly dark outside, and we wanted to get back to our hotel suite. The young waitress nodded and fifteen minutes later served our grilled chicken salad.

After eating, we sipped our Chardonnay and spent the remaining time in small talk, and soon Linda and I were grateful when we were back on the ferry, headed to our hotel. Once inside our suite, I turned and immediately locked the door. There was a slight chill in the room so I cranked up the heat and then without drawing attention to my actions, I went through the entire room, even the bathroom, to make sure we were alone. I walked back into the main part of the room and parted the curtains.

I peered outside.

Nothing out there.

No immediate danger.

No crows…

For nearly a minute I just stood quietly peering out the window, into the night, watching, listening.

The star-littered sky and the silver light of a quarter moon were the only things to see. Nothing else was out there.

Before the minute was up, I stopped *expecting* to see anything out there.

I drew a deep breath and felt a little better, in full control of myself; I no longer held worry, panic, and anxiety in front of me but instead, placed all three behind me, out of my mind.

I turned to Linda, who was looking sexy as hell, as always—waiting until the room warmed up—still dressed in a pair of black knee-high boots with a three-inch heel, tight black jeans, a beige turtleneck sweater, and a black sheepskin-lined jacket, wearing a beige cap with fur-lined earflaps tied under her chin.

I pictured her in those black knee-high boots, with those three-inch heels, wearing that black sheepskin-lined jacket—*and nothing else!*—and instantly became aroused.

Hard as steel.

Wearing a sly smile, I walked over to her. She responded with a sly smile of her own. She pulled off her cap, shook her hair free, and then threw her arms around my neck.

"Take me." Her voice was hardly more than a whisper as she passionately covered my mouth with hers. She pulled back and nibbled on my ear. "Take me now." Her words came faster, crowding into each other. "Take me, baby, take all of me, make me yours…"

Before another second could pass, our clothes, every last stitch of them, were peeled off and tossed to the side. Next to our shopping bags.

That night Linda and I made love like never before. I had truly made her *mine*...

CHAPTER NINE

'A Touch from Beyond'

It was 3am in the morning in our hotel suite when I got up from the bed and crept into the bathroom, mindful of Linda sleeping soundly. Dressed only in boxers, I gently closed the door behind me.

The bathroom door had a tiny privacy lock in the knob, which I engaged by pushing a silver button. After taking a piss, I decided to take a quick shower—in case Linda decided to 'make me hers' through the night. I finished my shower only when I had used every drop of hot water that my body could stand. *Fuck it, I wasn't paying for it.*

I stepped from the large shower stall; the first thing I noticed was steam clinging to the outer edges of the bathroom mirror, condensing into little beads of water that slipped and slid their way down the slick surface. I could barely see my image in the mirror. I tried wiping away the condensation, but it was useless. The more I wiped the cloudier it became. I began drying off and then slid on my boxers.

I suddenly felt a cool breeze.

Like a door or window had been opened.

The breeze was lightly scented with a lilac fragrance; it was pleasing to the nostrils. Like loving arms, the fragrance seemed to wrap and overtake me; it felt like a pair of soft hands caressing the back of my neck and skillfully feathering me with a towel, gently drying off the remaining dampness from my body.

Linda, I smiled.

I went with it, closing my eyes and finding myself moaning lightly as I experienced sensations that I've never experienced before.

Deep, sexual sensations.

Though it felt good, it felt a bit...strange...

Different this time.

Something I couldn't explain...

Slowly, gradually, I felt my boxers being tugged lower and lower down my legs, bunching at my ankles. My inner thighs and backside were being caressed and stroked with tender hands.

Again, it felt good but yet...*strange...*

"Damn, baby," I whispered, "what you doin' to me back there?" Instead of a reply, the sensations continued for half a minute or so then they stopped. Abruptly. I opened my eyes and that's when I heard a sound. A faint ringing. It was a sound I'd heard before.

Sleigh Bells.

A bit louder this time.

The sound soon became chaotic, darker, pitching lower—turning hollow, into an ominous tone.

Like a summons.

Seconds later I felt something come over me. *A different kind of sensation.* An ice-cold wind assaulted me, frigid enough to take my breath away. Without warning, I was shoved violently and stumbled back against the wall, grabbing the towel rack for balance. I frantically reached out for Linda in the fog-layered bathroom. Gasping in surprise, I realized she wasn't there.

What the f—

It was at that moment when I felt my mouth being squeezed and then something dry and papery pressed against my lips, in the form of a kiss. Something slid into my mouth, brittle and thorny. The taste was rancid. Putrid. Instantly, the inside of my mouth went as dry as powder, and my throat swelled so tight that I was unable to breathe or swallow.

Something pricked my tongue.

My heart pounded. Startled, I turned my head and tried to spit whatever it was out of my mouth. I hacked and coughed then wiped my mouth roughly with the back of my hand. I frowned, nauseous and feeling as if I were freezing to death because of the cold returning to my body.

I felt a presence near me.

Dangerously close.

I looked around with dazed eyes; I saw nothing. Nothing but steam and condensation coating the walls of the bathroom. I searched for something to arm myself with. I had nothing but my bare fists. I readied myself, nevertheless. Suddenly, the atmosphere as well as the eerie sound seemed to wound themselves tightly together and then both disappeared into itself, leaving only silence and stillness in its wake.

The air was no longer cold.

I gasped; my breathing was ragged as I swallowed hard and wiped sweat from my brow. The inside of my mouth was still dry, as if littered with shredded brown leaves, wads of cotton, and sandy grit. My entire body felt contaminated.

What the heck is going on?

Almost immediately I aimed my glance at the bathroom door. I distinctly remembered closing and locking it.

From the *inside*.

And it was still locked.

Linda could have not gotten in.

Nobody could have gotten in.

It was impossible.

Who or what had opened the door?

CHAPTER TEN

'*Mood, Behavior, Thoughts*'

Breathe deeply, I instructed myself, as I had done many times recently. *Pull yourself together. You're going to lose it if you don't. All of this was just in your head. In your mind. Nothing was coming for you—especially in your own home!*

I looked around the living room.

At the windows.

But hadn't something strange happened here? In my own home? Violently, I pounded my fists together. *Stop it! You're not afraid of a bunch of crows!*

But I was.

I worried of their return.

Even though nothing strange had happened for nearly a month.

I shook my head and then pulled myself up slowly from the sofa. A gust of wind hit the picture window, vibrating it. In my mind's eyes I saw a multitude of crows at the window, peering in, their eyes brimming with malice, poised to strike.

Enough already! I told myself, drawing in a deep breath.

It was getting late, and I had a busy day tomorrow showing several pieces of property. I drew another deep breath. Then, without even glancing at the picture window, I went directly to the lamp and switched it off. Then I made a loop through the rooms on the lower level: the kitchen, the dining room, the half bath, even the garage, rechecking all the locks and windows.

Like a frightened child trying to be strong, I walked through the darkness up to my bedroom. I brushed my teeth, washed my face, and then climbed into the bed, where I pulled the comforter up to my chin.

Something safe about the covers, I thought, trying to ease my mind. Slowly, I drifted off to sleep. My ringing cell phone on the nightstand brought me straight up to a sitting position. It jarred me like a pair of hands pushing at me, scaring the living shit out of me. I grabbed it immediately.

"Hello?"

"Hey, baby," Linda's voice came back. "Did I wake you? I know it's kind of late."

"No, I wasn't asleep just yet," I lied. I glanced at the illuminated face of my bedside clock. Nearly midnight. *Why was Linda calling so late?* "Is everything okay?" I asked. "There's nothing wrong, is it?

"No, everything is just fine," Linda answered quietly. There was a pause, and then she asked, "Baby, are you...okay?"

I instantly took a shuddering breath. "Why you ask?"

"Well, are you?" she repeated. "I need to know."

"I guess, I am."

"What kind of answer is that?" she asked sharply.

I hesitated, then said, "I'm afraid it's the best answer I have at the moment, baby…"

There was a long silence.

"What's going on here, Derrick? I thought you loved me."

"Baby, I do!" I shouted. I looked at the phone then realized Linda couldn't see me. I brought the phone back to my ear. "I love you with everything in me—with everything I got."

"Then tell me what's going on with you. You owe this to me, baby. Why are you acting so…so strange?"

"Strange, like how? Please tell me, Linda. How am I acting strange, as you say?"

"For one, when you spend the night with me, you're always jittery, like you're expecting someone to come knocking on the door. I've watched you get up through the night and peer out the windows. Secondly, when we're out, you're constantly peeking over your shoulders, like there's somebody stalking you." A pause. "Derrick, are you seeing someone else other than me?"

"Absolutely not, Linda," I said, slinging my legs from the bed. "I love you and only you."

"Do you…?" Her voice trailed off.

"Yes," I pleaded, sincerely and consistently.

Another pause. A bit longer this time. "I hope you do, Derrick, because God knows I love you."

"That's good to know, baby," I said reassuringly. "Because you mean the absolute world to me."

"And that's what I needed to hear." I could hear sniffling; she was obviously in tears. Rededicating our commitment to each other, we engaged in small talk, going over the busy days ahead of us. We promised to see each other in two days, over dinner at a restaurant near her place. But I had a much better place in mind. Afterwards we ended the call on a good note.

I laid back on the bed. Staring at the ceiling. *Acting strange, Linda said. Please. The poor girl didn't know the half of it.* I knew what it was. It was overload. And I knew all the symptoms of overload: nervousness, internal pressure, rage, despair, forgetfulness, paranoia, irritability, sleeplessness.

And I had all of them.

Every last one.

As I tried to drift back to sleep, I realized I'd forgotten one other symptom.

A major one.

I was scared...

CHAPTER ELEVEN

'Slowly Creeping Over the Edge'

My headache only worsened when I realized that the battery on my cell phone was on its last leg. Apparently I'd forgotten to place it on the charger.

I stared at the phone totally pissed, unwilling to accept any explanation other than I hadn't been sleeping well. I always charged my phone at night—same as I had for as long as I owned a cell phone. I wouldn't have forgotten something as important as that, and I hadn't. I had plugged the damn phone into the charger lying on the nightstand, beside my bed. Afterwards I turned the light off and went to sleep.

As always.

Hold up...

Maybe the charger itself wasn't properly plugged into the outlet and the phone hadn't charged.

Of course! That's what it was! Silly me!

It wasn't lack of sleep. Or the severe headaches I'd been experiencing. Or the fact that I was losing my damn mind. I was merely an idiot for not checking!

So now here I am, inside a vacant house, waiting to show some clients the property, assed out with a non-working phone. And my phone wasn't compatible for cordless charging in my SUV. I recall reminding myself that it was time for a phone upgrade.

Apparently, I hadn't listened. *Great...*

I walked over to the window and peered out. Located on the outskirts of West Garfield Park, not the greatest area to live in, or to be in, the houses in this neighborhood were extremely small, and many of them had a certain grayness—as if the people living inside had to choose between spending their money on repairing a roof rather than on a fresh coat of paint. The lawns were all kept up nicely, but still, this entire part of town had a desperate feel to it, of hopelessness.

The thought of being here without a cell phone was a little uneasy let alone not knowing what my clients looked like, or what kind of people they were.

Were they murderers? Wanted felons? Maybe I was being set up to be robbed? The old okie-doke.

I chewed my lips and swore softly. *Let it go, fool. Why are you so nervous, anyway?* But I couldn't shake the waves of uncertainty—at myself, at life, at wondering what would I do if the sun decided not to rise anymore. *Why was I even thinking like this? This is crazy! For the first time in my life, I'm living the best time of my life!*

I closed my eyes trying to focus on seeing Linda tonight, praying that it would counteract my rampant descent into hysteria. If I didn't, I would lose it, and my head would explode. I looked around, feeling my entire body covered in a cold sweat. *My dear God,* I had to ask myself, *what is wrong with me?*

CHAPTER TWELVE
'Deviant Behavior'

The crowd in the restaurant was putting out a steady stream of chatter, glasses clinking. Two waiters emerged discreetly from the kitchen, each carrying a plate of Kobe beef, both well done, with all the trimmings; another waiter carried a chilled bottle of *Dom Perignon* champagne. 1988, I believe.

I wanted this night to be special for Linda. It seems as if I was putting her through so much, so soon. Dressed for this occasion in a light gray two-piece suit with a bright yellow tie, I'd made reservations at one of the most elegant restaurants in the city of Chicago: *The Palm*.

The place was pure class—*six* stars on a scale of one to five.

The waiter outfitted in a white serving jacket, tall, polished and extremely professional, made a kind gesture of presenting the champagne to me, who I favored back with a subtle nod.

The bottle was pried loose with a festive pop.

The waiter then poured a bit for Linda and me to sample, while another waiter brought a silver bucket on a stand. After giving our approval, our fluted glasses were filled. He smiled warmly and then walked away, giving us time to savor the champagne as well as the ambiance of the place.

Grateful for the momentary solitude, I smiled at Linda. I handed her a glass and lifted the other one.

"A toast to us, baby," I proclaimed proudly. "Here's to three months of you making me the *happiest, most luckiest* man alive…"

At once, she nodded. "Yes, baby, and you have made me the happiest, luckiest woman alive in the process." In the same breath, she added, "Happy anniversary, baby, here's to three months."

Linda and I clinked glasses and we each took a long, savoring sip. "Damn, boy—this is simply delicious," she said with a smack of her lips.

"I'm so glad you think so." Placing my glass aside, I reached over and took Linda by the hand. She looked absolutely stunning in her dark burgundy blouse with a short matching skirt; her long, auburn-black hair was down and cradled her magnificent face; her makeup was flawless. I leaned in and kissed her hand, as intimate as if I were kissing her lips. She gazed at me, and I couldn't have looked away from her if my life had depended upon it.

All around us, there were muted voices, the occasional clink of flatware on china, and slight laughter feathering the air. The mingled scents of spices wafted on the breeze. We looked at each other lovingly. It was at this time when a band started playing in another room. I read Linda's expression instantly: *A restaurant large enough to hold a band? No way!*

There was a certain amazement in her eyes, that I would go to such an extent to make her happy.

Inhaling deeply, she looked around the restaurant and then eyed me dreamily. We traded glances, now speaking without the use of words. "I'm so glad we came here, baby," she finally whispered. "You really took me by surprise on this one."

"Absolutely nothing is too good for the woman who means the world to me," I proclaimed with a serious expression, still letting my gaze linger on her face. It was the picture of innocence and beauty. Everything about her was. I caught the faint scent of her perfume; *she smelled so good!* It was all I could do not to reach over the table and kiss her mouth passionately.

It was torture to want something, *someone,* so bad, and not fully have that someone to call your own.

I had to make her mine.

Permanently.

Forever.

If I had a ring on me, I'd ask her to marry me right here and now…

And it would be a strong marriage, too, this I knew; for keeps. Therefore, whenever we had a disagreement or argument, the both of us would make sure we'd call a truce before the day ended.

I understood, all too well, that Linda was a strong but fragile woman. She needed to know that I'd be there for her.

Always.

So, essentially, this period in the relationship was a trial run, a test for me, which I could only pass if I planned on sacrificing more pride than her—I had to climb any mountain—slay any beast, and when I had done that, I would have proven that I truly loved her, and that I would never harm or treat her badly as her former boyfriend had done. I would rather suffer the worst pain in the world than have Linda experience even the *slightest* discomfort when it came to our relationship.

I looked deeply into her eyes, almost through her.

As if on cue the band began playing a slow jazz tune, providing a soothing backdrop to a perfect setting. To a perfect evening. To the perfect woman. I couldn't help myself; I stood up from my seat and leaned over to kiss her.

That's when it happened.

A faint ringing danced in the air.

Sleigh Bells, I thought immediately.

I settled back into my seat. The ringing intensified. There was no denying it—*it was Sleigh Bells*. I sat there, in some sort of a stupor, a trance. Slowly, the ringing dispersed, fanning out everywhere around me. I could feel my heart pounding as if *something* were seeping into my ears, my head—like compressed air being forced into my brain like a balloon. I thought my head was about to explode. There was a flood of incredibly different things going on inside my mind—all at once.

Violently!

It became too much; I reached out and grabbed the sides of the table. "No," I uttered, fighting against *something*.

"Baby, what's wrong?" I heard Linda utter; it was like her voice was a thousand miles away. She placed her hands over my arms. Instead of answering, I gritted my teeth and looked around—still fighting the pounding in my head. To my horror, I saw nothing which resembled a restaurant. The tables, the walls, the people who were once seated around me—it was all gone! Even the sound had been sucked away—into some kind of vortex, galaxies away.

Everything surrounding me had gone *dark*.

I pulled my hands back and sat there frozen; I scrubbed a hand down my face. *What the hell...?*

I felt walls of some kind—closing in on me.

Something was coming...

Once again, I reached out and gripped the edge of the table. There was a pair of clutching hands wrapped around my arms. I looked up to see that it was Linda—again holding onto to me. Tightly.

"Baby, tell me what is going on here?" I heard her pleading. I looked at her; her eyes were dazed with confusion, wilting.

"I...I don't know..." I snatched my arms back and found myself gripping hers—holding onto her like she was a lifeline. The grip was incredibly solid. But I could still feel myself slipping away.

Drifting...

I didn't release my hold on Linda, and she...well, she wasn't about to pull away. She couldn't even if she wanted to. My grip was that strong. As tears formed in my eyes, I looked at her with a dire expression.

Help me, baby...

No matter how I worded it in my head, it came out sounding as if I were just short of vanishing. I could only look at her with frozen eyes, unable to explain what was happening to me. I knew I looked insane, an out-of-his-mind, out-of-control madman. I thrashed and squirmed as I felt myself drifting further away from reality.

Whatever it was, it had me, and it was *not* letting me go.

I shook my head violently from side to side. *No! Go away! Leave me be, dammit!*

It was no use. The vibration in my head only became greater. Nose to nose with my brain. Wrapped around my senses. Up and down my spine. Against the raw edges of my soul...

I gritted my teeth. *Shit!*

The chaos continued for a few seconds more then—*wham!*—just like that—everything came to sudden stop.

That's when I felt something blending into me.

Replacing me...

Moments later I felt as if I was settling into some sort of reprieve, which caused me to let out a long, exasperating sigh, and the internal pressure left my body like hissing gas, leaving me completely drained as well as bewildered. I fell back into my chair in a wasted heap—throwing my head back and moaning as if taking my final breath.

I felt so strange...

I really couldn't explain this feeling. But somehow, some kind of way...I felt *different*. It was like I knew who I was and what I was, but it was impossible to *feel* who and what I was.

I no longer felt like... *'me'*...

I'm assuming that all went well.

That I had made it through without any real issues. After a minute or so, I slowly opened my eyes. Somehow, despite my severe neck trauma, I managed to crane my head and take note of my surroundings.

There was darkness all around me.

No one was there.

It was as though I'd been locked in a dungeon.

Yet strangely, I now felt...*free*...

Truly free.

It was something akin to a prison cell, where the door had been summoned open, and I'd just been pardoned. Where I could interact with people.

Real people.

The outside world.

This world...

I recalled feeling this way some time ago, loving the feeling of being able to interact, to move about, to *actually* touch people in this world.

Again, this *other* world.

I found myself smiling, *Maybe I'd be lucky this time around. Maybe I could finally stay.*

I tried to swallow but it wasn't easy; my mouth felt parched and hollowed out. I brought my fingers to my lips and realized they were dry and chapped, nearly cracking. For some strange reason I was extremely thirsty—as though I'd been walking through a desert for days under a brutal, relentless sun. I saw that my clothes were still the same, still dirty, tattered, and weather-beaten, with the same holes in them. And my neck still hurt like a son-of-a-bitch from where it had been broken.

Apparently, my transformation wasn't complete.

Once more I looked around. That's when I cast my gaze on someone sitting across from me. It appeared to be a woman. A rather beautiful woman. Breathtaking. I peered harder, rubbing my eyes. My vision was still blurry when I dropped my hands but I was sure it was her. Not a hundred-percent, 'wouldn't bet the house on it' sure, but I was damn certain it was her.

I could *feel* it.

It was her...

I peered closer, deeper, more intensely. Her name still eluded me but the face was undeniable.

It was her!

And, *man-oh-man!*—was she looking good, as always! Looking like a pool of cool water! Incredibly inviting—clear, blue, quenching! Utterly refreshing! I could almost feel her waves crashing over me, spraying me with liquid haze! It had to be my lucky day; it just *had* to be! There's no doubt about it!—I'd just scored a double homerun!—obtaining the two most precious items *this* time around: renewed life and…her…

Yes…it had to be my lucky fuckin' day!

I looked at her hungrily, damn near salivating.

"I want you," I smiled.

In response, she played as if she hadn't heard me, appearing confused. "Baby, are you okay?" she asked.

I just stared back, now feeling myself smiling wickedly. I ran my tongue over my dry lips. *Bend her over, then one firm push at the small of her back along with a fierce thrust of my hips, and splash!—I could be deep in that cool water! Balls deep in this bitch!*

With that same frightened expression, she could only look back at me. *As always.* I locked eyes with her—wondering if she felt as amazing as she looked.

I had to know.

Now!

With a howling grunt, I reached over and grabbed her, hauling her up from the table and raising her into the air—sending slabs of meat and some other shit flying to the floor. I pressed up against her, forcing her body into mine, holding her tightly against my now engorged erection. Along with that terrified expression, there was sweat beaded up on her face. Up this close, I could feel the heat emanating from her body. I could sense every sizzling drop of fear.

She was afraid, I smirked. *Like always…*

I became hypnotized by every frightening gesture she made. I saw droplets of tears pooling in her eyes, spilling out and rolling down her cheeks.

The little bitch was crying...always fucking crying...

I grinned lustfully, again drooling at this point. There was a trail of sweat sliding onto her brow, and I brushed it away. She winced at my touch, and began shaking her head. I could only stare in amazement, in disbelief.

She was so pretty! Grown up to be so red hot! A real Bad Mama Jama!

I gazed up at her, her body still upraised and locked in my grasp. I knew what I had to do. I had to quench this burning thirst that was eating me up alive. I could feel the testosterone flooding my system. *It's been so long!* And I believed she also knew this.

She had to know...

I leaned in to kiss her. She turned her head and tried to pull away.

"Please, don't, Derrick," she pleaded in a low whispering voice, which sounded as though it belonged to a frightened child.

I looked at this bitch crazily. *Who the fuck is Derrick?* I frowned. My inner rage instantly crept up a notch and I shook her ass like a pair of dice.

"Derrick," she cried, her voice shaking with her body. "What's-gotten-into-you? Why-are-you-acting like-this? Baby, what-is-going-on? Please, tell-me."

I wanted to duct tape her mouth shut, not because I didn't want to hear her mouth—but because she almost made me laugh—*"Baby, what's going on here? Please, tell me."*—and laughter was not going to help me screw her brains out. In my manic rage, I smacked her across the face.

Hard!

She fell against the table and toppled to the floor. She made a sad attempt to get up. All I could see was a tight burgundy skirt riding up smooth, supple, stocking-covered thighs, revealing a pair of million-dollar legs, just staring at me. A smile was breaking across my face as I wondered—*did she have anything on at all, underneath that skirt?*

Best believe one thing: I would soon find out!

I watched her, at her feeble attempt to crawl away, trying to gain traction but her heels hindering her, slipping and sliding and shit. Just as she thought she was making a little leeway, I reached down and grabbed a fistful of hair—twisting and winding it until my clenched fist rested against the back of her skull. With those childish tears of self-pity, she looked up at me.

I laughed—*What?*—as my eyes burned into hers. She began lunging and kicking, twisting and turning, like a demon splashed with holy water. I yanked her body from the floor like a sack of garbage. Once again, I raised my hand—*turned it into a fist*—and smashed her face in good.

Several times.

She went flying to the floor and stared up at me, holding her bloodied mouth as well as the side of her head; her cheeks were puffed with malice, poised to strike.

Cocking both my fists at my side, this gesture made me chuckle, deeply. *"Bitch, please, you better stay down. If you know what's good for you."*

Hardheaded as ever, she tried to pull herself up. I shook my head, insensitive to her situation—pissed she hadn't heeded my warning. I started to bash her skull in but it was almost comical, entertaining, watching her actions as she tried to rise to her feet.

All I could see—*all I wanted to see*—was her shapely legs opening up for me.

"Get the fuck away from me, you crazy motherfucker," she seeped out, as she made it halfway to her feet.

I looked at her—*what the f—?*—my pride, my ego—both had just been assaulted. *I couldn't believe it!* This little cunt-bitch was actually talking back to me! After all the shit I'd done for her! *Oh, no, this will never do!* I raised the heel of my shoe and sent it flying into her left side, hoping I had damaged a few ribs. I kicked her a few more times for good measure then I plunged forward to finish what needed to be done.

As I tore at her blouse frantically with my hand, the other clutched and wedged between her legs, I felt a flash, an iron poker, as hot as oven steel, digging into my right cheek. Rising from the floor, I brought both hands to my face.

Somebody had fuckin' stabbed me!

The pain was searing and I yelled out, *"Keep that shit away from me!"* I looked around to see who or what it was but there was nothing there.

Not a damn thing...

I suddenly felt violated...disrespected. Instinctively, I balled both my fists and then took a defiant stance—ready to beat the shit out of the first thing I saw—man, woman, child, or beast!

You name it!

I could feel my lungs expanding and contracting fiercely as I peered around, as I held a vicious scowl; my fists became even tighter. I was ready to kill somebody! Anybody! Everybody!

Breathe deeply, I told myself after a second or two, as I had done many times before. As I drew several breaths that's when it dawned on me. I knew what was happening. I was being pulled back. Somehow, I wasn't strong enough to remain in *this* world. *Not just yet...*

The pulling became stronger, almost snatching at my shoulders, at my arms and legs.

"Enough already," I growled, drawing in a deep breath with an even deeper scowl on my face. *"I know the damn drill."* Before giving myself up, I made another sweeping gaze through the darkness surrounding me. I smiled. There was something about being in *this* world. It was nice and pleasant. Peaceful and relaxing. Calm and easy.

And weak as shit!

I could really do some things here.

Some really bad things.

Heinous, fucked up things…

Unfortunately, now was not the time.

The pulling came again. *"Stop it!"* I yelled in a rough, seething tone. I swear, sometimes I felt like a bug under a microscope—my every move being observed and documented. *"I'm leaving, dammit!"* I yelled out again. There was no use in arguing. It was time to go.

…to let myself go…

Raising both arms, as if surrendering to the cops after a long foot chase, I closed my eyes and let my body drift into nothingness, giving myself up almost obediently, without a struggle. Again, I knew the drill. I just wasn't strong enough to fight back.

Again, not yet.

There came a silence. And I could feel the space between *this* world and *myself,* separating. I felt myself melting further away, further and further still.

Until I was no longer… *'me'*…

Something suddenly came over me as though an ominous underlying spirit had just left my body.

I could feel myself being somehow…unchained; I felt…*free*…

As though *my* prison cell had been opened…

The darkness melted away and gave way to a brightness that seemed to hit me all at once, blinding me.

Spotlighting me.

The harsh brightness stung my eyes as I staggered and brought my hands to my face. I looked around. People were staring at me, wide-eyed, their mouths opened. Some got up from their tables and ran out. The rest stayed, but were backing away from me. Approximately fifteen employees in white uniforms and black bowties were watching me carefully.

Cautiously.

I can't explain it, but I felt more out of place here than ever before. I worriedly surveyed the room. I saw that our table had been somehow overturned. Our meal was scattered everywhere; to my left, the bottle of *Dom Perignon* had been shattered, as were the glasses. It was at that moment when I spotted Linda lying on the floor. She had her legs tucked underneath her body, half clothed, bloodied, looking extremely fragile and vulnerable.

Like she had been…*attacked*…

Someone had beaten her, badly.

A flush of compassion, of sorrow, perspiration and excessive rage washed over me. *Who could have done this to her?*

Linda stared up at me.

Disbelievingly.

Like there was a monster in the room.

Her emotional state looked even worse than her physical appearance.

Gripping her left side with strands of her hair clinging damply to her neck and face, she began scooting away from me, as though she was still under imminent danger. As though someone was still posing a serious threat to her well-being. I saw her chest rise and fall almost painfully as she glared up at me, shivering, trembling uncontrollably.

Something flickered in her eyes. Or maybe it was the expression that crossed her face, because her eyes widened as she looked at me.

Pitifully.

Like a wounded fawn.

And I was a ravenous predator.

I watched as a thin line of blood zigzagged down one side of her forehead. I wanted to reach out and comfort her. My heart was wrenching; I took a step towards her, extending my hand.

Almost instantly Linda flinched, drawing into herself, sheltering herself.

From me.

I looked at my hand and noticed that there was blood on it. On both hands.

That's when it hit me.

Tears flooded my eyes.

I realized that the reason Linda was lying on the floor all beaten and bloodied—*afraid of me*—was because *I* was the one who had done this to her…

CHAPTER THIRTEEN

'Unknown Variables'

No! I would not think about that now, I wouldn't start the morning with ideas on how to patch things up with Linda. There were too many other things to deal with: questions, doubts, fears, paranoia.

I sat at my kitchen table, gripping a glass of Crown Royal tightly like it was my only salvation; I was totally drained by the events of the other evening. I could not shake my apprehension. *What went wrong with me that night? How could I have done such a thing to Linda? I don't remember doing anything. How? And what about all the other things? The crows at my window? That bathroom incident in Michigan? What if these things were somehow connected? What if someone was secretly drugging me?*

I found myself frowning. *Could someone be hiding out and actually drugging me? And I wouldn't realize this until it was too late?*

My mind went back and forth as I tried to gain perspective. *No one was there or I would have seen them.*

Right?

Right?

The longer I sat there, the faster my imagination spun out of control. I took another pull of Crown, and caught a glimpse of my right hand.

It was still swollen from when I had struck Linda. I don't recall how she even made it home. Someone had probably called her an Uber. Most likely an ambulance. One thing was for sure: there was no power on earth that was going to convince her to let me take her home.

She wouldn't even look at me.

Who could blame her?

Hell—I wouldn't look at me!

Up to this point no police had come to pay me a visit. Neither had any complaints come from the restaurant. Hopefully things would stay that way.

At least until I could figure this thing out…

Once again I stared at my hand, nearly in shock. *I'd struck Linda…* Losing her was a horrendous thought. *How could I do such a thing to her and then not remember any of it?*

My brain was too fried to think about it.

About anything.

Fighting the urge to scream, definitely planning on getting roaring, stinking drunk—*seriously fucked up!*—I drew a deep breath and lowered my head.

"Dear God, Almighty," I said aloud. "Please tell me what's wrong with me. Please tell me I'm not losing it. Please, God, please tell me…"

CHAPTER FOURTEEN
'Crossroads'

Nearly a month had gone by, and Linda wouldn't accept any texts or calls from me. She even kept her voicemail filled so I couldn't leave a message. She eventually blocked my number. I didn't dare try to visit her. All of this made my days useless and uneventful, more than depressing; it was like I was kept alive with only the hopes of dying.

I might as well stick a knife in my chest or lodge a bullet in my brain. Somehow it seemed fitting. All my life I had so much pride and so little to be proud of. It was as if I'd been born with too many egos and now, it seemed, they were conspiring to destroy me. Had I been slapped in the face or kicked in the ass for my arrogance earlier in life, I might have scampered off into a corner and licked my wounds and turned out to be a better man, but I wasn't.

And now, it appeared, I was paying the price.

I thought of this as I hopped on the 9:50am flight to Las Vegas. It might have seemed a bit extreme, but I didn't have a handle on my life, and I was going stir crazy thinking about Linda.

And about me.

Approximately four hours later, the plane touched down. Thursday afternoon, it was seventy-six degrees at the airport in Las Vegas, and the dry heat emanating off the concrete felt soothing. I carried a light jacket in one hand, a single travel bag in the other. I had an

Uber take me to the Bellagio Hotel where I had reserved myself a nice room. Once inside, I took quick inventory: clean, a king-size bed, a lounge chair, air-conditioned, spacious. Microwave. Fridge. Coffee maker. The typical shit you'd expect for two-fifty a night.

I placed my jacket and travel bag in the lounge chair then flopped out on the king-size bed, staring up at the ceiling. Fuck the magnificent view I had. As I laid there, I felt stupid. *Flying nearly four hours— over fifteen hundred miles, dammit!—only to discover I was still dead on the inside. It was a long trip just to feel like shit.*

After an hour or so, I rose from the bed and took a long shower. I checked the time: 2:43pm. Las Vegas time. Instead of hitting the Vegas strip I decided to just remain in my room. I turned on the television, mainly for distraction, and surfed the channels. *HBO, ShowTime, Starz, Paramount plus, Cinema Max, ESPN*—there wasn't anything on I wanted to see.

I turned off the television and decided I needed something to take the edge off. *A shot of alcohol would do nicely.* I'd been on a drinking binge for a few days now, getting roaring, shit-faced drunk. Nearly nonstop. I thought better of it then said, *fuck it, I might as well.* I got dressed, but not only in clean clothes, I put on some *new* clothes. A silk shirt in a deep shade of blue I'd picked up while in Michigan. A pair of dark blue pants I'd been saving. A nice, little hookup.

For that special occasion with Linda.

Like I was ever going to have a special occasion with her now. I nearly laughed. *What did I think? That she was going to say that all is forgiven?*

For all I know, she didn't know if I were alive or even cared if I wasn't. I was completely fucked, and had been from the first moment I'd laid eyes on her. She was pure and innocent and I was filthy and no good.

It wouldn't have worked out in the end.

Face it, Linda was out of my league. I'd tried, and failed. Miserably. Fell flat on my damn face. *Hard!* Bump this! It was time to get roaring, stinkin', 'wake-up-and-not-know-where-the-hell-you-were' drunk!

Again!

I headed for the door. As I reached for the silver handle, my phone began to ring. I glanced at the display and stopped dead in my tracks. I couldn't believe my eyes.

It was Linda…

I turned and slowly took a seat on the bed. After the third ring I wondered if I should answer it. Or even if I *could* answer it. I was nervous, ashamed…and a bit scared. This was something I'd never expected when it came to Linda. Not ever.

And yet, I was.

Nevertheless, I answered. "Hello, Linda."

"Hello…" A long pause followed; it was like she didn't know what to say.

I couldn't blame her one bit. I felt like shit. I drew a few deep breaths to steady myself, to concentrate on breathing. I wet my dry lips. "Are you…okay?"

"No, I am not," she said tightly.

"I…I understand."

"Oh, really?" Hostility dripped from her voice. "What exactly do you understand? I'd like to hear it."

Though no one could see me, I shrugged hopelessly. *How do you answer that?* I swallowed hard, and said, "I guess, I guess I really don't understand anything, Linda. I don't know what's going on with me. All I know is I'm not the man you think I am. I would never hit a woman."

Like the cut of a chainsaw, she scoffed bitterly, "Oh, but you hit me, though. Hard. Several times. You even kicked me when I was on my knees. For a man who claims he would never hit a woman you really whupped my ass good. Even…even worse than my former boyfriend." She paused, then sniffed. "Why…why do men treat me so bad? Huh? What in the hell did I do to deserve this? Will somebody please, *please,* tell me. That's all I want to know…"

That statement.

That heartfelt plea.

It couldn't have hurt me more if somebody would have reached out and pressed a hot iron straight into my eyes.

"You hurt me, Derrick," she continued, "you hurt me really bad. But the hurt goes way deeper than the physical pain you caused me. You hurt my soul. My heart. The heart I gave you. That night, you literally crushed it under your shoes. You damaged me, Derrick, and I don't think I'll ever be the same. Do you know how that makes me feel? Do you have a fucking clue to what you have done to me?"

I stared blankly.

I did.

And I'm sure Linda knew this, too, what she'd meant about being damaged. She had helped me through so much. And I told her this. Many times.

"I'm so, so sorry, baby," I whispered tenderly. "Can we somehow put this thing behind us and start all over?" I knew the instant the words were out of my mouth that it was the wrong thing to say.

"Oh, that would be *so* easy to do, wouldn't it?" she snapped. "Show out, kick my ass all up and down in a restaurant for nearly a minute, and then try to force-fuck me afterwards—then say, 'Hey, baby, how's 'bout givin' a nigga a pass on this one, okay?'" She lost her temper. "Motherfucker, you are *damn* lucky that I don't press charges against your ass! You need to be sitting in a fucking jail cell right now!"

She was so right...

All I could do was close my eyes and take my medicine. Drawing a deep breath, I sighed and said it plainly, "You're right, Linda, I should be in jail after what I have done to you. I know...I know you must hate me now..."

"I don't," she said. "I don't *hate* you, Derrick."

I felt tears welling in my eyes. "You don't?"

"No." A pause. "I just know I can't be with you ever again."

"I...I understand," I said, my tone filled with regret, tears pooling in my eyes. "I messed things up with you, Linda. Big time. There's no other way to put it."

"Yes, yes, you did, Derrick..." Another pause, longer. "Maybe...maybe we can revisit things after you get some help. After you've talked with the proper people...if they're still any out there. Even then, I...I just don't know..."

With those words I found myself grinning stupidly, feeling hopeful—thinking maybe there just *might* be a chance of me winning her back. But there lay the problem: *How does one get help if one doesn't know where to even start?*

Whatever it was—wherever it was to be found—I'd do my very best to find it. *This* is what I promised Linda before we ended our conversation. I felt so much better just to know there was a chance to patch things up with her. A dim light at the end of *some* tunnel.

My spirits were renewed—soaring. It was simple: *Find out the real deal—fix myself.*

Not just cover it up.

Because I knew, all too well, that something was seriously wrong with me, on the *inside,* and I couldn't just apply a fresh coat of paint over rotting wood. That wouldn't cut it. Because whatever it was, it would eventually resurface again...

A series of knocks along with a voice announcing, "Housekeeping" woke me from a deep sleep. I scrubbed a hand down my face before I slid out of bed. The knocks came louder, more insistent.

"Hold on! I'm coming!" I barked. Stifling a fierce yawn, I walked heavily across the floor and peered through the peephole.

Judging by the gray-white outfit I could make out, it was definitely housekeeping, probably bringing the fresh towels that I requested. I checked the time: 2:15 am. *Why was housekeeping here so early?*

Though clothed only in boxers I made sure I was decent. I fumbled with the deadbolt and then cracked the door a few inches, and felt whiffs of cool air from the outside hitting my face. There was a dark-skinned woman standing just outside my door with a cleaning cart behind her.

"Good morning, sir, housekeeping," she smiled.

I nodded and opened the door. "Good morning," I said. "I really don't need my room cleaned. I just needed some extra towels."

"Won't take but a second to do both," she offered. "Unless you have company?"

Yawning slightly, I shook my head. "No, it's just me."

"Well?" She then peered at me defiantly over a set of rectangular square-lens glasses, snapping on a pair of latex gloves. It was like I couldn't say *"no"* even if I wanted to. And somehow, it was as if she *knew* this, too.

She was right.

I couldn't.

"Okay, you win," I sighed. "Please, come in."

With a curt nod, she stepped inside pulling a large cleaning cart behind her—filled with every cleaning product known to mankind, which shifted off-centered as the cart bounced along. There were also towels of all sizes, thin bars of wrapped soap and tiny bottles of shampoo, conditioner, and lotion. There were other things on the cart that I couldn't quite make out.

I slipped on a pair of jeans and took a seat in the lounge chair. "Do I need to step out?"

"No, sir, not at all," she smiled. "I can easily work around you." Her smile was a pleasant surprise.

"Okay," I said. "Have at it." I made myself a cup of coffee and watched the woman as she began cleaning the room. She was a short woman, around 5' 2", on the plump side. She looked to be of Haitian descent, like my great grandmother, with a semi-strong accent, but her English was pretty good.

It was hard to tell whether she was in her fifties or sixties, the judging even more difficult because of her complexion which was dark and smooth, like a Hershey chocolate bar. The roots of her hair were starting to show whispers of gray, but the rest was black as midnight in tiny micro-braids.

I watched as she moved with the efficiency of a well-oiled machine, intent on keeping her word. Surprisingly, she had a wonderful singing voice, finding joy in the simplest things. At every turn I smelled sweet cocoa butter coming off her body. I remembered Mama always wearing cocoa butter, saying she got it from her mother, and so on, and at times I caught Melody wearing it. I guess it was a generational thing.

After twenty minutes, before I could make myself another cup of coffee, she was nearly done—fresh linen and all; she peered at me while holding a handful of fresh towels.

"So, tell me, young man, are you going to be with us much longer?" she asked.

"I gotta about two more days left," I said.

"That's great. Have you had a chance to see all the wonderful sites Las Vegas has to offer? The shows? The nightlife? The casinos and restaurants?"

I smiled in spite of myself. "Actually, I've been cooped up in this room since I got here two days ago. I haven't set foot outside of this hotel. I just been ordering my food from the restaurant downstairs, via room service."

Raising a brow and propping a hand to her hip, she said, "Really? Las Vegas is sin city, young man, something for everyone. What about the pretty girls?"

I shrugged a shoulder. "What about 'em?"

"You don't like the pretty Las Vegas girls here? Again, there's something here for everyone." With that, the woman looked at me with a weird smirk. I noticed she had a repertoire of mannerisms, including one where she repeatedly cocked her left brow, like a question mark fallen sideways, and secondly, she twisted her mouth to one side when she wanted an answer to a question.

I looked back at her. "Not interested in any of these pretty Las Vegas girls. Not in the least." I caught myself. "And *no*—I'm not gay."

There was that brow-thing again, rising behind her glasses. "Never said you were."

"Good, because I'm not."

She laughed. "I really don't care either way. Your sexual preference is none of my business. Hey, I'm just an old cleaning lady, trying to make a living." She walked over to the bed. "Mind if I sit down? I've been traveling since early evening, nonstop, and I'm a bit tired."

I chuckled. "Have at it. I just had fresh sheets installed." Curious, I asked, "It's not even three in the morning. Why are you cleaning rooms this late at night? Or should I say, this early in the morning?"

She smiled. "I'm on a strange schedule. I go as needed. I saw your request for service, so here I am."

I thought it odd but smiled back anyway.

Doing a slow spin like a fashion model on a runway, she raised her short body and caught the edge of the bed with her big butt. "My name is Aphelia," she said warmly. "And what's yours, if you don't mind me asking?"

"Derrick. Derrick Archer," I replied. I stood up from the lounge chair and shook her hand. "Pleased to meet you, Aphelia."

"Same here." The brow thing again. "So, tell me something, Mr. Derrick Archer...what's a fine-looking young man doing in Las Vegas, all by himself, and not trying to have none of this fun?"

I lowered my head and then raised it again. Not sure *why* I was even here. I simply said, "I just needed to get away. Too much stuff going on in my life right now."

"Where are you from, Mr. Derrick Archer?"

Sighing heavily, I said, "Chicago, Illinois, the windy city."

For some reason my response brought a huge smile to her face. "Yes, I have been to Chicago Illinois numerous times, visiting my granddaughter. Although since she came to stay with us, her other family, I have not been there in over five years now."

I scoffed. "Well, you ain't missin' nothing."

She chuckled. "Oh, I am sure there's still a few good reasons for me to go back there again."

Once again I sighed and shook my head in frustration. "Good luck on your visit. As for me, personally, I'm not looking forward to going back. Some real messed up stuff has been going on back there."

Slowly, demonstrating a genuine concern, she leaned back on the bed, propped an elbow, and rested her head in her palm. "Care to talk about it, Mr. Derrick Archer?"

It was my turn to cock a brow. "So, what's this? You're a cleaning woman/therapist now?"

She nodded. "I'm a little bit of everything, Mr. Derrick Archer. You don't live to be my age without a little diversity. Now, tell me, what is troubling you, because that expression on your face looks awful."

Instead of saying anything I was stricken by a sharp pang of grief—a vision—as I thought of Linda. The longer I thought of her, the more my skin seemed to burn. *The things I'd done to her. The things she'd told me I'd done to her: A swollen face. A black eye. A split lip. Bruises, cuts, and scratches nearly everywhere on her body. A bruised rib. I had also pulled out chunks of her hair…*

Tears welled in my eyes. "I've done some very bad things," I whispered, releasing a stream of tears. "To someone that I love so much, that means so much to me."

"Like what?" a gentle voice came back at me.

I blinked rapidly, shedding more tears. "I hit her. No, hey, let's be real, I beat her up pretty damn bad. But the thing is…for the life of me, I…I don't remember doing this. I can't recall laying a single finger on her."

"If you don't mind me asking, Mr. Derrick Archer, do you do drugs?' the woman asked.

"No," I said, still confused. "Not really. I mean, I am a heavy drinker and I used to dabble with a little bit of weed and cocaine every now and then with the guys, but all of that stopped—*everything*—once I met Linda. I just can't figure out what could have sent me into a blacken rage to beat her the way I did."

"I didn't think you had a drug problem, Mr. Derrick Archer," she said. "You carry yourself too proud, too erect, and your body is strong and solid."

"Unfortunately, my mind isn't." With that, I grunted, rose from the lounge chair and began pacing the room.

"How deep does this thing go, Mr. Derrick Archer, if you don't mind me prying?"

"Believe me, you don't want to know," I sighed.

"Try me."

Chewing my bottom lip, I hesitated. *Should I? How would this woman react? Would she scream and then high-tail-it from the room? Who knows? Maybe it would help things, to talk it out with somebody...*

I stared at this woman.

This cleaning therapist.

She seemed genuinely interested, more concerned than anything, about my dilemma. I had faith in good people, and it seemed she was. Besides, I had to tell someone about the severe drama going on in my life.

This *thing* seemed unbeatable.

Finally, regarding this woman as my therapist, I explained everything that had been happening to me. From the very beginning.

The ringing of bells in my ears.

The strange sensations that followed.

The black crows at my windows.

A presence in the bathroom.

The unexplainable assault on Linda.

As I continuously paced the room, the woman's eyes followed me. Every step. Every turn and gesture that I made. I could *feel* it.

"Something unnatural is happening to you, Mr. Derrick Archer," she finally whispered.

I stopped dead in my tracks. It was as if the words had penetrated the darkness I was lost in. That horrible darkness...riveted with thoughts and pain and an explosion of wild screams I hadn't mentioned.

I suddenly felt a hand on my shoulder.

It was firm.

It was the cleaning woman, Aphelia.

Warm, strong fingers soon followed and caressed my neck, my cheek, and dabbed the moisture from my face and forehead. From my eyes. I felt my insides overloading and suddenly I began to weep, almost uncontrollably.

Finally, the day had come. I'd lost it. In front of a perfect stranger...

"No! No!" I heard myself screaming. Terror began stabbing through me. I felt myself shaking all over, sinking deeper into depression, with no way out.

"Shh, there, there," the woman breathed, still stroking my face and forehead, because it was probably all she could do. But it seemed to help. Like I was gradually swimming closer to full consciousness. Placing a hand to the small of my back, she escorted me to the edge of bed and carefully laid me back, grabbing my ankles and swinging my legs onto the bed.

"Lie still," she whispered, gently applying a cool, damp hand towel to my face and neck. It was unexplainable, but I felt a great relief wash over me. I suddenly felt exhausted, could barely keep my eyes open.

All I could remember hearing as I drifted off, were the words, "The help you seek, Mr. Derrick Archer, is here now. I believe I know what has happened to you…"

CHAPTER FIFTEEN

PART TWO

'Not Yet...'

Hell to heaven *then back to hell.*

My personal hell.

That was certainly a unique way to describe what I had been through I thought as the plane touched down at Chicago International Airport.

During my last day in Vegas, Aphelia, the cleaning woman and subbing therapist, had sat me down and told me...*things. Bone-chilling things.* Things that were both crazy and made perfectly good sense. *If that makes sense!* It left my head spinning. I was disoriented, in another world.

But the bottom line was I didn't know what to believe, which was okay with me. I could just shut everything out and hope for the best. Unfortunately, though, I had no choice in the matter. At some point I was going to have to face the reality of what was happening to me and deal it.

But not now.

I was not going to think about it now.

The stuff that I'd experienced—the terror, panic, questions, Linda, decisions—all were going to have to be put on hold until later, *dammit!* Just for a few days! Until then, I wasn't going to think about shit else—nothing except taking care of *me*, and working—go out there and do my best to wow the world! Or, at the bare minimum, spend some quality time with Melody and her two kids, to really get to know my little niece and nephew.

It seemed now more than ever, that I needed to be next to family. What little I had.

As I held on to that view firmly, I retrieved my travel bag from the overhead bin. I slung my jacket over my shoulder and exited the plane.

I was soon standing where I had started from, in the airport terminal, back in Chicago, amongst a multitude of people, millions. That *hurry, hurry, hurry* atmosphere of the city was undeniable. And to tell it, there was no place in this world I'd rather be.

For no reason at all, I found myself smiling brightly as I headed for long-term parking, to retrieve my SUV. I made my way to the escalator and descended to the main parking level. I headed to the exit doors when I realized there was a light ringing in the air.

Sleigh Bells...

This time it appeared quickly; there was no build up. *Shit!* I whipped around, inadvertently clearing a circle in the crowd around me with my travel bag. I looked around crazily—to my left, right, behind me, in front of me. From the corner of my eye, I caught a glimpse of my startled expression in one of the glass doors.

I looked wild and dazed. Like a madman gone over the edge...

But there was something else. In the air, approximately ten feet away, above me; it was a dark mist of some kind—a cloud, thin and wispy—advancing slowly towards me, steadily shifting, changing shapes every second or so, dispersing and reforming.

My heart threatened to pound its way out of my chest. I turned and saw the elevators, and made a mad dash to get inside one of them, only to find none of them available.

Apparently I was too late; everyone around the elevators appeared to be walking away and soon the area was clear. That is, I *thought* the area was clear. I felt a tug, as I turned and headed for the stairs.

Something was holding my arm.

Fiercely!

"Let go of me," I winced. It was all I could do to keep the panic out of my voice. Instinctively, I jerked my arm free and took a few defensive steps away until my back hit a wall. I soon felt a slick coolness in the air. It was the dark, feathering mist hovering over me. Left with no place to go, I held up my travel bag like a shield. The mist soon turned the color of black coffee as it floated down toward me.

My stomach dropped all the way to my feet. I looked around and spotted an elevator door opening. *I saw my chance!* With every instinct I possessed shrieking at me—telling me to *MOVE!*—I tucked my travel bag under my arm like a football and made a mad dash. I literally leaped inside the elevator just as the doors closed—tumbling to the ground like I'd been tackled. I gathered myself and leaned against the back of the elevator.

"You okay, sir?" a short Black woman with a deep scowl, asked. With her hands on her hip, she looked at me as though I was crazy, like I was having a nervous breakdown. Which just so happen I was having.

Sweating profusely, all I could do was look up. "I am now, ma'am," I gasped. "Thank for you kindly for asking."

Throwing my head back, I drew a deep breath and decided to stay put. Sitting right there on my ass. I couldn't rise to my feet anyway. I was frozen stiff with fear—still rattled and recovering from previous *things*. I stared blankly, thinking I'd been caught by total surprise on this one. This made me realize a few things: I could not allow myself to become relaxed and complacent. Not for a single moment. A single second. Secondly, I had to be aware of the sights and sounds which brought terror into my life at a moment's whim.

Starting with those ominous *Sleigh Bells*.

And lastly, it was Aphelia; I had to adhere to everything she had said. No matter how crazy it sounded. It was clear now that I needed to. Because I did *not* have a handle on this thing.

No matter how confident I felt.

In the soft lights on my bathroom mirror, my image disturbed me: dark circles under bloodshot eyes. Skin a bit slack and gaunt, a serious shave needed. I was use to a reflection that could make most women drool: handsome good looks, nice skin tone, a great smile. Now the person looking back at me seemed like a stranger, a man on the verge of turning into a zombie.

Until all this shit happened, I never believed the old sayings about dark spirits, other worlds, demonic possessions, none of that bullshit.

I believe it now.

I believe in all those things now. I believe that there are actually things that go *'bump'* in the night. I believe there just might be things hiding under the bed, or in the closet, waiting to get you while you slept, that demons do roam this world. You name it, I believe it. But I didn't have to accept it. I'd have to fight back. Find out why these things were happening to me.

As I had done with Aphelia, I began to reevaluate my life, backtrack what I had done to warrant this type of bewitching placed on me. Once again I started with my adolescence. I never did anything bad in my youth. Never hurt anyone or stole anything worth mentioning. I skipped school a few times and got into a couple of after school scuffles. Smoked a little bit of weed here and there. Talked shit with the guys and snuck out to a few parties when I shouldn't have.

But that was kid shit.

I wasn't a bully, or that weird little boy who stayed off to himself. One who liked to pull the legs off insects one by one with tweezers, then burn them to death with a magnifying glass. Again, I did normal things.

And I loved the girls.

Girls.

When it came to the girls, *any kind,* I loved them all. Lord knows I had my share. I definitely made my rounds. A few I liked, some I tolerated—the rest got the middle finger.

It was pretty much how I had treated all women, most of my life.

Was I being cursed because of this?

I could try to explain to myself that what started all this was an act of karma, but that wouldn't be quite accurate. That was more like an act of stupidity. Call it a part of growing up. Maybe even a cry for help.

Whatever, it was just me being a man.

A good-looking man who had a winning package. In every way. In every department.

But I've got to say, when I look back on my life, the way I treated and felt about women, I had to marvel at what an arrogant asshole I was. But never once had I laid a hand on a woman.

But I had with Linda…

I'm not going to deny that when it came to Linda, I got what I deserved. But the things I had done to her—it just wasn't in me—who'd ever expect something like this?

I loved that girl! And still love her!

I had a bad feeling about this, and the cold, unalterable feeling twisted my gut; it was draining me; I had very little strength in me to fight an ever-growing sense of doom, that black, malignant cloud hanging over me, and with every second that passed I found that cloud a little darker, hanging a little lower.

I couldn't help but think of a shitload of other old sayings. Cautionary proverbs: be careful what you wished for, because you just might get it. The pride goeth before a fall. The apple doesn't fall far from the tree. That lies walk on short legs. That all that glitters ain't fuckin' gold. And then there was that last one I recalled: that misfortunes seldom come alone.

Somehow all of these tied into my situation. I thought of psychics, premonitions, fortune-tellers, extra-sensory perception, reading tea leaves and the lines in the palms of your hand—it used to be all bullshit to me. But I believe it now. I wasn't even a theatrical man, giving into melodrama.

But once again, I believe it.

I believe all of it now…

CHAPTER SIXTEEN

'No Rest for The Weary'

It was Wednesday morning. I stared at the Keurig machine and decided against getting my usual third cup of coffee. I really didn't need more caffeine right now and got a bottle of water instead. I headed out the door, got into my SUV, and made my way towards a prime piece of historical property, an Oak Park home, located in an upscale part of Chicago. Well, at least the homes were upscale. Just beyond a few blocks it was rough as hell—every man for themselves.

The property was listed at nearly two million dollars. My commission would be well worth it.

At this point in my life I hated my job, truly despised it, so the thought of losing it wasn't exactly bumming me the fuck out. My mind just wasn't in it anymore. On the other hand, it wasn't as if I had a backup plan in place, and the money was great. Plus, I could pretty much set my own hours. There was no choice but to stick it out. Like Mama used to say, *'don't throw out old water until you've found new'*.

I knew what it was.

I didn't know what I wanted. My mind was all screwed up.

Half an hour later I was sitting in front of the property—a five-thousand-plus square foot Historic home, built in the early 1900's. It was a three-level home, with large windows and no shutters, white and gray-looking, all wood, old school—looking as though it belonged on a movie set from *The Amityville Horror*.

Just what the hell I needed.

I stared at the 'For Sale' sign listed in the front yard as though it were a *'Do not enter'* warning, that something sinister was waiting inside. I was grateful it was still early in the day, with plenty of sunshine beaming down, ridiculously cheerful.

Dressed in an expensive two-piece suit with a new overcoat I'd recently splurged on, I walked to the front door. After opening the lock box and retrieving the front door key, I let myself in. I closed the door and looked around. The inside was very nice, spacious, with both old and new amenities, real hardwood flooring throughout the home.

There were six bedrooms and five bathrooms. All had been updated.

But no matter how beautiful things looked on the outside as well as the inside, the place still resembled a haunted house on steroids.

Nevertheless, with the price being more than fair for the area, not to mention the scarce listings in this area, I was certain that the place would be an easy sale.

Nope.

After showing the property to what seemed like everyone and their mother, I couldn't have been more wrong. It seemed no one could secure the proper financing. This happened from time to time in the real estate industry. I was prepared for this; I was pumped full of strategies—go on the offensive: get better loan rates, better terms, offer incentives, get the seller to lower the price—whatever it took.

Until then, the home would just have to sit on the market until that moment happened.

Because the listing belonged to me, I gave the home a quick inspection. Afterwards I locked up and then got into my SUV and drove away. Over the weeks I kept myself purposely busy. Between the gym and working insane hours, I was constantly on the move. In addition, I was spending long hours, late into the night, every night, doing Internet research on my predicament.

Some of the things I found out were quite disturbing.

Like Voodoo.

Curses.

Possession.

Black Magic.

Things that Aphelia had touched on. But nothing pointed to why this was happening to me. Which did nothing but cause me sleepless nights. Some days I was running on pure fumes. A couple of times, on long, traffic-thick drives home, I almost fell asleep at the wheel.

Luckily, as though *something* or *someone* had nudged me, I was suddenly jolted awake, stopping myself at the last second from veering into the lane of oncoming traffic or slamming into the car in front of me.

For this I was thankful.

I was also thankful for something else.

Nothing *strange* had happened to me lately. For nearly a month. I was beginning to think the worst was over.

Hopefully it was.

But I knew I couldn't drop my guard.

Not for a second.

CHAPTER SEVENTEEN

'Whispers Of Warnings...'

I spent the better part of my day in the office, working the phones, so to say. I had a nice little cubicle near the back of the building with a decent street-level view of the outdoors. Leaning back in my chair with my cell phone clamped to my ear, I worked on my real estate leads, touching base with several potential clients. A big part of my job was listening to their problems, both real and exaggerated, therapist-style, which was a bit nerve racking considering I had my own problems to deal with.

Most of the time all I heard was pure bullshit.

I sifted through a few more leads when I got a call that someone was very interested in seeing the large Historical home, which had been sitting on the market now for nearly three months. The only drawback was they needed to see the property first thing in the morning, and a pipe had burst in the kitchen and the place still needed to be cleaned up. I checked the time: 4:48pm.

I leaned back in my chair. *Maybe I could stop by the place and tidy things up a bit if needed.*

By it being mid-April the days were still somewhat short, and it was quickly getting dark. I decided to make my move and drove as fast as I could over to the property. In less than an hour I arrived and pulled in front of the house, where I found myself staring at the 'For Sale' sign on the front lawn—still looking as if it were brandishing a gun at me—telling me to 'keep the fuck away'.

Was this an omen? I thought.

As the shadows of the evening melted the fading afternoon light, I got out of my SUV and noticed that the air had grown chilly. I purposefully avoided looking at the 'For Sale' sign as I opened the front door and hurried inside. I immediately locked the door behind me. I turned, and the aroma of pine-scented disinfectant hit me like a ton of bricks, brutally assaulting my nostrils.

Flicking on a light switch, I glanced around. The place was clean and tidy, pretty much as I remembered the last time I was here. I went into the kitchen and found this area also neat and tidy. Apparently, the pipe issue had been dealt with.

After going through the entire house and finding everything presentable, I decided to call it a day. Or night. Depending on how you look at things. I headed for the door and was suddenly halted in my tracks. I drew a deep breath, exhaled slowly, and glanced around—remaining still and deeply uneasy.

Something *odd* was in the air, gradually mounting and gaining strength, as if seeping from the walls both above and below, into a cascading avalanche. I heard a sound. It was a strange, eerie sound. A *gurgle-sputter-hiss*—like water backing up in a sink.

It came from the kitchen.

Rushing into the kitchen, I checked out the sink. Which was double-sided. There was no sound to be heard. Certain it was coming from the sink I turned on one of the faucets to check the water pressure. No water came out. I tried the other side, to no effect. That's when the watery noise returned.

Again, above me.

Around me.

Below me.

The character of the sound had changed, no longer a *gurgle-sputter-hiss*, but now more like a faraway raging babble of an angry, destructive river. Approaching closer with every passing second.

For reasons I couldn't explain, I tried turning on both faucets—hoping somehow it would alleviate things. It didn't. In fact, it seemed as if it only made things worse; I could feel the pressure of *something* coming.

That's when I heard it.

Sleigh Bells.

Hundreds of them.

Thousands or maybe millions of them.

Loudly.

I thought my brain was about to shatter. I covered my ears with my hands but to no avail; the *Sleigh Bells* were brutal and unmerciful. In spite of the sounds plaguing me, I thought I detected a voice mingling in the air. It was low, gravely—less than human—spewing out not-quite-decipherable words as if they were gobs of thick phlegm.

Yet, I did manage to make out the words: "*You...you...you...*"

Sweat drenched my forehead, and I immediately made a tight fist with my right hand—ready to swing at the first thing I saw—human or not. I began easing away from the kitchen and made my way to the front door, which seemed a mile away. The garbled voice followed me, my every step.

"*You...you...*"

The words sounded not only *creepy* but infinitely strange, imperial, nearly demanding. It reminded me of something...someone...

Could it be...?

No. It couldn't be... My imagination began to ease away from me. *What I was hearing couldn't be—*

I shook my head.

It was nothing.

Nothing but ordinary hallucinations.

Delusional fatigue.

Made-up bullshit.

With every passing second, the sluggish, distorted words spoken into the air became clearer, "*You...you...*"

But I blocked them out still not quite following the meaning. In my frustration I banged my fist against the wall, and I was surprised to hear myself emit a half-stifled cry of desperation. I needed to pull myself together. After all, as terrifying as the voice was, it appeared to represent no real threat to me.

Did it?

Even as I posed that question to myself, I was overcome by the conviction that I must not listen to the voice seeping into my ears, my head—that somehow, I would be in mortal danger if I understood even one word of what was being said to me. Yet, as crazy as it was, I still strained to listen, to wring clarity from the muddled voice.

"You..."

That one word was undeniably clear.

"You...will..."

The hideous, mucus-clotted voice was speaking somewhat clearer.

"You...will...never..."

The voice appeared to be drawing closer. Coming toward me like skittering crabs. Seeking contact.

Something about the voice was...*damaged, enraged.*

Slowly, gradually, the same way it came, the voice began fading away, drifting into nothingness. The ringing of the *Sleigh Bells* soon followed. The strength of the raging water also dissipated into a free-flowing swirl, leaving the house completely silent, leaving me standing there, alone, with a blank expression on my face.

I couldn't explain it but the experience left my insides shriveled, yet, aware and on full alert. I knew it wasn't over. *Something* was still here. *Resetting itself, ready to come at me again. Even harder, perhaps for good.* Knowing I was about to be in for the fight of my life, I readied myself with balled fists.

But something told me I wasn't going to win, that if I wanted to survive, what I had to do was make it to the front door and run. That I would only be safe then. And that's just what I did. I turned and bolted out of the door, somehow remembering to place the key back into the lockbox. Afterwards, I jumped into my SUV. My palms sweating, I started it up and sped away—stomping and mashing on the gas pedal as if it were a scurrying cockroach.

To keep from hitting a row of parked vehicles, I grabbed the wheel with both slippery hands and pulled roughly to my left, missing them with only a few inches to spare—so close that I expected to hear the tearing of sheet metal. I swerved around a few more cars and then I went for broke—punching the gas pedal and taking off like a launched rocket.

The only sounds were the rumble of the engine, the hum of the tires, my ragged breathing, and the pounding of my heart. I took a peek in the rearview mirror. Though it was no longer in my view, there was *something* about that house. I had the strangest feeling that I would come back to it.

Whether I wanted to or not.

CHAPTER EIGHTEEN

'Deadly Embrace'

"*Are you okay,* Mr. Derrick Archer?" asked Aphelia, over the phone, desperately worried.

As I checked the last door lock to my townhome, I answered with my cell phone pressed tightly to my ear, "I believe I am now." Fear and urgency had made my alcohol-induced voice both slurry and shaky. I took a seat on the sofa, in the living room.

"So, tell me, what happened this time, Mr. Derrick Archer," Aphelia demanded mildly.

I drew a haggard breath, and said, "Along with those freakin' sleigh bells, there were watery sounds coming from the walls and then a voice appeared from out of nowhere." My own words scared the shit out of me and I turned my head sharply, as if I heard something. Just outside my living room window.

"What kind of voice was it?" asked Aphelia.

"I really couldn't tell you. It was distorted, sort of muffled and cloudy."

"Was it a man's or woman's voice?"

"I honestly don't know."

"It's very important that you try to think. Now, was it a man or woman? Take a serious guess." There was an urgency in her voice.

I took a quick pull of Crown Royal to wet my lips, to calm my nerves. "If I had to guess, I'd say it was a woman's voice, but husky like a man's."

"I see..." A long pause followed.

I felt my stomach clench. *Why does this not sound like good news?*

"Why? Why does the sound of a voice matter?" I said hurriedly, to keep Aphelia talking to ease the out-of-control beating of my heart.

Ignoring my question, Aphelia instead asked, "How long were you seeing the woman you were dating, Mr. Derrick Archer? This Linda woman?"

I swallowed. "Not very long. A few months, maybe. In fact, we were celebrating our three-month anniversary of being together."

Another long pause. "Do you trust this woman?"

"What do you mean?"

"Do you think she would hurt you? Bring harm to you in some way?"

"Like how?" I cradled my glass of Crown and brought it to my chest. I felt nauseated, dizzy.

"I asked this because it's become very obvious that you have been cursed by something…by someone."

"By Linda?" I gasped, cold sweat drenching me in waves. I cradled the glass tighter against my chest. "I find that extremely hard to believe. Linda is such a sweet, innocent person. I couldn't see her hurting me. Or anyone, for that matter."

"The same could be said for you, Mr. Derrick Archer, yet you brought hurt to her. Serious hurt from what you've told me."

"Yea, yea, I did…" I babbled, shutting my eyes tightly.

"Hell hath no fury like a woman scorned. Have you heard that saying before, Mr. Derrick Archer?"

I blew out a deep sigh. "I have. But I just can't believe Linda would do such a thing. I mean, I didn't scorn or push her away, not in any kind of way."

"Has there been anyone else that you may have scorned or ticked off in your travels? It's very important that you try to remember."

With those words I glanced around the living room—going through the women in my life like a mental rolodex.

"Think, Mr. Derrick Archer," prodded Aphelia, "think hard. Your very life may depend upon you remembering."

I did try, and in the process, I discovered to my surprise that my posture had changed; my body was in the same position as before, but my muscles seemed to have tensed.

That's when it hit me.

Janet!

Almost instantly my stomach cramped.

Janet…

I was positive. The way things had ended between us—the look in her eyes that said I couldn't outrun them.

As I sat there on the sofa, ice-cold terror shot through my veins. But being terrified wouldn't help me. Calm, clear thinking probably wouldn't, either. But it was all I had, so I fought back the terror and went with the calm-and-clear thing. *Maybe it wasn't her. Maybe it was actually a man's voice that I heard. Or something not even human. Maybe it was an alien. A being from another planet. Another dimension.*

I drew a deep breath, thinking furiously all the while. Coming up to one conclusion: Janet.

It had to be her...Janet...Janet...yes, Janet...

I wasn't sure—but it seemed by me just *thinking* her name something weird was beginning to happen. I could actually *feel* a hand trailing my cheek. I was positive she was here—sitting next to me—looking at me. I felt myself cringing, resisting her attempts to lay her hand over mine. As if on cue, as though I knew it would happen, my hand was gripped tightly, almost brutally—in a vise, steadily tightening. I snatched my hand away, sending my glass of Crown flying across the room.

It was so unexpected!

"Mr. Derrick Archer, are you okay?" a voice came back to me over my phone.

It was Aphelia.

I couldn't answer. My voice had locked up.

That's when I caught wind of a chilling sound.

Sleigh Bells.

I hurled the phone across the room and covered my ears. The ringing bore down hard on my shoulders. All of a sudden, like the wind had shifted, the ringing stopped. I looked around and then caught sight of my hand.

The one that had been touched…

Without warning the tightening came again, harder, and the knuckles of my fingers started turning beet-red and blood began to swell at the fingertips. The pressure became unbearable and I could feel my entire hand starting to become brittle, crumbling. At the same time the seething voice emerged once more.

"…You…will…never…be…hers…"

All I could do was jerk and pull at my hand and scream at the top of lungs. And that's exactly what I did; I screamed and screamed and screamed, until my voice nearly gave out.

"…You…will…never…be…hers…"

It was my last coherent thought.

From out of nowhere I was struck violently across the face, then my head, and felt my body falling to the floor—seemingly landing into the murky embrace of a swampy mud pit. Gradually, in slow stages, I could feel myself, my very soul, sinking, being pulled under.

Further and further. Deeper and deeper. Until everything went black…

CHAPTER NINETEEN
'A Small, Well-Deserved Victory'

As I sat in the booth inside Manny's, a small deli cafeteria near downtown, I wondered why I had chosen this place. Why was I even here? One glance at my hand as well as the pounding in my head told me the reason. It was terror. I needed to be around people. I felt safe here. My townhouse no longer provided the peace and security that I needed.

But was it just my townhouse?

Everywhere I went, I seemed unable to escape this unexplainable presence and influence. Another 'visit', another terrifying 'calling'—this repetition of madness—and it would be over for me. It was like I was on a sinister treadmill that I couldn't get off because I didn't know how to—that it would only stop when my heart stopped beating.

I sat there staring out the window, stirring my coffee with my spoon, the occasional *ping* of the spoon striking the sides of the cup putting me into a hypnotizing trance. The morning sky was beautiful, delicate and graceful in both composition and color, so unlike the *ugliness* going on inside of me.

Which seemed to be getting uglier and more of a struggle by the second. Hard and merciless. If it were possible for it to get any worse, it would. I could feel it coming.

...for me...

I checked the time on my phone: 10:45am. Aphelia would be calling me soon.

Hopefully.

I really needed to hear her voice. Now more than ever. She understood my predicament. It was obvious what the trouble was: I was cursed. *Marked*, as she called it. Either way, I wouldn't have to constantly explain my predicament to her, and for that I was more than grateful.

Somehow, it seemed as if she had a grip on this thing. At least outwardly. She appeared self-controlled, deliberate, and quietly obsessive on helping me through my situation. She was never impulsive, combative, or volatile, like me.

Another difference was Aphelia knew when to discard things where I held on to *everything*. She told me to forget about Linda, at least for the moment. She knew I was still in love with her, and that would be a huge inconvenience right about now.

A serious hinderance.

And she was right.

I needed to stay focused, to listen to everything she had to say. I guess we were a team now—we needed to question and challenge everything going on around me—even each other, if need be; we needed to weed out what wasn't solid or didn't fit, until only the truth remained.

Even if I might not like the truth.

I sat straight up in bed.

Even though it was 3am, when I was usually out for the count, I was sleeping roughly in my room at the Holiday Inn Express, just outside the city. Maybe I had been dreaming, having my usual round of nightmares, or maybe I was waking up and my imagination had subconsciously gone on a journey.

To another world, maybe?

Either way, I was all messed up.

Bottom line: I was afraid. Scared shitless. That's why I chose to stay here. I was afraid of my townhouse.

Whatever this thing was it knew where I lived.

Where to find me.

I made an effort to control my breathing so I could sleep. I'd been waking up a lot like this lately, feeling all tight inside, out of breath. I tried my version of mental discipline to ease the tension, getting tough with myself. *Stop worrying, you big pussy, you and Aphelia are going to figure this thing out! Man up, fool!*

It didn't work.

I fell back on the bed with my eyes wide open.

In a few days Aphelia will be by my side. To help me. For this I was extremely relieved. I drew a deep breath and felt I was breathing okay now. I tried to relax, even though I was sure *something* had awoken me. It felt like a gentle presence, lightly irritating me, perhaps keeping me from sleeping. I told myself it might have been anything.

Or nothing at all.

Slowly, I drifted back to sleep. Back to my safe place. Once again, not sure when, I was awakened by something. Something soft, probably a moth, had brushed my forehead, and I swiped at it with my right hand, not really expecting to make contact with anything. Wearing nothing but boxers I slid out of bed and walked over to my third-floor window; I parted the curtains and peered out into almost total blackness.

For some reason the parking lot lights weren't on. A sliver of moon provided the only light in the parking lot below. Otherwise, there was no movement of light or shadows. I rubbed my eyes giving them a minute or so to adjust, and then I peered through the parted curtains once more—still thinking it was strange to see no parking lot lights anywhere.

I figured, *so what,* I didn't need light, since I was hiding out like a chicken-shit mushroom in a dark motel room, and being in this dark room, I wasn't afraid of light giving me away. *Besides, why was I even worrying about this? I was safe. There wasn't anything outside that could get me…*

An odd sensation came over me; beads of sweat began forming and trickled down my bare chest and back. Not giving in to this strangeness, I made myself relax and let weariness close in on me again.

Everything's gonna be okay, I told myself. *Just fine. So, calm down, all right? Aphelia will be here soon. So, in the meantime, take your scary ass back to sleep, okay?* I nodded, then let the curtains fall back into place. Sighing deeply, I turned from the window and headed back to bed.

That's when I heard something.

Coming from the outside!

My eyes flew open.

There was no doubt about what I was hearing. It was the unmistakable ringing of *Sleigh Bells.* Very faintly. Just outside my window. Adopting a low crouch, I crept back to the window and peered out; I shifted my weight and glanced in all directions over the sill. That's when I spotted a black four-door sedan.

A Crown Victoria.

A police-looking car.

Very old, from the early seventies, pulling into the parking lot. Faint moonlight glimmered off the hood and fender. Along with the car being lowered a few inches, I could see that all the windows had been blackened out. From my point of view, it looked like a phantom image floating on air.

Sinister looking.

It was like the car didn't belong here, not in this parking lot. Not in this time period.

...not in this world...

Another sound!

It might have been a car door opening and shutting, as boldly as possible. I peered closer, and my heart started racing.

Somebody had just gotten out of that Crown Vic, all right.

I spotted something easing away from the car and then looking up at my third-floor window. *A late-night guest, maybe?* It was hard to make out but the person didn't resemble *a person.* It was more of a reptilian creature that somehow learned to walk upright. It stood as erect as a man, wearing tattered clothing, rags, dusty with holes everywhere.

The frame was black and rail-thin, intimidating yet fragile-looking—as if everything *evil* had been sutured together—genetically flawed. I saw the head leaning to one side, shifting and bobbling, as if the neck had been broken.

It was a horrendous sight which stole my breath. A hideous *thin-thing*—both terrifying and less than human. From what I could tell the narrow torso had been gutted open, and the intestines were sliding about as it moved. Each step caused more bubbles of entrails to burst in its guts.

I could only stare in horror.

In the vague, grayish light, I saw the head sling upward and toward me. I could see its eyes; the yellow-red brilliance shimmered in the sockets. Flickering. With a blood-sodden body wearing makeshift clothing—looking like a lone, forgotten scarecrow in a cornfield, it stood stiff and stared up at me with a bizarre, festering hatred. I couldn't see a face—it was deleted, erased, completely wiped away—there were no facial features to be found.

Just eyes...

I watched as the gaunt-like creature pointed a finger in my direction.

Straight at me.

It shrieked with murderous disgust as wisps of smoke rose around its frame.

We stared at each other, in a heart-freezing confrontation, and my breathing became labored.

I knew it had come to kill me...

With its tethered clothing flapping in the breeze, it moved from sight, just out of my view; I saw that the ground had been stained with blood, which resembled slow-expanding puddles of spilled oil. Piercing the night and echoing off the window, I could hear a wet, guttural snarl.

It was coming for me!

Shaking, weak-kneed, I slowly backpedaled away from the window to where my jeans were wadded up on a chair. I hurriedly slipped into them, then yanked a dark blue hoodie over my head. I thought about going barefoot, then changed my mind and took the time to work my feet, sockless, into a pair of sneakers. Hot sweat was pouring off me, stinging the corners of my eyes.

I had to get the fuck out of here.

I picked up my travel bag from off the floor and held it in my left hand while I dug out my key fob from my jean pocket with my right. I walked over to the door and threw back the security latch and then the deadbolt. Very cautiously, I pushed down on the silver door handle and with a trembling hand, I slowly pulled the door open a few inches.

Sultry hallway air flowed into my face, carrying the fetid stench of a backed-up sewer. *It was near!* I knew. Yet I could see nothing outside but an empty hallway. I glanced to my right. To my left.

No movement out there.

But the putrid smell appeared terrifyingly close. Growing closer still. I had to make a move. I heard a door being opened down the hall. *Maybe it was just a guest getting some ice, or a late-night snack. Something like that. Then again, maybe not...*

For a brief second I thought maybe I was dreaming all of this. Or perhaps my mind was just playing tricks on me. Maybe the stress of being dog-ass tired had finally gotten me the best of me. Had me worked up over nothing.

Seeing things.

Hearing things.

Once again, maybe not...

Either way, I wasn't about to go back to sleep! I was getting the hell outta here!

I stepped all the way outside the door, into the hallway, moving cautiously with every step. My breathing was temporarily put on hold as I made my way to the stairwell. Fuck that fuckin' elevator. Holding the key fob to my SUV tightly in my hand, I flung my travel bag over my shoulder and slowly opened the stairwell door. Sweat coated my face as I began creeping down the stairs. I ran into an enthusiastic couple making out in the stairwell, the woman pressed tight against the wall and making gasping sounds.

Y'all better fuckin' run! I wanted to tell them.

Edging around the young couple, I made it to the ground floor and grabbed the door handle—squeezing it so hard I felt it digging into my flesh. In my left hand, I still held my key fob tightly.

I noticed the smell wasn't as strong as before.

Maybe the creature was at my room, on the third floor, already kicking the fuckin' door in and searching for me—pissed off that I wasn't there.

That was it!

I had outwitted that damn thing!

Like a bolt of lightning I opened the stairwell door and headed for the first exit door I saw. I punched through it and ran like my life depended on it. I made it to within fifty feet of my SUV, then used the key fob to unlock the doors. A dim light came on inside. I straightened up and moved faster, not worrying now about the *Sleigh Bells* ringing even louder in my ears. I opened the door, threw my travel bag inside, and swung myself up behind the steering wheel.

Wham!

A powerful thud hit the hood of the SUV like a huge cinder block. What it was I couldn't begin to tell you. I peered out of the side window and soon saw what it was. An air conditioning unit. Torn from the wall and then heaved out the third-floor window.

From my room.

I reeled back even as I reached forward to hit the ignition button. *Sleigh Bells* began ringing out of control all around me, and the stench of the creature began punishing my nostrils.

Ignoring all of it, I slammed the shift selector into reverse, twisted the steering wheel, then stomped on the gas. Tires screeched as the SUV did a 180-degree spin. The SUV stopped and was still rocking as I rammed the selector into drive and headed—pedal to the fuckin' metal—for the exit leading to the main road. The engine roared as I hunched over the steering wheel—as I gripped it with sweat-coated hands. About half a mile down the road, something made a loud *clunk* on the right side of my SUV. A panel being struck. Like a brick had been thrown at it.

Only I knew it hadn't been a brick.

There was a vehicle beside me.

It was the black Crown Victoria. Dangerously close and looking like something straight out of a nightmare. I looked over and all I could see through the tinted window was a pair of red glowing eyes.

Jesus, help me! It was that hideous-looking creature!

I made a quick, screeching U-turn and my right foot mashed down on the accelerator even harder. The engine roared violently. *This damn thing could really move!* I thought as I felt myself being pressed backward in my seat. I hadn't a clue as to where I was going but knew I had to keep on driving.

Like a bullet I surged forward, into unknown territory. The Crown Vic held its ground, hanging with me, not letting up. My SUV took several bangs as the

Crown Vic tried to run me off the road. I pounded the accelerator as my SUV roared and sped along. The Crown Vic fell back a bit but seemed to be moving closer, darting from side to side, driving hard to keep pace.

Within a mile or so I saw what I needed, a small, blue and white sign indicating a turnoff ahead. As I blew by it, I couldn't read what it said but I put light pressure on the brake pedal, getting ready.

Then there it was on my left, an opening to a side street. It wasn't much more than a narrow strip, but enough of a road to make my escape. Just enough. I yanked the steering wheel hard to the left and the SUV leaned hard and went up on two wheels. Then it dropped back perfectly onto the narrow road. As soon as I straightened it out, the road became rough and unpredictable, full of potholes, bumps and dips. The SUV got tossed around; I felt the top of my head hitting the headliner.

But this is what I needed. The kind of road where I could go but a low-slung car couldn't. The bumpier the better.

Nevertheless, there was still a pair of headlights in my rearview mirror. The road began to wind, seemingly moving in closer on either side. But I didn't lose control of the SUV, or my head. I was learning a lot about my driving skills. I could become a regular badass when I wanted to.

I clenched my teeth and followed the SUV's headlight beams, tromping harder on the accelerator when I came to a straight stretch of road. The SUV responded as if it were alive and born for the challenge. I continuously picked up more speed and momentum as I surged forward. The ringing of the *Sleigh Bells* as well as the Crown Victoria were still present but were flitting this way and that way in the darkness, and were soon well behind me now.

There was nothing ahead but dark road, all smooth, and soon I came upon the faint white lines flickering away into the night, on the pavement. Which meant the road had become civilized, widening and opening its arms for me meaning freedom was here.

After a while, I chanced a glance in the rearview mirror and saw only a pair of fading headlights. Which may or may not be the Crown Vic's.

A few seconds later I looked again and saw only blackness.

I backed off a bit on the accelerator, driving more carefully. My breathing was ragged, and my heart was beating as if it might break through a rib. I knew I wasn't free from my curse, but *dammit*, I couldn't help but let out a loud whoop as I pounded the steering wheel! I'd shaken that hideous, scarecrow-looking motherfucker!

Dust in the wind, bitch!

But even in the midst of personal victory, I could only shake my head and sigh. This incident only showed me how worse things were really getting. How much they were steadily progressing.

That the worst was yet to come…

CHAPTER TWENTY

'Struggling To Stay Hopeful'

Too many close calls.

After arriving to Chicago, Aphelia waited outside the airport terminal, standing off to herself. It wasn't long before I picked up her in my SUV, and then we immediately hit the interstate, heading to a destination that Aphelia had suggested. A place where we could regroup and plan. Hopefully it will be a safe place.

For some strange reason there was no address to this destination. I had to check with Aphelia every now and then for updates and directions. According to her, there was about seventy-five miles left to go, then we'd be just shy of the meet up point, the rendezvous, located somewhere in Lexington Kentucky. The plan was to stop there, make contact with someone that Aphelia trusted, then all three of us would head back to Chicago.

The place where it had all started.

Realizing all of this was bit too much to ask from a woman that I barely knew, I tried over and over to convince Aphelia that this was my problem. Not hers.

Aphelia wouldn't hear me.

She would not allow me to go on living—surviving—in such horrific circumstances. It wasn't right. Not when she might have a solution to my dilemma. She claimed she had one. But it would take more than just her. She had an associate, a man named Danial, from somewhere she never mentioned, who claimed he had intense knowledge of my curse—and had assessed and assured her that he could help in some way.

Hopefully...

As I drove I couldn't help but notice the big ass dent in my hood, not to mention the ones on the passenger side. How could I explain this to the insurance adjuster? I couldn't. He'd never believe me if I told him the truth anyway. I can see it now: *"Well, you see, Mr. Insurance Adjuster, it's like this: I was being chased by some phantom creature that was driving a car, an old Ford Crown Victoria—who was out to kill me because of a curse that I've been plagued with. Why, I couldn't begin to tell you. Anyway, he, she, or whatever it was, was trying to run me off the road, but thank God, I did manage to get away. In the process of making my escape...well, as you can see, this is what's left of the SUV..."*

The end results: the insurance adjuster would look at me crazy, like I had lost my damn mind—probably thinking I was strung out on some kind of drugs. I had to shake my head; I even chuckled.

Then I grew serious.

Very serious.

I thought about the hideous-looking creature pursuing me. *What was that damn thing? Why was it after me? Why was it so hellbent on killing me? What did I do?* Deep shivers went through me and I shook my head; I had to block it out! I gripped the steering wheel tightly, hunching over the wheel, flexing my fingers as I drove ten-and-two. My mind then drifted to this Danial guy.

What if he couldn't help me? What would become of me then? Would my life end up with me running from something I couldn't outrun?

I could only hope and pray that this man *could* help me. As it stood, I didn't know how long I could go on—looking over my shoulders, peeping around corners, afraid to sleep, jumping hysterically at every little sound—leery of the shadows around me.

Even my own.

Lord, let there be a solution...

Still driving ten-and-two, still gripping the steering wheel as if my life depended on it, I continued down the interstate. I had to use the restroom, badly, but I wouldn't stop. Instead, I turned south, as Aphelia suggested, then I would turn off at an exit in approximately twenty-two miles, then skirt around some back roads and by then we should be there, just before dark.

I gripped the steering wheel even tighter.

Danial better be waiting for me!

It wasn't supposed to intrigue me; but it did. This wasn't what I expected. There was no denying that I was blown away by what I was seeing. And it made me wonder, *did this stuff really work?*

In the kitchen sitting at a small table, I watched this guy, Danial, our contact, as he mixed an array of powders together in a large bowl. Dressed in beige khakis with a matching top, he was tall, slim, hard-muscled, hard-faced, with a dark complexion, sixty-eight years old, ten years older than Aphelia, who I just learned was his wife. His eyes were his most arresting feature.

Cold.

Black.

Humorless.

I saw that his hands were enormous as he poured a green liquid into the bowl. He began stirring the liquid and powder together. The mingled scents of exotic spices hung in the air. He then took a small tree branch, the size of a man's arm, and broke it in half. Taking out a large sharp knife holstered at his side, he began sharpening one end of the branch. Once done, he started sanding the branch. I could tell he enjoyed this part. With the aid of his knife, he steadily used more and more finely-grained sandpaper as he shaped the end into a gradual, tapered point.

For almost an hour he sanded the rest of the branch, idly chanting and meditating, humming to himself. The rhythmic sound of the sandpaper on wood was slowing as the branch took shape in his hands. It resembled something akin to a miniature spear when he was done. An oversized dagger. Smooth and sleek.

"Hand me the flask," he grunted at Aphelia, who sat at the table beside him—dressed in a large black dress which covered her body. Her hair was wrapped in an orange turban. Smiling warmly, she handed him the small leather flask. It was obvious that she loved and admired her husband. However, the same couldn't be said for his feelings towards her. At least outwardly. He seemed to harbor powerful and complex feelings for her, but he gave no indication that he felt anything except companionship.

Now, his assistant.

He also seemed to harbor nothing but contempt for the rest of the world. Not once since arriving at the well-kept, very old stucco home, had I seen him smile. I could tell he was a very serious and driven man.

And I'm not going to lie; this is what I needed to see. Somebody who was dead set on helping me with my situation.

I watched as he poured the green-black liquid into the flask. Sitting the bowl down, he looked over at me. His eyes were chilly as ever. "Drink some of this," he said.

I sat up straight. His voice was direct and clearer than it had been since I met him—since he first began to use his strange talent for creating this concoction. He claimed it would gradually strengthen me, rid my body of spiritual contamination, and provide my soul with sharper insight. I swallowed nervously as I rose from my seat at the table. Taking the flask with shaky hands, I nodded. I raised the flask to my lips, saw what looked like vapors around the rim, thought about what I was about to do, and placed it back on the table.

Seeking reassurance, I looked over at Aphelia. In response she nodded with a smile, telling me to trust in her, her husband, the process.

Should I? I wondered. I looked deep in Aphelia's eyes—the same for Danial's, her husband. In hers I saw an earnest truthfulness, so convincing that perhaps she'd made a believer of me. In him, I saw a sense of urgency, that time was being wasted.

Precious time.

He carried the look of a man with a deranged mind yet with a brilliance of the unknown. Almost immediately I began to panic. *He knew something that nobody dared to tell me!* Once again, I shook it off and then peered down at the flask.

"Drink it," he demanded. "Drink it now."

With those words I felt my heart sink. I slumped back into my seat. I took several deep breaths—forcing myself to relax—to regroup my sanity. For some strange reason I knew the choice was clear, without hesitation or doubt, virtually without thinking about it another second.

I needed to drink it.

I glanced over at the two people who were watching me very intently. Aphelia and Danial. Especially Danial. Who was extremely impressionable. As well as knowledgeable.

He believed in strange powers. In this strange concoction I was being asked to drink. And I could also see that the events of my situation had left a haunted look on his face.

In his dark eyes.

That the worst was yet to come.

There was no other choice.

I had to drink it.

There was no other way out of this thing.

CHAPTER TWENTY-ONE

'Here To Help'

A few days had gone by.

It was getting late as Danial, Aphelia, and myself sat at the kitchen table, in my townhouse. Danial, always dressed in beige khakis, looked directly into my eyes as he explained to me: some people—people whose lives have been affected in some terrible, unspeakable way—keep it all inside, they bury their secrets, hide the pain, the whole cliché. They seek refuge, shelter, relief, some kind of way to help them cope, live, and deal with whatever it is that they are going through.

And I was no different.

At times I chose to walk the mean streets alone. I'd grab a bottle of Crown Royal, rum, gin, or whatever, and drown my sorrows—discussing my problems with no one. Not very macho; kind of solo-bitch-like, but there you have it.

I stayed silent as Danial spoke. When he got to the point about curses, my curse, in particular, I let out a small groan and closed my eyes and kept them shut for a very long time. When I finally opened them, I asked, "What's the next step for me?"

"We wait," Danial said, his voice deep and strong.

"For what?"

"For your tormentor to make a move."

I thought about it, shaking my head in worry and disbelief. "That could be days, weeks, months."

Danial appeared unfazed. "I know this," he said. "But we have no choice. I must see—firsthand—what we are up against. Only then can I plan a strategy."

I sighed. "And what if you can't come up with a plan? A strategy. What then?"

"We will, Mr. Derrick Archer," Aphelia chimed in as she peered over her rectangular reading glasses. "We most certainly will. You must believe this."

With those words all three of us went silent. My mind, usually so active, was numb, as it had been for a while lately. I just didn't understand what was going on. I wondered how these two people could explain things to me so that I would understand. I stayed still, waiting. Finally, I asked Danial, "Do you believe we can beat this thing? Or should I say, *me?*"

He nodded stoically as he pressed the palms of his hands together, steepling them. "We can. But first we must determine how deep your curse goes. If what you have told me is true, I'd say you're about mid-point in your crisis."

My eyes immediately bucked. *Mid-point? Fuckin' mid-point!* I tilted back in my chair as though the words were jabs at my chin. *What in the hell did that mean?*

I had to ask. "What exactly is 'mid-point'? And what happens after that?" I turned and saw Aphelia's eyes getting misty.

"We will cross that bridge when we get to it," Danial said firmly. "I need to understand just what we are dealing with; how strong this curse is. Once that has been revealed, we'll talk about it then. Otherwise, we're wasting our time speculating, okay?" He pinched the bridge of his nose with his thumb and forefinger. "I'm tired." He stood up from the table and left the kitchen, saying he needed to rest.

I sat back in my chair, nodding slowly. "Okay. Rest easy, Danial, sir, and thank you for everything."

"It's going to be all right, Mr. Derrick Archer," smiled Aphelia as she placed her hand over mine, also rising from the table. When I looked over at her I saw tears streaking her cheeks. "It's going to be all right," she repeated in a whisper.

All I could do was nod as she left the kitchen. Leaving me alone. Alone with my thoughts. With my chin in my palm, I sighed heavily and stared out the window. "Jesus," I muttered.

Why me? What did I do?

I felt myself losing it.

Again.

Deep breaths, I told myself. *In and out. In and out. That's it. Slow and easy. Horrible as this thing is, you're still alive.*

I thought about calling Linda, just to hear her voice. At the very least, her voicemail recording. I wondered if she was still blocking my calls. Probably was. Once again, I sighed, heavily; I wanted to cry; just break the fuck down and cry like a baby. But I wouldn't. I couldn't. I reminded myself once more, as horrible as this thing was, nobody had died or been seriously hurt.

Except Linda…

But I was sure she was on the mend. For that I was more than grateful. But there was something that kept nagging at me; I knew—*felt it*—that there was more to this thing. Something *far*…and in a sense, *very close.*

Something I was overlooking…

CHAPTER TWENTY-TWO

'A Mother's Love'

Approximately three days passed and nothing eventful had happened. Though I remained restless, constantly on edge, Aphelia remained cool, calm, and upbeat—and with Danial—*ready!* I wondered how they could do it—this wasn't even their problem!

I watched them every morning, before the day started, how both would meet in the living room. They would bow deeply, facing each other, as they fell into their customary roles: Danial led, Aphelia followed. They started with meditation. Both loved meditating, as I intently witnessed. Each would sit in the lotus position, palms tilted up, hands resting on knees, back straight, breathing through their noses—forcing the air down, letting their abdomens do all the work.

I tried doing this in the privacy of my bedroom, thinking it might help things. But I couldn't quite get the hang of it. My mind, even during less chaotic times, wandered. I got fidgety. I guess this just wasn't my thing. Focusing, breathing properly, while in your zone. I liked the gym better. Running the treadmill all out for thirty minutes straight. It was the most tiring activity in the world. Don't believe it? Try it, just five minutes. You'll see.

While Danial and Aphelia were doing their thing in the living room, I sat at the kitchen table drinking my coffee.

It was Tuesday, and the morning sun speckled the floor as well as my face with drops of sunlight. At times it stung my eyes; I didn't seem to mind. It felt good. I stared out the window. An hour to kill before I started my day with Danial and Aphelia by my side. My two-week vacation from my job was quickly ending. I had about a week left. I'd probably put in for more time. Another week at the most.

But what then?

What if this shit lasted for months? For years?

I didn't want to think about it.

I didn't want to think about anything.

No, way too much of that already.

I wanted to just sit here and let the sun melt over me. For some reason I thought about rich people. *Did they have the same problems as poor people? What really went on behind the walls of those mansions?* I shook my head and let out a deep sigh.

Again, too much thinking...

I stared out the window for a long time without registering anything. About half an hour went by and suddenly I felt a strange sensation coming over me. A light flutter, dancing and flickering over my face, around my eyes and ears.

Like a moth.

I'd felt this before. When I was awakened at the Holiday Inn Express motel. Just before encountering the thin, man-like creature.

I thought it strange.

This flickering and fluttering.

Eventually the sensation went away, as quick as it came. Once again I peered out the window, staring out at the morning ahead of me. Particularly at the trees and the birds. That's when my vision blurred, my eyes reflecting on another image, creating a visual echo of something, *someone,* I could not make out.

Finally, I could. Nearly knocking over my coffee, I sat upright in my seat.

It couldn't be, is it?

But it was…

…it was her…

Wednesday had come and gone without incident, nothing happening. It was in the wee hours of Thursday morning when the sound of *Sleigh Bells* blew me out of my sleep like a shotgun blast! My hands clamped over my ears until I thought I would squeeze my head in. My heart pounded heavily in my chest, and I screamed out in agony.

At the very top of my lungs.

But oddly, I couldn't hear the sound of my voice. Not a trace of it. I knew I was screaming but it was as if I were screaming on the *inside.*

Then, as though things were steadily compounding, I discovered that everything inside me had seized up. My entire body was frozen. I managed to move my head and noticed that the *Sleigh Bells* had suddenly fallen silent. Leaving the room also silent. Motionless and still. Like a bright moon in a dark sky.

It was more than unnerving.

The only sound now was the steady echo of footsteps that were approaching my bedroom door. Just *outside* the door. Sharp and direct. Shoes against cool marble—walking through an old museum at night. Since my vocal cords were useless along with the rest of my body, I couldn't move or yell out for help.

I stared at the bedroom door.

...footsteps coming closer...

Whatever the cause of it, I was certain it wasn't the Sleep Fairy about to throw pixie dust into my eyes to coax me back to sleep, nor was it Danial or Aphelia coming to check in on me.

Something *evil* was close at hand.

Something unimaginable.

It always was...

Somehow, I slowly managed to move and eased from the bed, all the while keeping an eye on the door. A choice was facing me. Walk over to the door and open it—confront whatever it was head on. See if it's anything at all. End this bullshit right here and now!

Like I was receiving a slight nudge in the back, I took a step towards the door. Then another. To my dismay, my body had once more seized up; I couldn't move.

Lord help me…

I said this, but again the words formed without sound. Then suddenly all around me, the *Sleigh Bells* returned—full volume—and blasted relentlessly in my ears. Even louder than before. Like never before. I became disoriented, yet I could feel things happening.

To my left, beside my bed, the drawer of the nightstand was snatched open by *something*. Slammed shut. Snatched open. Slammed shut. Snatched open. The next time it shut, it stayed that way. That's when I spotted my cell phone resting on top of the nightstand. *Something* was drawing my attention toward it.

Use it!

Use it now!

Somehow my body unlocked and then in a rush, I grabbed my cell phone and called Aphelia. I found a voice and yelled for help. Afterwards I threw the phone aside. I took a step toward the door. Unexpectedly, it swung open as if urging me to leave—then a second later it crashed shut as if a strong gust of wind had closed it. It opened and closed itself repeatedly, as though a tug-of-war was going on.

I backed against a wall, afraid to move.

"Mr. Derrick Archer!"

Aphelia and Danial were on the other side of the door, briefly visible as it swung open. They were staring at me, in shock. I pried myself from the wall and reached out for them.

The door closed with even greater power than it had before—flew open, shut, open, shut.

Danial tried to come in as the door opened again, but it slammed in his face. The next time it opened he wedged a foot at the bottom, threw his entire weight on the door, and forced his way inside.

The door stopped moving.

That's when something like a hissing shadow seeped inside the bedroom, through the door, through the walls. The ceiling. Almost immediately I could feel a warm, muggy draft. It hung in the air like wet laundry and carried the undeniable stench of a swamp. It was a smell I remembered, both consciously and subconsciously, and probably would never forget for as long as I lived.

Not ever.

However, I was shocked to hear the drone of insects: biting flies, mosquitoes, crickets—again, things from a swamp.

Between the overwhelming stench as well as the incessant insect noises, things around me became ominously *evil*. I could only hold my breath as I gazed around me.

Bouncing from wall to wall, floor to ceiling, I saw a dark silhouette of a person flashing and darting around me. Without warning I was slammed in the chest—*hard!*—which sent me flying across the room into another wall. I'd just had the wind knocked out of me. Afterward I slumped to the floor like a crumpled ragdoll. Slowly, still dazed, I pushed up on my knees and crawled toward the open door.

"Derrick!" I heard Danial yelling out. "Above you!"

I looked up, only to hear something flapping over my head like a wind-tossed flag. I didn't wait to see what it was; I crawled even faster towards the door. Which suddenly slammed shut. I looked around me in a frantic state. I heard something swooping down and then that's when it happened; my neck was encased by a pair of strong arms; I was twisted—my spine bending in a way it was never supposed to. My head was violently jerked back and my legs went splaying in mid-air from underneath me.

Somehow I managed to squirm out of it and instantly felt relief. I coughed, wheezed, waited a few seconds, then pulled myself into a corner. *Something* was watching me. I could *feel* it. Frantically, I looked up, down, left, right. All around me.

Nothing.

Yet *something* stood in the shadows.

I saw it.

A silhouette.

Once more fear overtook me and locked me in place as the room became stock-still. Seconds later I heard that unearthly voice again.

"You…will…never…have…her…"

"Who…who are you?" I asked.

Nothing.

"Who are you?" I repeated. In some way, by some miracle, my body began loosening up. My breathing was easier too, more controlled. I opened my mouth and looked over at Danial, who nodded his head, urging me to go on.

Once again, I wet my lips and continued, "Who are you? Please, tell me. What do you want…?"

"You…will…never…have…her…"

Not sure of what to say or do, I slowly rose to my feet.

"You…will…never…have…her…"

I felt my hands balling tightly into a fist. *Enough is enough!* My blood was seething with anger and began to boil. "Who are you, dammit!" I demanded. "I'm sick of this cat-and-mouse bullshit!" I felt myself becoming bolder. "Go fuck with someone else, you hear me! Cause I ain't afraid of you!"

Wrong thing to say, I knew, *but hey…*

It was.

Like a ton of bricks something came crashing down violently over my head. The pain was so intense that my knees hit the floor. Soon afterwards I felt a kick in my stomach which sent me into a retching rage. A pair of hands immediately seized me—tugging and yanking on me, in several directions—stretching my body out—trying to pull me apart. Then like a punching bag, I felt my body being pummeled by vicious blows—uppercuts, jabs, hooks, sucker punches—raining down on me—unyielding, mercilessly. I begged it to stop.

It wouldn't.

The blows kept coming harder, relentlessly. I felt another kick to my ribs, then my stomach. Several more. I tried to shield myself but something had snatched my head back so hard that I thought my neck was about to snap. I honestly thought I was about to die.

But then I felt something put itself between me and the blows. Like a shield. But it was pulled away so the beating could continue. For what seemed like hours I experienced pain from nearly everywhere on my body. I could feel myself about to blackout.

Suddenly the blows came to an end.

As though a wall had been erected.

A stronger shield.

"It...is...over..." a kinder, gentler voice announced, seemingly from above.

It was at that moment when I experienced a strange, baffling sensation melting over me. I soon felt a hand. Cradling and touching my face softly. Stroking my cheek.

"It...is...over..." the voice came once more.

Swallowing hard I looked up and saw a pair of silhouettes hovering over me, near the ceiling, peering down, as if deciding my fate, then both vanished into the darkness, each going in separate directions, leaving the room, once more, eerily quiet.

Bruised, battered, aching everywhere, I raised up on my knees, clutching my sides and my stomach. Pain was searing all over me. Yet I did experience a wave of relief that I couldn't explain; it was like something had set me free; like something had come to save me, when I could no longer save myself.

I looked around and saw my chance.

In a maddening rush I rose from the floor and bolted from the bedroom. Once outside the room I collapsed to my knees, desperately blocking out the pain as well as the hellish experience I'd just been through. The one I had somehow survived.

I found myself breathing shallow; it hurt trying to breathe any other way. At the same time, as my ribs throbbed, pulsated, and ached, I recalled a peculiar feeling that I had experienced.

A certain wall that had been erected.

Then there was that *other* voice.

The kinder, gentler one. The softer one....

I compared it to the vision that had come to me earlier, while sitting at the kitchen table.

*It was her...*I uttered. For reasons I couldn't explain, I became overwhelmed with emotion.

It was her! It was her!

I tried holding it in. Tried hard not to give in to my rising emotions. *Dammit, I tried—continuously! I tried with everything in me! With all my might!*

But I couldn't stop it...

I began to shed tears. Which soon blossomed into deep, bone-wrenching cries, full-body sobs. Just when I thought I couldn't cry anymore, something came over me and touched me. As before it was a kind, gentle touch.

A soft, warm touch.

The touch of a mother…

"It's you, isn't it, Mama…?" I spoke in a light whisper. "It…it *is* you, Mama. I…I *know* it is. I can *feel* it. I can feel *you*. You…you came to see me earlier. And…and it was you who just saved me now. Wasn't it, Mama?"

Though no answer came, there was nothing in the world to convince me that it wasn't. Slowly, as a hand trailed my cheek, I found I could breathe a little easier. I even managed a smile. It was a faint smile. But a smile, nevertheless.

"You…will…be…hers…" were the last words that I heard before the warmness finally vanished.

Realizing it was Mama—*and it was!*—I cried and sobbed without pause or letup. This time around, my voice was no longer contained and bottled up inside of me. In the midst of my cries, my sobbing, I heard my voice coming through loud and clear.

Both on the inside as well as the outside…

CHAPTER TWENTY-THREE
'A Jogged Memory'

After opening the door, Melody gave me a hug which lingered well past 'brother-sister' status, I felt, and then she led me inside her home, straight into her kitchen, where I leaned against the wall. Her dog Saber came trotting into the kitchen closely behind us. Surprisingly, he gave me a slight nuzzle with his nose. He then looked up at me with dark, searching eyes, seemingly understanding something wasn't right with me.

Or maybe it was...

I could only stare back with mild curiosity. Normally the dog wouldn't come anywhere near me. After giving my hand a few licks, he collapsed by my feet and lowered his head on his front paws. I squatted down and gave him a series of pats and strokes on the top of the head. His tail wagged briefly then went limp. It was like a truce had been made.

I caught Melody smiling; it was a small but grateful smile. I wasn't sure but I thought I caught a tear before she turned away...

After fixing us both some coffee, we took our usual seats at the table.

"I haven't seen or heard from you in a long while, lil Bro," Melody said. With her hair pulled up into a bun, arms folded tightly, she sat back in her seat and looked at me with an expression I perceived as both worry and irritation.

"I know," I replied with a long sigh, frowning a bit. "And I apologize. I...I have no excuse for this."

"Is there something wrong?" she asked innocently. "Are you in some kind of trouble?"

Some kind of trouble... I sighed, this time with a chuckle. *Now that's the world's greatest understatement if I ever heard one!* I scratched my forehead with an extended finger. "You wouldn't believe me if I told you," I said.

Melody leaned over and placed a hand over mine. "What is it, Derrick? Does it have anything to do with why your car looks like it's been through hell and back?" She watched me very closely, with narrowed eyes.

"I've been cursed by something," I said bluntly. *"Marked,* more like it, at least that's what the two people waiting in my SUV parked outside call it."

Melody frowned as she sipped her coffee. "What two people? I didn't see anybody when you got out of the car."

Once more I chuckled. "Damn, girl, you better leave that weed alone. Both of them were right there with me when I pulled up. There's a lady in the front seat and a man in the back seat. I'll introduce them to you if you'd like."

Adding more sugar to her coffee, Melody shook her head defiantly. "Well, I didn't see them, and no, I don't want to meet anybody looking the way I am." She gave a stern look. "And for your information,

Bro, weed ain't got nothing to do with your eyesight. If anything, it helps it."

"If you say so." I leaned back in the chair and drummed my fingers on the table, all the while exhaling and shaking my head. "Jesus help me…," I found myself uttering.

Naturally, this brought serious concern to Melody's face. "Derrick, what in the hell is going on? You look like shit, your car looks like shit. For heaven's sake, you better tell me something."

I couldn't say anything, not just yet. I took a sip of coffee instead and closed my eyes, thinking all of this was still a dream. A nightmare. I could feel my head swelling to the levels of utter agony. Somehow I managed a smile as I shook my head. Then I opened my eyes and stopped smiling. "Something or somebody is out to get me," I whispered. "Somewhere down the line I screwed somebody over good, and now I'm paying for it. Plain and simple."

Melody looked at me curiously. "Who? Is it a woman?"

I had to shake my head with a smirk. "Of course, it is, Sis. Who the hell else?"

Melody leaned back in her chair and once more, folded her arms. Rather tightly. "Lord have mercy, what did you do this time, boy?"

"I didn't want to be with her," I shrugged, still not wanting to believe it could have kick-started all this shit. "I slept with this woman—*one time!*—and then told her simply that I didn't want to be with her."

Sighing long and deep, obviously reliving things from her own past, Melody said, "How did she take it when you said you wanted to end things?"

That caused me to scratch my head. "Surprisingly, easy. Sure, she had some foul shit to say to me, but then she seemed okay, like it was no big deal. She even gave me a parting gift, a memento of our brief time together. Go figure..."

As soon as the words left my mouth, my body went rigid; I shifted roughly in my chair and spilled a major portion of my coffee on the table. Melody had to act quickly to avoid a lap full of coffee. *"Dammit, Derrick!"* she yelled—nearly spilling hers.

"That's it," I uttered warily. "It has to be..."

"What?" she demanded. Shaking her head, she reached over and pulled out a half-dozen napkins from the holder and blotted up the spilled coffee. She rolled her eyes and then said, "What is going on here, Derrick? What *has* to be?"

"Before leaving," I began, with sweat beading up on my forehead, "this woman gave me a jewel. It was strange, small, no bigger than a pebble, but very expensive looking. It was dark but the inside seemed to glow, like there was a light in the center."

"So, where's the jewel now?"

I felt my brows furrow. Then it hit me. *It was still in my overcoat pocket where I'd placed it. Wrapped in a green handkerchief...*

I rose abruptly from my seat and looked at Melody with crazed eyes, smacking the table. Rather hard—*wham!*

As a result she choked on her coffee. "What the fuck, Derrick!" she sputtered—her tone was designed as angry but came out more like a frightened plea. "You better tell me something, dammit! You're starting to scare the living shit out of me!" Without warning she reached out and took me by the arm, as though she was suffering from the same shock as I was. I could see her chest rapidly rising and falling—dragging her blood pressure through levels of stress it wasn't designed for.

I opened my mouth to explain then hesitated. I wanted to say something but decided against it. I knew once I let the genie out of this bottle, I couldn't put it back in. Plus, I didn't know if this jewel thing meant anything at all. I thought about it. *Nope! I wouldn't say a word to Melody. Sometimes, shutting the fuck up was the best thing.*

It was enough.

I forced a timely smile on my lips to ease the situation, as well as the pressure in my chest. Including Melody's. I leaned over the table and traced a finger along her right cheek, my usual deep voice now light as a feather, "Your little brother is going to be okay. I think I've found an answer to my problem."

In response, Melody leaned back in her chair as if I'd given her a slight shove. When she recovered, she nodded her head slowly, still unsure of *anything.* "Okay, lil Bro, if you say so…" she eased out. "You call me later, you hear me? No more of this disappearing, going-ghost crap, you understand?"

I grinned with a wink. "Fosho."

She sighed. "You'd better." Then she whispered, "I love you, Derrick."

Her words, *"I love you, Derrick"* hit home like never before. I looked directly into the depths of my big sister's eyes, which were misting with tears. Soon tears came and formed rivulets on her cheeks.

Something was wrong, I could hear myself saying. *She was hiding something from me.* Slightly unnerved I stared at her. *Something was definitely wrong...* She didn't mean to cry but was powerless to prevent it. Somehow, for some strange reason, I was right there with her, feeling the exact same.

"I love you, too, Melody," I managed to ease out. I vowed to keep my emotions in check; tears welled up anyway. I was becoming a real wuss these days. I desperately wanted to tell her something about my plight but it seemed as if there was something that was much deeper on her plate than she was telling me. I also wanted to tell her that Mama had come to visit me.

To save me...

Shutting the fuck up, I reminded myself. I smiled warmly at Melody and kissed her forehead, then I bent down and gave Saber a pat on the head. Afterwards I turned from the kitchen and headed outside. That's when the strangest feeling came over me. I felt antsy, anxious. The way a young army recruit would feel before going off to fight in his first *real* battle. His first war. Or the way a person feels when they're about to embark on a long journey to the unknown. And that's exactly how I felt.

On both.

...on a long journey to do battle...

To where or who to do battle with, I hadn't the faintest idea. I just knew I would be going soon. Sometime in the near future. I didn't know if I'd even return from this journey.

I turned around only to see Melody peering at me through her living room window, through the parted blinds. *Would I ever see her again?*

I didn't know and because of this, I had to hurry to my SUV before I turned around and told Melody everything.

It was late in the evening, and Danial and Aphelia were crashed out in the adjoining bedroom. I hadn't heard a sound.

It was funny.

I never did. Not even a peep or a snore.

They were definitely sound sleepers.

I had to admit it was nice having those two around. They were like parents coming to visit. I found I could sleep better, more soundly than I'd ever slept, a strange, tranquil sleep settling over me like a welcome blanket.

I hadn't mentioned anything to them about the jewel that Janet had given me. Not yet. Earlier that day, after leaving Melody's house, I did check to see if it was still there.

It was.

However, something about the jewel had changed. It was still the same size and color but the strange glow in the middle had intensified, almost to a pinpoint of light, like a distant star. The sight unnerved me. Thinking it could burn a hole through the center of my palm—skin, bone, ligaments, nerves, and blood vessels being vaporized—I hurriedly wrapped the jewel with the handkerchief and tucked it back inside the overcoat pocket.

My first thought was to tell Danial and Aphelia about the jewel, but I hesitated. It was a big piece in this puzzle and certainly worth bringing up, yet I was curious at the same time. I wanted to see for myself if a simple jewel could cause such chaos in one's life.

My life.

Plus, I needed to prove that I could handle things myself, by myself, if need be. That I didn't require a couple of senior nurse maids to look over me like I was a little kid who constantly needed his nose wiped.

Man up, I told myself, slightly ashamed. *There is no reason to scream and cry at every little thing. Real men don't call for help without a reason. You'll be wearing bras and panties, lipstick and lace, if you don't pull yourself together!*

Nevertheless, as I lay in my bed, I felt uneasy. I stared at my bedroom door. It was closed.

I was trapped.

Claustrophobia started to set in. I wondered if I should open it. *Should I? Could something be waiting for me, on the other side?* I stared at the door, harder. *Who was standing there?* My mind went back and forth; my imagination spun out of control.

Stop it! Stiffen your backbone! I fumed, once again scolding myself. *There's nothing there! So put some steel in your balls!* I did. However, despite my thoughts, I had to get up out of bed and check things out for myself. I had to see if anything was there waiting for me, just beyond that *closed* door. Otherwise, I'd be a chicken-shit wuss for the rest of my life.

Do it, fool! I shouted at myself. *Do it now!*

I threw back the covers and crept out of bed. I moved forward, slowly at first, and then unable to control the impulse, I ran to the door, flung it open, and walked into the hallway in one big rush.

Nothing was there…

As expected, it was dark. *But, dammit to hell, nothing was here!* I found myself smiling. Hard!

I had worked myself up for nothing!

My imagination had nearly caused me to shit my boxers! *For what! Not a damn thing!*

Stifling a chuckle, thinking that I was indeed a true idiot, I decided to grab a late-night snack. I was about to head down the stairs when a hand came down on my shoulder. My knees buckled and I grabbed the rail for support. My breath was trapped in my throat. I couldn't utter a single sound. I—

"Mr. Derrick Archer, are you okay?" An arm circled my waist, supporting me. "I'm sorry if I startled you."

"Aphelia." My voice shook. "I…I didn't see you."

Aphelia carefully straightened me up. "I thought you might have been asleep. I'm so sorry," she repeated.

"It's okay," I grinned. "And it's me that should be sorry. At times I forget that you guys are here with me."

Dressed in a long burgundy duster with a burgundy bonnet over her head, always smelling like sweet cocoa butter, Aphelia smiled, "Well, since we are both up, let me fix you something to eat." As if on cue, she did her brow thing. "Are you hungry, Mr. Derrick Archer?"

I looked back at her. Just being around her was comforting, in an endearing, almost childlike way. "I am, Aphelia," I said. "Actually, I'm starved."

Smiling brightly, she patted my shoulder. "That's a good sign when your appetite is strong, Mr. Derrick Archer. It means your anxiety level is low." She tipped her head. "Now, let's go get some food for your tummy."

With those words I glanced at Aphelia. She could have been—*most likely was*—an angel sent from above to watch over me…

The rain sounded like salt pellets as it pummeled the windshield of my SUV. Off in the distance, flashes of lightning strikes streaked the dark skies. Peals of thunder added to the atmosphere. I use to like these types of storms. It reminded me of summertime nights during my childhood. The rain, the thunder and lightning, all of it made it easy to sleep. And dream. But now it could mean something else.

Something hideously terrifying.

It was late afternoon and under normal circumstances I wouldn't be out in this kind of weather. Unfortunately, I was running low on food and toiletries at my place, and with two other guests to look after I had to do what was needed. Feeling emotionally as well as physically drained, I stopped in the local Walmart and got what was needed: coffee, creamer, eggs, milk, juice, bottled water, various meats, bread, and an array of toiletries. It was funny; it seemed as though I were the only one using and eating up everything.

It was like Aphelia and Danial barely touched a thing, food or toiletries.

I loaded up everything into my SUV and headed back to my place. About halfway there, my cell phone began to ring.

It was Linda.

Without hesitation I immediately answered, and over the phone, she spoke softly, and I couldn't make out all the words. She sounded concerned. Worried. She wanted to see me.

Now, if possible.

At first I was hesitant. I was taking a chance with this solo Walmart run as it is. I'd be pushing things even further by going to see Linda. No one knew I would be heading over there. And if I had told Danial and Aphelia both would be against it—*fiercely!*

Still, something worried me. Bothered me. *Why had Linda called me out of the blue? Was she okay?*

Did she have something to tell me? Was someone holding a gun to her head?

Needless to say, my mind went everywhere—like ping pong balls in a dryer. Oddly, I thought about the weather around me—coinciding with Linda's call. It seemed…unwise…chaotic. *Was it an omen? Maybe I should wait until the storm passes. But I wanted to see Linda. Desperately! But there were too many unknown variables.*

Whatever.

I had to follow my heart and not my mind.

At least this time…

Making a sharp U-turn, I drove hard and fast to see Linda. I wanted to talk to her. Sure, we could have probably talked over the phone but I knew a phone conversation wasn't going to fix anything. I had to see her, then we'd talk. Maybe I hadn't made it clear to her about how badly I needed her.

At least I could explain to her in person that—through everything—both real and *unreal*—that I still loved her. I could only hope and pray that it wasn't too late.

As the dark, bloated sky released a deluge of rain on the windshield and all around me, I drove even faster…

CHAPTER TWENTY-FOUR
'A Well-Needed, Unhappy Moment'

Forty-five minutes later I knocked on Linda's door.

Fifteen seconds after that she opened the door, her face softening when she saw me. Dark circles framed her eyes from what I believed was lack of sleep or grief. Same as me. A mixture of sorrow and happiness battled within me.

She was there.

Standing in front of me...

She looked gorgeous. Naturally gorgeous. No makeup. Dressed in gray sweats and a sleeveless tee shirt. Her thick hair had more shine than usual, and the skin of her face glowed as if she'd just emerged from a deep, blue sea—after a refreshing plunge. Every little thing about her was staring back at me, for me to see and appreciate.

I couldn't control myself; I reached over and touched her face lightly. In response, she opened the door wider. She wasn't smiling, but her eyes told me she was pleased to see me.

"Come in."

She closed the door behind me and I took a few steps inside. Almost immediately I turned, and we embraced, breathing in deeply. She'd recently showered, the smell of soap and water, her hair still damp.

After nearly five minutes, I slowly pulled back. "How are you doing?" I asked, thinking that it was a dumb question after what she'd been through over the last few months. But I needed to talk with her, to hold her, to let her know that I was here for her, whatever she wanted or needed.

"Not good," she whispered.

"Is there anything I can do?"

"Hold me."

I did, rubbing her back with my hands. I could feel her heart beating rapidly against my chest, then slowing as she relaxed. I ran my hand absently through her hair, wishing I could take all her pain away.

She sighed in contentment, stepping back and giving me a half smile. "How you doing, Derrick?"

"Better now," I grinned tightly.

"Me too." I could see tears welling up in her eyes. She touched the side of my face, her expression full of want and desire even though she'd never admit it.

I wanted to take her, make love to her, protect her and keep her safe, under lock and key.

Time, I said, catching myself, *give her time…*

Linda wanted the same, I could tell, but like I thought, she needed time. She leaned in and kissed me lightly on the lips, then rubbed the stubble on my face. "Damn, baby, you really could use a shave."

Scrubbing a hand over my five o'clock shadow, I smirked, "I know, I know. I just haven't been taking care of the little things. Too occupied by the big ones."

Her face wilted. "Are you really okay?"

"I'm going to be fine," I said. Emotions hit me hard—like a ton of bricks. I turned away, squeezed the bridge of my nose to stop the tears. *Dammit! Why was I always crying!* I asked myself. Crying wouldn't help things, and I wouldn't allow it to happen.

Linda gently took me by the chin, forcing me to look at her. "We're going to get through this, baby," she whispered. In response I kissed her forehead, holding her tight.

"I love you, baby," I sniffed as I swallowed hard. It became too much. *I knew it...* The tears finally broke through, and Linda held me fiercely. Soon both of us were sobbing like two little kids separated from their parents. Simultaneously, we pulled back and stared into each other's eyes, thinking—*We could take away our pain for a few hours...*

...if only for a moment...

Little did she know I would take *all* her pain away if I could. Standing there, I felt myself losing control. I pulled Linda to me and kissed her hungrily, trying to slow down my urgency, but Linda wasn't accepting any of my patience.

"It's been too long." She pulled my earlobe into her mouth causing me to lose focus. *She was right! It had been too long!* I missed her every second that I couldn't be with her. I hugged her tightly then lifted her up and carried her into the bedroom. I threw her on the bed.

Almost immediately, Linda peeled off her sweats and tee shirt and threw them aside. Her panties were next. My insides burning up, I ripped off my clothes in a fury. I leaped onto the bed where Linda and I engaged in a hard, torrid grind. With tender hands, she began stroking me; I couldn't think at all.

She was right! I heard myself screaming over and over and over again—*It had been too long!*

Linda leaned back and gapped her legs—inviting me inside—begging me, and I plunged in—holding my breath as I tried to pace myself, but Linda kept moving, her hand now cradled my head as she kissed me, her tongue mimicking our urgent lovemaking.

"Oh, Derrick—"

"Linda—"

She wrapped her legs around me and arched her back, sinking me deeper. We both were coated in sweat; Linda from climaxing hard, me from trying to hold off. Her voice went up into a muffled scream, and it was all I could take. I felt everything in me being released. Afterwards we lay there breathing heavily, side by side, holding hands, staring up at the ceiling; we didn't move for quite some time. Then I leaned over and kissed her, tasting her sweat, lust, and love. I stroked her soft cheeks as I hovered over her, as she laid beneath me.

Gently, I whispered, "I promise never to hurt you—"

"Don't," she stopped me. "Don't say anything…"

"But I have to," I pleaded softly. "Baby, I need to."

"Please don't, Derrick," she sniffed. "Not until this is over." A pause. "I think...I think you should go now. Please, baby, please just go...without saying another word." Her eyes wilted, and her expression, bit by bit, became saddened, like it was melting before me.

Please, baby, she seemed to be saying, *please leave me with this moment...*

My breath snagged. I didn't want to leave the warmth of her body or the bond we were sharing, but I knew I had to respect her wishes. Sucking it up, I slowly slid away; I even managed to smile. It wasn't easy. There was no kidding myself: the fast, hot sex was *great!*—but seeing and holding Linda was even better.

Slowly, yet quickly, I got dressed. Showering was out of the question. It would just prolong things. I looked over at Linda, who was laying on her back with an arm draped over eyes and an arched knee slowly swaying back and forth.

The pain was killing me.

And obviously her.

I wanted to say something. Something meaningful. But I didn't.

I reminded myself to keep my word, as Linda had requested.

Just leave...

...without another word...

CHAPTER TWENTY-FIVE
'An Unexpected Step Closer'

8:45pm.

I drove slowly along the main street until I reached the Langham Hotel. As I approached the garage entrance, I swallowed nervously. But it was too late at this point. I'd come this far and there was no turning back.

Linda meant too much to me.

I had to know.

I soon found a spot to park my SUV. After shutting it down, I slipped an antacid tablet in my mouth. I'd been anxious from the moment I woke up this morning, and the more I thought about Linda the worse it had become.

I know I should not have come here but I *had* to. Once again, I'd magnified the situation by not telling Danial and Aphelia about my intentions or whereabouts, sneaking out while they were asleep. I even turned off my phone. Now my stomach was in a knot. I reached into my glove compartment and slid out a pint of Crown Royal from up under some papers. I screwed off the top and took a long pull, then another, and felt no remorse for doing so, then slid the bottle back into the glove compartment.

After popping a few mints into my mouth, I grabbed the door handle but didn't get out. Instead, I sat back and blankly watched as a few guests came and went. A couple of times I was almost tempted to just drive away.

But I thought about Linda—more than myself, and once that had taken hold firmly in my mind, I couldn't let it go. Although I admitted there might be a certain degree of risk—*even danger!*—I had to see this through.

I never felt more positive of something in my life. Still, I hesitated, struggling with myself. I finally shook off the shivers and exited the vehicle. Dressed in dark blue sweatpants with a matching hoodie, I walked over to the elevator and summoned it. Once inside the elevator carried me to the 17th floor. I exited the elevator then walked down the hallway.

I tried to be brave—sure-fire and confident. I even smiled, realizing that there was some abnormality about the smile. It was fake as hell. The kind of smile people make when they told themselves to smile; it wasn't a reflection of true inner emotion.

This is so messed up, I sighed deeply.

I soon arrived at my destination.

Room 1726.

Janet's place.

Resisting the urge to cross myself I drew another deep breath. *GOD be with me,* I heard myself saying. Then slowly, I raised a hand and knocked softly on the door. Thirty seconds passed, and no one had answered. I began to sweat. *Fuck this!* If no one answered this time, I'd kick the damn door in.

I knocked again, harder.

Nothing.

It was agony. I couldn't stand here another minute.

A few seconds later, I heard the lock being disengaged.

Salvation, I sighed.

The door was opened. By a man, approximately 6' 4", around twenty-three. A white man. A good-looking white man, who had thick, dark brown hair, flawlessly tanned skin, and shockingly crystalline blue eyes. He had on a pair of tight jeans which showed a massive dick print, and the gray sweater he had on molded perfectly to his athletically-carved torso.

He looked like the *Ken* doll from the *Barbie* collection. Except *this Ken* was packing like a muthafucka!

"Can I help you, sir?" he asked. His voice was deep and sultry, and I had to admit, *silky smooth.*

I swallowed. "Is Janet available?"

"Yes, she is. But she's kind of busy at the moment. May I ask who's calling?"

Again, I swallowed, easier this time. "I apologize for my unexpected intrusion. My name is Derrick. Derrick Archer. I was hoping to have a brief word with Janet, if I may. I guarantee it'll be very brief."

The man had a lopsided grin on his face. "You must have gotten your days mixed up, too, huh? I usually bang this old broad on Wednesdays and Fridays."

"Pardon?"

"Aren't you here to—"

"Who is it, Justin?" a faint voice inquired from inside the apartment. Judging the graveness to it, I knew it was Janet. She was probably naked.

"Some guy is here asking to see you, babe," the man threw over his shoulder. He turned to face me. I knew right off his *molded* attire was no accident. He made it a point to dress this way. Every day. It was his way of advertising, to showcase his package. Confidence was not something he lacked.

He was a younger me, I thought. *Except he was white...and had a couple of inches on me. Both in height and probably in length.*

It wasn't long before Janet came to the door, wearing nothing but a burgundy robe and an unpleasant look on her face. As usual, her face had been overly done up with clownish makeup. Standing by her side, her beau Justin, smiled and threw an arm over her shoulder; he began playfully nibbling at her earlobe.

With a disgusted expression Janet batted at his face then pushed him away.

"Go wait for me in the bedroom, Justin," she bit out. "I'll be there soon."

"Sure, babe, anything you say." He gave Janet a quick peck on the cheek and walked away. Behind her back—where he was certain she couldn't see him, he winked at me, then pointed his index finger at her—pretending to gag himself with the same finger.

What an asshole, I thought. *Again, just as I was...*

With her eyes rolling, I saw Janet sighing, as if she knew some stupid stunt was going on behind her back. *It seemed as if the mockery never stopped...*

Almost immediately her expression changed as she walked up to me. "How can I help you, Mr. Archer?"

Dead set on my reason for being here, I reached into my hoodie pocket and gave Janet back the jewel she had given me. "I believe this is yours."

She looked at the folded handkerchief with the jewel inside. "May I ask why you are returning it, Mr. Archer?" she questioned with a raised brow.

"I just don't want it," I said.

"It's worth a small fortune, Mr. Archer. Did you inquire about its value?"

"No. I never took it out once you gave it to me."

"May I ask why not, Mr. Archer?" She sounded a bit disappointed.

"Because it isn't right to accept such a gift from someone I barely know." I looked at her and shrugged mildly. To show no disrespect.

"I see." Slowly, she folded back the handkerchief and picked up the jewel inside. She examined it with a curious expression. "This was one of the priciest from my collection, Mr. Archer. I'm surprised that you are returning it. Most of my constituents usually keep theirs."

"I suppose I'm not like most," I said.

"That you are not, Mr. Archer," she grinned slyly. "So now what? What happens to you and me?"

"Absolutely nothing," I said through clenched teeth. "You go your way and I go mine."

Calmly, Janet shrugged. "I thought that's what we had done, Mr. Archer. To be honest, I never expected to see you again." She cocked a brow. "Something else is going on in your life, isn't it, Mr. Archer? Something off the beaten path has brought you here."

I stared at her with direct, piercing eyes. She seemed too cool; too blasé; I couldn't help but wonder if she really had been playing with my life all this time.

Or was there something else?

Nevertheless, thinking she *was* toying with me, I said harshly, "I think you know what brought me here, Janet. I think you know *damn well* what brought me here."

Very easily, she responded, "Honestly, I do not, Mr. Archer." She stepped closer to me and seethed, "Listen to me perfectly clear, Mr. Archer, I am a woman who does *not* play foolish games. I can buy most anything I want, and as you can see, I can buy the best fucks in town. Now, don't get me wrong, you made me feel *damn* good—better than I ever have—but not you nor *anyone else*, for that matter, will have me begging for your companionship. Do I make myself perfectly understood, Mr. Archer?"

She glanced at the clock on the wall, then back at me. Overwhelmed by her words, which sounded genuine, I merely nodded. I was certain that this woman wasn't the cause to my dilemma.

"I apologize if I came off as rude and accusing, Janet, I truly am," I whispered. "And I'm also sorry for disturbing your evening." I don't know why but I took her by the hand and kissed it gently.

"All is forgiven, Mr. Archer," she said, light as a feather.

"Thank you, Janet," I said sincerely. "You truly are a wonderful human being."

"Who you foolin'? I'm more like a rich, over-the-hill floozy with an insatiable sex drive," she said, hiding a grin. She reached out and stroked my cheek; she could sense my anxiety. "Take care of yourself, Derrick, I hope you find what it is that's troubling you…"

My heart skipped a beat; I swallowed hard. It was the first time I'd ever heard her call me 'Derrick'.

"Good night, Janet," I uttered. My voice wavered more than I would have liked. Once again, I kissed the back of her hand as my eyes briefly locked onto hers. There was no response from her. She simply turned and walked away, where I saw her disappear, into her bedroom. I could only let out a deep sigh.

I looked around.

The jewel meant nothing…it was simply a gift…

Though it was time to leave I debated on what to do. There was a beehive of things going on in my head. Separate things. Collective things.

Deciding there was no reason to be standing here, I took a deep breath and left Janet's apartment. When I made it to my vehicle I just sat there. A wave of despair overtook me. *The avenue I thought was the right one ended up being closed!* Suddenly I pounded the steering wheel with both fists.

"What the fuck is going on with me!" I yelled out. As if I were expecting a response, I went silent. I yelled again, more loudly, which brought nothing but more eerie silence. I started to yell again but my throat had gone dry and my mouth was parched.

I started up my SUV and headed for home—before the silence was broken. By *other* things. Things that I did not want to hear. Or see.

Or *feel*.

A mishmash of sights and sounds—starting with those fuckin' *Sleigh Bells* and all that other *otherworldly* shit that usually followed.

I pressed harder on the accelerator. I prayed that I would make it home.

Before anything *did* happen…

CHAPTER TWENTY-SIX
PART THREE
'*A Secret Revealed*'

"You're not going to tell me where you have been?" Danial asked me harshly. He had both his fists perched on his hips.

"I told you already: just a drive," I said. "What's the big deal?"

"You have been *marked*, Mr. Archer," he said. "Doesn't that concern you? Why didn't you tell me or Aphelia where you were going?"

"I just needed to get out," I frowned. "This shit ain't easy to deal with. You don't know the strain I've been under. The shit is overwhelming."

"We had an agreement," he gritted out, with a definite bite to his tone. "We have sacrificed a lot to aid you in your time of need. It is clear that you are not taking this matter seriously."

I turned and walked up into Danial's face. "Oh, trust me, *sir*—I am. You have no clue how much shit I have to deal with."

With that, Danial turned away. He stood there for a long moment with his back facing me. Finally, after sighing deeply, he dropped his head. "I do know, my son...believe me when I say I know precisely what you're going through, firsthand," his voice light as air. He turned to face me. "You see, I was once *marked*, as you are now."

I could only look on, hoping my mouth wasn't hanging open.

"It is true, my son," he said quietly yet sternly. "It happened to me a very long, long time ago."

I swallowed. "Please, Danial, sir, please tell me what happened."

"No. I promised myself that I would never go over that hellish experience again," he stated with conviction and anger. "You just have to trust and believe that I did."

"I do." I reached over and patted Danial on the shoulder. "And I'm sorry, sir, I should've let you know where I went." I looked over at Aphelia who was sitting on the sofa. "I sincerely apologize to you also, Aphelia. I was wrong, I realize this now."

"It's okay, Mr. Derrick Archer," smiled Aphelia. "No harm done. I'm glad you made it home safely."

"If you don't mind me asking: where exactly did you go?" Danial inquired, raising a more-than-curious brow.

I couldn't answer. Instead I just stood there, tightening my mouth, looking around the living room, staring out the front window, into the night.

...*thinking about fuckin' crows*...

I caught Aphelia looking at me, who moments ago had a warm expression on her face, now wearing a look of concern. "Where did you go, Mr. Derrick Archer? Please tell us."

"I…I went to see someone," I whispered with a sigh.

"I can't hear you," Danial said.

"I went to see someone who I thought had cursed me," I said, clearing my throat.

"Who?" Danial asked forcibly.

I took a seat on the sofa next to Aphelia. I felt ashamed for my actions, both past and present. "It was a woman named Janet," I said calmly. "I met her at a hotel a while back and one thing led to another and we slept together. Just that one time. I broke things off with her a few weeks later."

"Why did you end things?" asked Danial. With a perplexed look on his face, he walked over to me.

"I just didn't want to go on seeing her," I sighed. "I was wrong for seeing her in the first place. I was seeing lots of women during this time, exploiting them for whatever I could get. Most likely masking the insecurities going on inside myself. I…I was wrong for doing this, I see that now."

"So, your conscience was bothering you, I take it?" Danial asked firmly, like a father chastising his son.

"It was, sir. Very much so."

"And how did this Janet woman take it when you said you wanted to end things?"

"It was somewhat cordial. She even gave me a jewel as a parting gift." I couldn't help but think I'd been saying the same thing to Melody.

Danial slowly paced the room, looking as if he were a lawyer, cross-examining me. "And what happened when you went to see her tonight, Mr. Archer?"

I wet my dry lips. "I returned the jewel to her."

"Why, may I ask?"

"I thought it was the reason I was being cursed. *Marked*, as you call it."

Mulling over my words Danial turned serious. *Extremely serious.* "Understand this very clearly, Mr. Archer: no single object can curse you. You, unfortunately, have been *marked* by something far worse." He began pacing the living room again.

Following Danial with my eyes, I was speechless. For a second I almost felt like leaping through the living room window, or simply finding a gun and blowing my damn brains out. "What is it?" I asked anxiously. "What the hell is this thing? Please, tell me."

Danial stopped pacing; he stepped over to me and placed a hand on my shoulder. "A spirit has *marked* you. From what I can conclude from your last encounter, it appears to be an extremely strong and violent spirit."

Where did I pick up this spirit? I could feel blood rushing to my head; my scalp was burning. With a feeling that was a mixture of confusion, anger, pain, and nervousness—not to mention being scared shitless—I slunk down on the sofa and threw my head back.

This shit was too much to handle...

I had to ask.

"Can I beat this thing?"

Surprisingly, Danial actually smiled. "If I beat it, Mr. Archer, then you most certainly can."

"How?" I pleaded, feeling somewhat hopeful.

Danial tapped the side of his head. "With intelligence," he said, still smiling. "We find out where this spirit originated from, what the purpose is, and then we either give it what it wants, or we banish it away forever. Hopefully, the latter."

It was odd. Strange. I gradually began to follow Danial's line of thinking. *I needed to zero in on why I was being tormented—instead of focusing on 'what' was tormenting me...I had to dig to the core of this thing, find out what was the meaning of each visit. What the common thread was.*

I suddenly felt renewed.

"What's our next move, sir?" I asked, rising to my feet.

"We wait, as usual, my son," he replied tightly, steepling his hands together. "In the meantime, you need to take in as much nutrients as you possibly can from the concoction that I have made for you."

I sighed, then chuckled. "Do I have to? That stuff tastes awful and on top of that, it gives me the shits something terrible."

"Better out than in," Danial smiled. *He really did have a great smile,* I thought. "It's going to be a tough fight, Mr. Archer, and we need to remove as many spiritual impurities from your body as we can."

"...removing impurities..."

The words echoed in my head; they haunted me. *I remembered hearing the same exact thing from an old guy at my gym. Something about sweating, how it was God's way of ridding the body of its impurities...*

I wondered if it was the same thing.

I caught myself staring at both Danial and Aphelia, with a totally different light burning inside me now.

There was hope.

A light at the end of this *dark* tunnel.

I couldn't help but think that *somehow, in some strange way, everything was slowly coming full circle...*

CHAPTER TWENTY-SEVEN
'Fear Me Now'

Sometimes the confinement of my townhouse was too much to handle; it made things all that much more painful. Harder to breathe. So I jumped at the opportunity to get some fresh air, like I jumped at every opportunity to do something to keep my mind and hands fully occupied.

This time it was a brief outing. Suggested by Aphelia. Just the three of us. Me, Danial, and Aphelia. A simple cruise around town, to soak in a few sights to take the edge off; it would do a body good. For all of us.

Especially, Danial...

Like a pit bull on sentry duty, always dressed in beige fatigues with his trusty, homemade dagger strapped to his side, he remained forever vigilant, cautious, leery, focused—relentlessly watchful of every little thing and because he was like this, it was bittersweet; I knew I was protected but knew I had to be protected from *something...*

Firing up my SUV, we hit a few side streets and then I decided to head downtown. Though sunset wasn't technically for another twenty minutes, it was already dark when I made it downtown. A fierce storm had come through the previous night and had dumped nearly two inches of rain on the city, leaving the streets slick and reflective, like those in the movies.

Feeling like an Uber driver as well as a tour guide, I threaded through the main streets of Chicago. It was Friday evening, and there were tons of people in cars and also walking and milling about, enjoying all the pleasantries of Chicago's nightlife. A lot of the people walking were paired up, or double-dating, appearing to be out-of-towners, and from what I could tell, at nearly every turn, there were plenty of selfies and group pics being taken.

The towering high rises, the iconic landmarks, the unique architectural designs—everything stood out defiantly and proudly, regal and majestic; I could tell, even in Danial's face, that he was impressed and overwhelmed by all the sights.

And I had to admit, even after all these years, so was I—even though I had experienced these very same sights a thousand times.

After a couple hours of showcasing the city, we all decided to grab some burgers from a fast-food restaurant, in and out through the drive-thru, then head back to my place. After placing our orders, I hit the interstate and headed home. Danial soon went silent; I knew the day had finally caught up with him; he was out like a light in the back seat.

Aphelia, wearing a light shade of red lipstick and smelling as usual of sweet cocoa butter, was the complete opposite, sitting next to me in the passenger seat—chatting in my ear about what a wonderful time she was having.

Considering...

"Are you feeling better now, Mr. Derrick Archer?" she asked, smiling brightly.

"Much better, since I'm out and about," I said. Smiling, I gripped the steering wheel firmly as I said, "I was thinking that maybe, before my vacation ends, you can show me how you and your husband twist and contort your body like pretzels every morning. I tried it over and over and all my body ever does is cramp up."

Damn...

Almost immediately I shook my head. It was lame of me for saying that, and I knew it. This whole situation was jacked up, and I'd made it ten times worse by mocking someone's rituals and beliefs.

Apparently, Aphelia took no offense as she grinned, "As with anything, Mr. Derrick Archer, it takes time to stretch and relax your body." She patted my hand. "My husband and I have been doing this for more years than you would ever believe, trust me. Just keep at it, you'll get there. Besides, you're so big and strong and handsome anyway."

"I guess." I peered into the rearview mirror to see that Danial was still out like a light. "You two guys really seem to be happy," I said.

Seizing the moment to nod in a whisper, Aphelia leaned over and grinned, "We do what we must to keep each other happy, Mr. Derrick Archer, sometimes more, but never less. But it isn't always easy. My husband can be a very difficult and stubborn man. In a marriage, you must give and take, but unfortunately, I do most of the giving." The corner of her lips quirked as she did that eyebrow thing over her reading glasses. "One day you will have a bride, and I'm sure it will be this Linda woman that you care so much about, and then, Mr. Derrick Archer, you will understand precisely what I am talking about."

With those words, I peered at Danial. I knew he was a good man who handled his business like a real man should; after all these years, I could tell he still retained a soft spot for his wife, which he unknowingly from time to time, took shameless advantage of.

I nodded my head slowly. "I hope you're right about me and Linda, Aphelia, trust me, I am really hoping as well as believing. I just like to hear it coming from someone else from time to time."

"That's good to know that you are a believer, Mr. Derrick Archer. Just keep your trust in GOD and you will be well on your way..." Stifling a yawn, Aphelia slid down a little in her seat, resting back against the headrest. She pushed her glasses up her nose and folded her arms over her chest, sighing deeply.

She was tired.

So was I.

Mentally, I joined her, sighing deeply and sliding down in my seat. I was so tired I felt practically boneless. So tired I felt practically brainless. It took real effort to stay awake. Getting comfortable was probably a mistake, but the hell with it. I figured after wolfing down a few of these greasy sliders I could treat myself to a hot soak in the tub. Afterwards I'd pop a couple of sleeping pills, jump in the bed under some nice, cool sheets, and sleep like there's no tomorrow.

All that was needed was having Linda butt-ass naked under those sheets with me. *Damn, now that would be the way to close a day out!* I grinned.

A few minutes later the interior of the SUV became silent as a tomb; I was alone with my thoughts. For some strange reason, I thought about Janet. Instead of feeling despondent, disappointed, rolling my eyes or being hard on myself over the situation, as expected, I felt relieved. It was one less thing to worry about. For that I was more than grateful.

My mind then shifted, and my gaze slid from the road ahead of me over to Aphelia, who was fast asleep. This tiny, round, power-packed woman was so special to me. I loved everything about her: her caring nature, her upbeat, unwavering attitude, her bluntness, and above all, that adoring scent of sweet cocoa butter which seemed to cling to her body.

Naturally pure, sweet, delightful and innocent. Straight from Mother Earth...

It was her trademark signature.

After turning off the interstate, I waited patiently at a traffic light. I remembered blowing through these damn things like a madman. The light soon turned green, and I headed on. I was approximately twelve miles from home when suddenly I thought I heard something.

Miles away.

I sat up in my seat and glanced around, waiting with bated breath as I peered over the steering wheel.

In the distance, I caught a glimpse of something faint. Shifting, moving. It was far away but seemingly closing in fast. I could only pray it wasn't what I prayed it wasn't. Once more I glanced around, up, down, side to side, seeing nothing this time, nothing but night lights, buildings in the background, stars, the moon—hoping all of it might give me a little badly needed encouragement, that there was nothing else, but I realized it was just wishful thinking.

The faint glimpses came again, appearing sharper this time. Followed by a faint sound. A familiar sound. Coming in clearer.

It was time to face the truth.

Sleigh Bells.

The sign of bad things to come…

I looked right, left, confused. In a rush I reached out for Aphelia as I gripped the steering wheel. I grabbed her arm and squeezed it, shaking her violently. "It's happening, Aphelia!" I cried out. "Wake up Danial! Now! Please! Wake him!"

Her eyes popping open in shock, Aphelia looked over at me and then unhooked her seatbelt. With shock still in her eyes she turned in her seat and seized Danial by the collar.

"Danial, wake up! It's Mr. Derrick Archer, he's…he's being attacked again! Wake up, Danial!" Her voice cracked badly.

The *Sleigh Bells* were soon on me like a tightening vise. I fought against the ringing in my ears and somehow managed to keep the vehicle in a straight line. There was still traffic, but it was light. As I drove, something strange began happening to me.

Something I hadn't experienced before.

It came over me in increments.

The first symptom was a stinging sensation somewhere up inside my nose causing a wave of violent sneezes. Initially, I thought something had flown into my nose, maybe a fly or mosquito. Maybe even a gnat.

I was sure it was a gnat.

The irritation rapidly progressed from my sinuses into my throat, which was now sore, especially when I tried to swallow. To make matters worse, I smelled something putrid in the air, the stench of a sewer. A foul-tainted swamp. I began to cough uncontrollably, which hurt my throat as much as swallowing.

Looking as if she'd seen a ghost, Aphelia's eyes widened after I let out a particularly explosive cough. There was black phlegm everywhere—looking like stirred-up muck.

Again, something from a swamp...

As the seconds dragged on, I became extremely bothered by a stiff neck. I tried to rub my neck muscles but it didn't help. Even the fabric of my hoodie seemed to be magnifying the discomfort. It felt as if I was being choked by a pair of hands.

Extremely strong ones.

What in the hell had me?

A shaking chill interrupted my thoughts. Once again, a sustained bout of coughing followed.

More phlegm.

Black, muddy, smelling horribly rancid.

I tried to hold it in and nearly blacked out.

"Expel everything inside you," encouraged Danial. "It will keep your body less contaminated."

All I could do was nod, and let out another round of explosive coughs. To my horror, I saw the black gobs I had spewed from my system. Chunks of it. Most were the size of pebbles, some big as a fist. I could see a team of gnats and mosquitoes mingling in the muck.

Danial was right. We were dealing with contamination. *Inside of me!* It was shocking just looking at it. It was not merely bacteria contamination, either.

If only it was that simple.

God, if only.

I stared at the slimy, mucus muck—covering the steering wheel, parts of the dashboard and bits of the windshield—looking like freshly-laid tar.

I could only shake my head.

That putrid shit had come from me!

The thought was horrifying!

I had gone well past 'mid-point' ...this I knew. I had to be careful. This thing I was dealing with was now in its advanced phase. I was dealing with spiritual intrusion. Something *unholy*. A darkness capable of spreading throughout my body and seeping deep into the soul. Devouring me. It could eat—

Don't think about it. Don't. Don't!

I coughed a bit more, this time bending down and spewing up everything inside me, the best I could. More and more of that putrid, dark-looking shit came out. When I finally got my breath, I looked up; I thought I was seeing double.

Triple!

I couldn't believe what was coming at me, in nearly every direction. My worst nightmare.

Crows!

Millions of them!

A steady stream of shrieks, caws, and more shrieks pierced the air as crows began peltering the vehicle—sounding as if it was travelling through a hailstorm. The constant *pecking* was nonstop—not letting up for a second. It wasn't long before the windshield began surrendering to the assault—creating a web-like, jagged network of cracks and zigzags. I could barely see where to guide the vehicle. The side windows were next to receive a relentless beating.

Things weren't about to get any better, I knew.

The ringing of the *Sleigh Bells* grew louder and caused my hands to shake. The vehicle pitched from left to right—feeling as if the tires were about to give out. I started to pull over. But Danial didn't think it would be wise. He suggested shelter, that we needed to be indoors somewhere. I didn't know whether this was wise or not but I knew it made a ton of sense: the crows would soon break through, and it would be over for us.

I became hopeful. *Maybe the crows would suddenly stop and go away, as before?*

I got my answer as even more crows flew in, the assault coming faster, brutal, more furious than ever. Again, not letting up for a single second. Aphelia screamed out in a twisted yelp—scrambling to crawl into the back seat to be with her husband, who pulled desperately to help her. The chaos heightened as the front windshield began to cave in. It was undoubtedly clear we were about to die.

It couldn't end like this, could it?

I needed to take action, not wishful thinking.

My mind went into overdrive as I forced myself to think. *A safe place? But where? Where? Where?* It was too far to drive to my place—the windshield would never last—and all the businesses appeared to be closed. *Where then, dammit! Where?* My eyes wandered aimlessly in my head.

Then it me!

The Oak Park home!

It wasn't too far!

I could be there in less than five minutes!

Feeling I could make it there I punched the accelerator, and the SUV leaped forward. Not giving up, the crows scattered and reformed in hot pursuit—traveling single-file in a *whoosing* formation to maximize their relentless attack, with dead-on precision. I managed to put a little distance between us.

Several minutes later, I pounced on the brakes and the vehicle came to a screeching halt, in front of the large Historical home. This time, I was more than pleased to see the 'For Sale' sign still perched on the front lawn. Because I had overshot the home, I backed up and pulled into the driveway. Seconds later, all three of us leaped out of the vehicle and headed for the front door. I grabbed the lock box and frantically tried to dial in the correct combination to retrieve the key stored inside.

After several attempts the lock box opened, and I snagged the key and inserted it into the lock. My hands were shaking so badly that I dropped the key. I couldn't believe it! *I had dropped the fuckin' key! What the f—!* I bent down and searched frantically but couldn't see where it had fallen.

It was so dark!

Dropping to my hands and knees I reached out blindly for the key. Aphelia joined me while Danial kept watch over us.

"Hurry," he said, trying to keep panic from his voice. He didn't need to tell me. I heard it. *The crows.* The *whooshing* sound building and rapidly increasing in volume, until it would be deafening.

And then it would be too late…

There was no key to be found.

I stood up and thought about kicking the fuckin' door in. That's when something strange happened. Stranger than I could ever imagine.

It was the key.

It had somehow risen from the shadows and was suspended in the air in front of me. I couldn't believe or understand what was happening. Slowly, I held out my hand and waved it back and forth over the key to make sure there wasn't a string or a wire there.

There wasn't.

I began sensing a warmth melting over me as I stood there. It was a peculiar warmth that tingled my skin, starting at the feet and traveling upward. When it got to my face, the tingling intensified. I felt something cupping my right cheek.

I knew then what it was.

More like *who* it was.

It was Mama…

"Grab it!" shouted Danial. "Grab the damn key and use it! Now!"

I did, and my hands shook like Jell-o as I bent down to insert the key into the lock, turning the doorknob simultaneously. The three of us rushed inside and I slammed the door behind us.

The violence followed shortly after—crows shrieking and striking the door with manic determination and hatred—as if being mocked. Aphelia cried out as she backed away. I, too, wanted to scream but my voice was weak, and I was salivating so much that any speech was nearly impossible.

Marshaling whatever strength I had in me, I walked over to Aphelia and embraced her tightly. I began consoling her; this time it was *me* telling *her* that things were going to be okay.

But my efforts were in vain.

After speaking a few more words I started to retch, horribly, violently. Moments later utter terror descended over me as my body was racked by a series of rapidly advancing seizures that nearly doubled me over. I soon felt another presence. A tingling in my ears, all over my body.

It wasn't *Sleigh Bells*, hands, or fingers.

Not this time...

It was an odd yet familiar sensation. A sound. The cries of a swamp: Crickets. Bullfrogs. Buzzing flies and mosquitoes. The warning sound of a rattlesnake. *Yes*, the very distinct sound of a rattlesnake.

Another sound emerged, something I had never heard before, and it pierced and burned inside of me like a knife dipped in lava.

It was laughter.

Not comedic laughter.

Not joyful laughter.

It was a dark, menacing laughter. Filled with soul-searing terror and hatred. I stood there frozen stiff—stricken by the unknown—something of pure, unrelenting *evil*.

And it was coming at me...

...for me...

Different this time...

Appearing more powerful...

...coming to overtake me...

Closing in fast!

Like a huge 747 plummeting to earth, there was no way to stop it.

I looked up at Aphelia, then over to Danial. "Run," I said. *I was right...* I felt sick, my heart raced; it seemed as if a portal—the very bowels of hell had been ripped opened—and I was being sucked in; I could feel myself dissolving, fading away, being tugged violently.

...by something...

"Stay away from me," I now warned, in a scalding whisper. "Hide somewhere, please. Something is coming, I'm telling you, it's coming—so run and hide, dammit. Because I...I can't stop this thing—"

My stomach suddenly clenched up; it was that noxious, swampy odor inside me, building up. I tried not to gag as the smell rose and spread inside me like a mushroom cloud. The walls around me soon let loose with another round of ominous sounds.

More laughter.

More presence of swarming insects.

The air became exceedingly humid. I was wet, and getting wetter by the second. I knew this was it.

It was no longer coming...

It was here!

With pleading eyes, tears now streaking down my cheeks, I looked at Danial and Aphelia. Both appeared confused and extremely frightened.

I couldn't blame them.

I knew I looked ghastly.

Somehow, I found the last ounce of strength in my voice and hollered out, until my vocal cords nearly snapped, "It's here! For the last time, *damn you*—run and hide!"

CHAPTER TWENTY-EIGHT

'Once Again, A New 'Me' Surfaces'

Even as cold sweat drenched me, I took care to breathe—*in, out, in, out*—in the slow rhythm of a deep sleep. All the while I watched through the tiny slits of my eyelids, as the horrible, elongated silhouette seeped through the doorway, bringing pure *evil* with it. Just behind it, I could hear the cries of crows, cawing out frantically, constantly striking the outside door and windows with a clattering *thump-ticking* sound.

Once again I was frozen stiff, with sweat dripping down my back, and could only watch—hoping and praying that this blacker-than-black silhouette wouldn't come in my direction, wouldn't come anywhere near me.

But it did.

In, out, in, out, I told myself. Lying as still as death, steadily breathing in that set rhythm, I stared as it came closer. I couldn't help it; I fell to my knees and started to shake.

The shadowy mist swirled, ever-changing, and then it congealed, looking like a column of dense smoke. That's what I wanted to believe: that it *was* just smoke. Soon a repellent, horrendous odor hung in the air as the now blood-dark mist writhed, and then took on a human form. My mind went wild; I had never seen ghosts and hobgoblins in real time; that was for weaker minds.

But now…

I stared in horror and shock as the mist became more defined. Moments later it resembled a man. Just out of focus. Tall, thin, clothed in tattered rags, dusty and moth-eaten, looking like a weathered scarecrow—carrying the same, overpowering stench of a swamp—which permeated the air, suffocating and choking the air, stifling it.

It was the same hideous creature that had come for me before. Only it looked more…complete…

This time there was no place to hide. No SUV to outrun it. Soon it would seize me and kill me, all before I had a chance to stand and fight back.

My breathing snagged—*in, out, in, out…*

Slowly, the thin silhouette advanced in my direction—I prayed like never before. *Don't let me die. Please, Lord, don't let me die. Make it…make it go away. Please…*

My praying appeared useless, falling on deaf ears as it approached closer and closer, closer still. I spotted a single gold earring in the thing's left ear. Which glittered brightly. I also spotted something else which caused me to shutter even more. The thing's chest—it was ripped open, with the ribs shattered and peeled back—exposing internal organs.

A beating heart.

Lungs that expanded and contracted.

Twisted intestines, veins and vessels that appeared to be moving, pumping blood.

I wondered how such a thing was possible.

But I knew I wasn't dealing with normalcy. Things that could be easily explained. I was looking at an apparition from another world, another dimension—therefore *anything* was possible.

Gradually, like a creeping fog, the silhouette came closer—all the while staring at me; this time it had a face—hideous-looking yet human-like. It might have been in a trance except there was a fiery spark in its eyes.

I felt something drifting over me, hovering, descending. As it crept lower, I felt *something* surging through my body. Simultaneously absorbing and blending into me. Pushing what was left of me to the side.

...outside...

A terror unlike anything I had ever known—*yet familiar*—twisted my stomach, tightened my throat. I tried desperately to rise up; I got as far as my hands and knees but my chin was forced violently to the floor. I was purposely being held at bay.

Call it crazy…but I could almost hear a jail cell being slammed shut…

I knew undoubtedly what was happening to me.

The feeling was undeniable.

I was being replaced…

Once again, my time to shine had come, as I had known sooner or later that it would. As always.

You can't keep an evil man down, I smiled.

On that pleasure-inducing note, I slowly rose to my feet. I squeezed my eyes and looked around. I could feel my brows knitting in a fierce yet confused manner. I was in another place—another time. In a house that wasn't mine. The place was fuckin' huge—a mansion—it was old and creaky and smelled faintly of cocoa butter.

I hated that fuckin' smell!

It appeared that I was alone, but I wasn't sure.

I would have to explore the entire house to be certain. *Every fuckin' inch if I had to! Every room, closet, cubby hole—every nook and cranny! And I would kill anyone I encountered! Anyone! Everyone! I'd thoroughly smash their skulls in! Rip their spleens from their backs and crush their organs with my bare hands! There would be no survivors!*

Snarling, I peered into the darkness—my heart pounding, my breathing like an enraged bull—nostrils flaring. This house—there was a reason I was here. Of course it was! *But what? Why?* Once again I peered around. Then it hit me. I was close…the house was a gateway. I wasn't just imagining things. This house was the path to something!

But what?

To where?

Which fuckin' way to go?

With severe frustration and malice overtaking me, my eyes scanned everything around me. The room was dark. The entire house was probably dark, too, and quiet.

Too fuckin' quiet.

Every room was most likely this way…empty, dark, soundless.

Again, *too* quiet.

I tilted my head.

My ears picked up a sound, a movement. *Was it real or just some bullshit…?* My breathing stopped as my eyes swung blindly in the direction to where it had come from.

Upstairs.

I heard it again.

This time it was for real.

There was someone in the house…

CHAPTER TWENTY-NINE
'A Mission of Pure Hatred'

The rooms of this house were massive; so was I.

Though I was considered thin and unintimidating in my former life, I now possess a phenomenal degree of strength—which gave me a *huge* advantage over everyone.

Anyone!

There wasn't a single person alive who could stand in my way. *"Let a muthafucka try!"* I chuckled loudly as I checked one of the upstairs bathrooms.

I was now an ancient enemy that hadn't merely surged up from out of nowhere—*fuck that!*—I had risen from the previous stables of bad asses: dictators, rulers, fascists, emperors, authoritarians, kings—murderers, assassins—which a world should be built on!

And soon—I'd be higher than all those fuckers! Mightier! Obviously I was much more stronger!

I didn't think I'd make it to this level.

But I had.

It cost me a lot.

A whole lot...

But hey, you had to give up something big to gain something even bigger.

Right?

Right!

Severely irritated, I mashed my teeth together, grinding them, when I found the bathroom empty. I was more than pissed. I wanted to *seriously* hurt someone! And before it was all said and done—someone *would* be hurt—torn apart, crushed under my heels. Not tomorrow, not in a few days or perhaps the *next* time I was set free—but *tonight!*

I looked around. Nothing. Not a sound. The only noise was the creak of the hardwood floors as I shifted my weight on it. I crept down the hallway, stopping every second or so to detect movement, or sound. A shifting shoe. A muffled cry. Held breath seeping through fingers, clutched tightly over somebody's mouth. I cocked my head, listening intently.

Carefully.

Nothing.

Fuck...

I was getting restless, and to be honest, bored. My time in *this* world was precious, and I didn't want to waste a single minute—*a single second!*—chasing my own ass. I headed further down the hallway and entered another bedroom, a smaller one, facing the front of the house. Through the windows I could see a portion of the street. It was nearly deserted. Only the trees moved, leaves fluttering in a soft wind. I smiled mildly as I spotted my car parked on the front lawn.

My black, four-door Crown Victoria. *I loved that fuckin' car! Always have, always will!*

I craned my head from left to right, still peering out the window. There was nothing else to see. Nothing but a white, piece-of-shit SUV in the driveway, looking like it had been through a war zone.

The crows had done well, I noted with a tight nod. Once again, I found myself smiling mildly as I stared at the SUV. *You got me the first time, you son-of-a-bitch, but I got you the second. Now look at your ass—all dented up and shit—ready for the junkyard. Call the tow truck, somebody!*

Grinning evilly, I turned from the window. I checked the bedroom only to find it empty. I cursed and then left the bedroom and crossed over into another one. Much larger. I took a step inside. That's when I heard something, coming from behind me. My heart racing, I turned and poked my head just outside the bedroom door. I swiveled my neck, which at one time had been broken, and tilted my head and listened.

Once again, nothing.

Not a damn thing.

Wait...

Another sound.

It was distant and brief, but it sounded like a muffled welp of a woman; it wasn't merely a welp or even a nervous chirp; it was the sound of terror, of panic and alarm, coming from downstairs. *Someone was hiding from me,* I grinned. *Someone was shitting and pissing in their pants—hopefully good!*

...maybe it was her...

Then I could have her alone in this big ass house! All to myself! Just me and her! No interruptions!

Now sneering heavily, feeling a sexual surge searing through my body and swelling in my testicles, I headed toward the stairway, all the while opening and closing my hands tightly, making solid, damaging fists. I began my gradual descent down the stairs, slow step after slow step, keeping my ears and eyes vigilant for the slightest of sounds.

The *tiniest* movement.

I made it to the main level and looked around. Nothing. I hated to admit it but deep down, I was growing impatient, becoming more and more bored. It was like a childish game of hide-and-seek, with nobody playing but me!

What kind of shit is this!

I was not to be played with!

As I was about to raise a foot and send it through the wall, a thought hit me. *Maybe this house was a dead-end. Leading nowhere. Maybe it wasn't the gateway I thought it was. The one I'd been hoping for.*

Frustrated, growing further impatient, I decided to check out the kitchen, then the pantry next to it. About halfway there I heard movement in the living room, at the rear of the house.

Then a noise emerged, from upstairs.

Was that possible...?

Unless...

I slowly nodded. *Yes. There were other people in the house. More than just her. People who wanted to stop me from what I'd been doing! But they couldn't! They wouldn't! I'd kill all of them! Every last one of them! Then it would be just me and her.*

...forever...

I found my face torn between two expressions: frowning...smiling... *Yes,* I whispered, finding the common ground between the two. *I'd kill them all. Then, once again, it would be just me and her...*

...the way it should be...

...forever...

After realizing I wasn't alone anymore, I decided to follow my instincts. I turned and crept back toward the stairs. I was sure somebody was up there. And now they were boxed in. There would be no place to run. No place to escape.

Except through me!

I felt an evil smirk locking in on my face. It was time to end this fuckin' hide-and-seek game.

Suddenly, as I headed toward the stairway, I wasn't the least bit bored.

CHAPTER THIRTY

'Three-Quarters There'

With the possibility of someone hiding from me, and soon to be killed, I found I could hardly contain myself. I had even reached the point where I did a little shimmy as I approached the winding stairway. Which seemed to have a million steps.

I climbed each step one at a time, slowly, in the normal *human* fashion, knowing damn well I could seize the stairs five or six steps at a time! I was forever getting stronger; I had unmeasurable power surging through my body.

When I reached the top of the stairs I sensed something was wrong. I hadn't felt it downstairs because the intensity just wasn't there. But now that I was upstairs, it was different.

I looked around.

Something seemed odd.

I became a bit unsure of myself, of which way to proceed. A little confused even. I started questioning my judgement. This shouldn't be happening. By this time I should have been up to full strength—at least close to it—developing a total awareness as well as a collective consciousness of everything around me. A built-in compass, a self-driven GPS, to point me in the exact direction.

Maybe I still had some growing to do?

With a sense of panic that I didn't understand, I could feel my heart beginning to race. My fear was that perhaps I was harboring some disastrous gene that couldn't manifest itself. In that case, I wouldn't be allowed to complete the full transformation. I gritted my teeth. *Those black fuckers lied to me! I'd sold my soul for nothing! I was cheated! Why those—*

Feeling myself losing it, I took a deep breath and reeled in my emotions. I smiled. *I would deal with those fuckers later. One by one. And, boy-oh-boy, would I make them pay dearly, severely...*

But right now I had a job to do. *To finish!* Once more, I looked around.

Nothing.

Yet...something.

Something had just been here...

I quickened my pace and headed into the bedroom I'd just left, finding it empty, as before. I was more surprised than anything to find the room empty. I was sure someone was just in here. *And judging by the smell in the air, I'd been right. Somebody was here!*

The aroma was undeniable.

Fuckin' cocoa butter!

I turned and gazed at the open window. I walked over to it and looked down at the ground outside, just below the window.

Disturbance.

Footprints.

Then my eyes went up to a tree next to the window, and I saw a large branch.

It became obvious.

Somebody had escaped through the window, aided by the tree branch. And now they were gone. *Fuck!* I could feel my chest rising and falling with mounting anger; it became too much; I let out a shriek which echoed throughout the entire house. In a rush, I left the bedroom and charged down the stairs—immediately coming to a halt—finding the front door open!

I'd been tricked!

How?

I was fuckin' invincible!

Naturally, because I *was* invincible and *had been* tricked—outwitted, I wanted to kill somebody—*them!*—*anybody!*—*everybody!* My nostrils flared as my eyes landed on the front door.

That opened door.

Like a raging bull, gritting my teeth and slitting my eyes, I became totally engulfed with anger. I drew back a solid fist and began punching the walls—every one of them! I smashed windows, cracked countertops—kicked the railing on the stairs—ripped sinks, toilets, and pipes from every bathroom—I practically shook the foundation of this fuckin' place—screaming and yelling at the top of my lungs—making a shitload of noise!

Then suddenly I stopped.

I found myself calming down, breathing easier, becoming deeper in thought rather than rage. I knew anger wasn't going to get me anywhere. It wouldn't do me any collective good. None, whatsoever.

I still had some growing to do.

I realize that now.

A well-honed consciousness rarely expresses anger. I'd been outwitted and didn't know how to handle it. Case closed. I needed to be smarter. Start thinking with my head instead of my fists. I began to worry. I thought I would have been *there* already.

But I wasn't.

Maybe three-quarters there.

I just needed a little more time, I smiled, yet feeling a tad disappointed. *Yea, that's all,* reassuring myself, *just a little more time. Maybe a few days more...a week or two at the very latest...*

It was at that moment when I decided it was time to leave. To let myself go.

...back to the abyss.

...back to my domain.

...back to my own world...

Conscious of my thoughts and actions, I closed my eyes and allowed my body and mind to shut down, to give themselves up—to melt into myself, so my body could vaporize and thin out, so it could fade and fade and fade, fade further still—until I was just a shimmering mist—drifting from this house and floating seamlessly to my Crown Victoria, still parked outside on the front lawn, where I would slither back inside, behind the wheel, and drive off...severing myself fully from *this* world—but only for the moment, *dammit!*

I just needed a little more time, I reminded myself as I felt myself thinning out more, drifting more, becoming a whispering, sooty nothingness.

...just a little more time...

Just as I was about to retreat into the final shades of pitch-black darkness, I picked up the faint sounds of a siren, in the distance.

A vehicle was approaching.

Several vehicles.

Police vehicles.

Coming in fast.

Most likely coming here. I'd made too much noise taking out my rage on the house, and somebody had called the cops.

Fuckin' concerned citizens!

But I could care less.

Not one bit.

I was already in my car and driving away...

CHAPTER THIRTY-ONE

'My Deepest Fear Comes to Light'

Out of breath, staggering up the street, I vomited three blocks away from the Historical Oak Park home, mere seconds before the police pulled up. I walked a few more blocks until I hit a main street, where I made my way to a small, abandoned building, under renovation. I leaned against it.

My head was spinning out of control as I looked around. It had to be close to midnight. Feeling extremely nauseous again, I pitched forward and puked my guts out. A couple of homeless men looked up and applauded. Finishing up on a dry heave, I gave them a wave, acknowledging my peers.

Welcome to 'Chi-Raq', ladies and gentlemen—the rough side of Chicago. The part of the city that no one wants to talk about!

I had to get out of here, before I got robbed and then killed. Then robbed again. I tried my cell phone, but the signal was weak. Clutching my stomach with one hand, I jogged further up the street, about a half mile further, until I reached an alley next to a vacant lot. I tried my cell phone again and saw all the bars standing tall—an amazing victory, *considering*...

I dialed Aphelia. As always, there was a strange, hollow ringing on the line whenever I called her, yet, it was a wonderful, sweet reassuring sound. She picked up on the third ring. "Mr. Derrick Archer, are you okay?"

"Yea," I said. "And you…are you and Danial, okay?"

"We are," she replied joyfully. "I jumped out the window and Danial escaped through the front door."

I closed my eyes tightly and thanked God for sparing them. "That's great to hear," I sighed heavily. "Tell me, where are you now?"

"We're at a restaurant about five miles from that house."

"Can you guys take an Uber back to my place?"

Naturally, there was hesitation. Both were probably wondering if I was *really okay*. Then Aphelia said, after a few seconds longer, "Yes, we can do that."

"Okay," I breathed. "You guys know how to get in. Go there and I'll meet up with you soon, I promise you."

Aphelia's voice took on a harsh tone of concern. "What about you, Mr. Derrick Archer? Where are you now?"

With that, I looked around. My head was still clouded and my ability to clearly think wasn't the best. But I knew I was still not in the best place to be. Just across the street from me stood a few young bruthas—eyeing me like I had just cashed a check. To the left, there were some seasoned bums, licking their lips as if I was a dropped sandwich. I met all their gazes and did not look away until they did.

I was not in the mood for some bullshit. And definitely not tonight!

And definitely not from *humans!*

I assured Aphelia that I was okay and that I would see her and Danial soon, an hour at the latest. Shortly after, I called an Uber, and a mid-size SUV pulled up in the promised fifteen minutes. I hopped into the backseat, said "hello" to the female drive, then threw my head back. I prayed she wasn't a talker. I just didn't have it in me at the moment.

Thirty-five minutes later, the Uber dropped me back to my place. When I stepped through the front door an explosion of grateful cheers greeted me. It was Aphelia—flying across the living room and hugging me tightly, nearly in tears. I hugged her back, with tears welling in my eyes.

I looked over at Danial, his hands steepled, sitting stoically on the sofa. He appeared unemotional, as always, but of course he was also pleased to see me home, alive, in one piece.

If I weren't mistaken, I thought I saw a tear forming in his right eye. He quickly turned away. I couldn't help but choke up on the inside. Still gripping me tightly, Aphelia broke down and started crying. Loudly. The wuss that I was I joined her. It soon became *Bose* stereo crying. It wasn't long before Danial let his tears loose, though he remained calm, reeling his emotions in before they ran rampant.

The entire scene was touching, filled with genuine love. One of those moments where you didn't think such a moment could exist. But it did. Though they weren't my real parents, I didn't look at it this way. They were there for me—through thick, thin, and whatever! Say what you will, but who wouldn't want to be loved like this?

What happened next was more than odd, more than strange. As if nothing had happened that night, *just hours ago!*—the three of us headed into the kitchen engaged in meaningless chatter—meaningless on topics or purpose—while Aphelia fixed me something light, yet filling to eat: a huge deli sandwich, with chips and pickles on the side.

It was like she knew I was starving and needed strengthening.

And I was. On both counts.

After eating, we all talked a bit more and then Aphelia went silent, as if she'd run out of things to say. She had a wonderful ability to know when to back off. Danial soon fell silent. He folded his arms tightly over his chest as he leaned back in his chair.

The spotlight fell on me.

Both wanted to know what was going on.

With me.

Inside of me.

They listened in silence as I began to explain. I told them that I felt another spirit inside me, pushing me aside and locking me away as it took over. That I felt like a mere spectator in my own body, unable to say or do anything to control or stop it. That I had no conscious or awareness of what was going on.

Both had concerned looks on their faces.

Who could blame them?

Unfolding his arms and then leaning forward, Danial asked, "Before this spirit invaded your body, what exactly did you see?"

I thought a bit, chewing on my bottom lip, then I said, "I remember seeing some sort of man, a couple of times. The first time was at a motel, a Holiday Inn Express, just outside the city. He came to me wearing old, beat-up clothes and driving an old Crown Victoria. And then it was tonight, he came to me wearing the same beat-up clothes. Only this time, the clothes didn't look as bad, like it was a Goodwill upgrade..."

"Go on," nodded Danial.

I thought a bit more, then added, "The first time I saw him he didn't have a face, this time, however, I could clearly see facial features: dark complected, narrow, beady eyes, and a long, hooked nose, like a hawk of some kind. He also had an earring in his left ear. A gold one."

Danial stayed still for a moment. At one point he frowned. He then stared directly into my eyes. "Anything else you may have overlooked or forgotten?" He reached over and gripped my hand. "Derrick, my boy, I need to know everything."

I leaned back in my seat and exhaled heavily. My mind worked frantically—trying desperately to recall anything I might have overlooked or outright missed. The *tiniest* thing. A few of the same details hit me: Once more I told him about the hideous swamp smells, the *Sleigh Bells,* the voices—coming from the invading spirit as well as from my mother. I mentioned about the two forces pulling at me.

One to save.

The other to destroy.

Once again Danial leaned forward, resting his elbows on the kitchen table. He steepled his fingers. He did that a lot. It looked good on him. Still holding the steeple, he bounced his forefingers against his lips. "Aphelia, honey, it's getting late. I think you should go to bed," he whispered without looking up. "Please, honey, would you mind?"

"Sure, darling," she nodded as she rose from the table.

Releasing his steeple, Danial made a small waving gesture with his hand. "Thank you, honey, I'll be joining you soon." Without another word spoken, even to me, Aphelia left the kitchen, leaving the two men alone to talk. I knew then it was about to get serious.

I was right.

After a minute or two, after making sure that his loving wife had truly gone to bed, Danial asked me for something to drink. And not just a simple 'everyday-common' drink: juice, milk, pop, bottled water. Not even the bottle of Chardonnay I kept for Linda.

No.

This man wanted liquor.

Strong liquor.

The best I had on hand was my good old standby: Crown-*muthafuckin'*-Royal! Several pints, still in its trademark carrying bag.

He told me to pour him a shot—straight—nothing to water it down with, which meant no ice. I did. For both of us. After knocking down several healthy doses of Crown, nearly a bottle to himself, Danial slowly began dropping his guard. Reaching to his side, he pulled out the dagger he'd made and laid it on the table. He looked up at me, tight mouthed, patting the dagger gently with an opened palm.

"It's going to take this dagger, my son. The dagger that I made for you." With a serious look now etched across his face, in his eyes, his voice dropped to a seething battle cry, "It's going to take this dagger, along with the help of your mother, for you to defeat this thing. Trust me, I know."

I could only look on with a blank expression, accompanied by a gaping mouth. Slowly, gradually, ingesting even more and more Crown Royal into his system, Danial began telling me things.

Things about his past, on how he'd found himself cursed.

Marked!

Recalling his story and trying to remain calm were not his forte. The feelings on his own personal entanglement could only be labeled as: "appallingly hellish". When he finished, I felt as though I had been through *his* personal hell and back. I stared blankly at the walls, nearly shell-shocked.

This can't be real... I heard myself repeating, over and over. *It...it can't be...it just can't...*

Yet, somehow, it made sense. Perfect, logical sense. At least in Danial's case it did. *But what about mine?* I needed to check out my situation, my own personal dilemma, to see if it applied to me.

I hoped and prayed that it didn't.

I looked Danial dead in his eyes, as if to say I needed final confirmation.

"Linda?" I whispered.

A slow nod from Danial. "Yes."

"Are...are you sure, Danial?" I seemed to be pleading, hoping for a different response. "Are you sure? Tell me, *dammit,* are you for sure!"

Another slow nod.

Almost instantly I stopped breathing as I melted into my chair. Once again, I stared at the wall. I went numb. It felt as though an ice pick was being slowly inserted into my ear, the sharp steel piercing my brain, gradually being twisted to maximize damage.

After months and months of struggling with this—countless weeks, days, nights of being tormented, having nervous breakdowns after nervous breakdowns, being afraid of my own shadow—it was finally coming to a head.

Linda...

Her name stung. I didn't want to believe it. I wanted to scream, maybe even cry. But I couldn't either way. There was still hope.

I would have to talk to her.

Ask the right questions.

Probe her brain. Deep yet carefully.

Get her to open up, whether she wanted to or not.

I had to know one way or another.

I drew a deep breath and held it.

For quite a while.

I found myself gasping as though I knew at some point that I had to exhale and breathe. I wondered if I were unconsciously trying to kill myself.

Gradually, I gave my lungs a reprieve and exhaled as I closed my eyes. Leaving me with one final thought. One I wished I could erase from my mind.

Linda...

I didn't want to believe this...

CHAPTER THIRTY-TWO

'Perfect Timing'

It was Saturday evening, around 8:30, when I decided to call Linda. I could only hope she would answer. There was so much that I needed to know. So many *dark* things needed to be brought into the light.

I gripped my phone and paced back and forth in my bedroom, in a slow, relentless gait, nervous and wondering if I could make it through this thing. I felt myself panicking. And that was unacceptable. Panic bred carelessness, and that could blow everything.

Linda may freak out and ask me *'what the hell's this all about, Derrick?'*, and then shut down.

Never to speak to me again.

Then all would be lost.

For me as well as for her…

But I wouldn't allow this to happen. If worse came to worse, I'd just blurt everything out to her—tell her exactly what's been going on with me. *She would believe me, then! She had to! She was part of this! She'd seen—firsthand—what I did to her!*

I don't know. I just don't know…

Maybe I was grasping for hope. Going way out on a limb. Deep down hoping and praying that maybe Linda wasn't really a part of this. That maybe Danial was wrong. I could feel myself getting cold feet. I thought about backing out entirely. Pounding a fist to my head, I felt myself losing it—I didn't need this shit! None of it, you hear me! None of it!

I dropped my head and then shook it as despair began taking hold of me. It seemed as if my spirit to go on was fading away. *Like I didn't care either way...*

Fuck it, maybe I'll kill myself. End all this bullshit for good! *Cut my throat! Slit my fuckin' wrists and wait to bleed out while I lay in a tub of warm water! Overdose on some pills! Find a gun and blow my damn brains out! Lay on a set of railroad tracks until a train came along and sliced my body in two!*

I knew I was being a bit dramatic and even foolish, as Melody often told me I could be, but even the craziest person finally got tired of knocking on a door and not getting an answer, of hoping patiently and then hoping some more, only to come up empty handed. Or maybe I was simply giving up on past hope. And grasping for new hope. Something I could count on this time around.

But wasn't this new hope?

I stopped my pacing and sighed heavily; once more I hung my head. One thing became clear: even if something did come out of this, good or bad, I knew my life would never be the same. I'd experienced too many things to try to live a normal life. Things that no man should ever have to experience, or witness. Ghoulish, hellish things. *How could a person rebound from something such as that?*

I shook my head.

They couldn't. It was impossible...

Increasing despair, the steadily progressing feeling of hopelessness, the thought of losing this battle—all of it caused me to turn slowly toward the bathroom. I just stood there. In sort of a daze. Looking at the bathroom. I knew I had a bottle of sleeping pills somewhere in the medicine cabinet. Something that would knock me the fuck out so I could leave this world. Then I wouldn't have to worry about a damn thing.

I'd be free.

Free from it all...

I closed my eyes and imagined myself after taking a shitload of pills and then leaving this world. I could already feel myself floating. Actually *hearing* the winds and the skies calling out to me. *The feeling was so euphoric!* All the pain and anxiety were being washed away as I started my journey. I even saw a faint glimmer of distant light as I made my way.

Light meant happiness. A beginning of something new...

I found myself smiling. I knew my transition was at last coming to a close. A peaceful ending. I would no longer be associated with this cruel world.

It felt so good...

Then, as I gradually opened my eyes, reality hit, and it all came crashing down. I looked around. Finding myself standing in my bedroom. Back to the *real* fuckin' world. One plagued with problems, heartaches, worries. Ghouls and hobgoblins. Spirits and demons. Everything and then some.

I want to go back to the light, I could hear myself saying. I turned and found myself staring at the bathroom. *It was calling me...* I knew what I had to do. Where I wanted to go. Where I *needed* to go.

...back to the light...

Because I had never *really* thought about taking my life, that I had done so now, was proof that it needed to be done. I turned and headed for the bathroom.

Smiling.

That's when something strange happened.

It was my cell phone. It was ringing in my right hand as I stood there. I looked down and saw that it was Linda. She was calling me! I nearly fainted.

It was a sign, I knew.

I realized I was breathing heavily, from Linda's call to the thought of what I was about to do. Thank God, I hadn't. In mere seconds I would have. What in the world was I thinking of?

Testing, testing, I could hear God saying to me.

My faith in God grew ten-fold in just that moment.

With a pounding heart, I answered the phone, feeling a heck of a lot stronger than before. "Hello, Linda, I…I was just fixing to call you…"

CHAPTER THIRTY-THREE

'Bracing Myself'

Linda and I chatted for quite a while after I answered the phone, not about my problems, not about hers and not about getting back together. About nonsense, about a neighbor of hers who has eight cats, about international headlines, the crisis overseas, her job, my job, movies that were streaming. We were like a couple of twelve-year-olds who had just discovered the telephone.

I told her that I was driving a rental until I bought another vehicle. *Never explaining the reason why.* I told her about how much I laughed at the selfies we took nearly everywhere we went. How beautiful she always looked, how I always appeared as if I was drunk or high, an image from a practical joke.

What I didn't tell her was the pictures of me and her, no matter how bad I looked, got me through some rough times.

Nearly forty-five minutes had gone by, and Linda and I had been talking nonstop. She appeared relaxed. And that's what I wanted. The time had come when I no longer felt obligated to stall things, as I had earlier.

In fact, I went straight for the jugular.

"So, tell me about your parents, Linda. You never really talk about them." I eased back on the bed and propped a pillow behind my back; I closed my eyes, to allow my mind to erase anything that may cause distractions.

"What do you want to know?" she asked, in an amused tone.

"What type of parents were they?"

"Well," she paused, "for starters, my mother was a stay-home mom. She ran the household like she was running a business. Everything was in order, from the cleaning to the cooking to the washing, making sure we all were properly cared for. She'd read to me nearly every night before I went to sleep. When it came to my dad, he was a hard worker. A really hard worker. He put in nearly fifteen hours a day working as an engineer for the airline. Most of the time I only saw him on the weekends. But still, he was the best dad ever, both him and my mom. We'd go to church every Sunday, no matter what." She hesitated, then sighed, "It was the worst day of my life when they were killed in that car accident. It was a simply horrible accident, too. Gruesome. I…I didn't think I could ever smile again. I…"

I heard sniffles; Linda was crying, reliving that tragic moment in her life.

"What about the people who took you in after that?" I asked, trying to hurry her through this time.

Linda sniffed harder and exhaled through an open mouth. "Well, that would've been my uncle Leonard Hayes, my dad's older brother, and his wife Rachel."

"What kind of people were they?" I asked, sitting up a bit.

"The complete opposite of my mom and dad, let me tell you," she said, sounding a bit angry.

I cleared my throat and swallowed. "Like how?"

"Well, actually, to be real, Rachel was kind of okay. She worked a ton of hours at Walmart. She would buy me little things every time she got paid. Gym shoes, earrings, dresses, blouses, jeans, things that were on sale, you know, things from Walmart where she could use her employee discount. Which didn't matter to me. I guess that's why you always see me in sweats and tee shirts to this day. It's what I've become." She stopped, sighed, then whispered, "I used to feel so bad for Rachel. She'd be so tired from working."

I found myself nodding. "I see, and what kind of man was your uncle Leonard?"

After a slight pause, she bit out vilely, "That man was a piece of freshly-laid shit, and that's putting it mildly. It was hard to believe that he and my dad were brothers. That ugly, hooked nose, snake-looking motherfucker was a straight-up bum. A real loser. Rachel used to argue with him every time she got home. He never cleaned the house, stayed drunk all the time, and couldn't hold down a job for more than a month. He'd steal from her purse and then head straight to the bar. Some juke-joint back in Louisiana. The only reason he wanted me there was so he could get a Social Security check for letting me live there."

My heart ached. "I'm so sorry you had to go through that, Linda. I can imagine it was a bad time in your life."

"Bad time? Bad time? Please, you don't know the half of it." A pause came. For nearly ten seconds.

"Hey, baby, you still there?" I urgently asked.

"I am," she whispered at last. Another long moment of silence came, again on her part. I knew then something was on her mind, like she was once again reliving a bad moment.

"Linda," I eased out, carefully and tenderly, "is there something you're holding back and not telling me?"

"It is," she replied bluntly, as she drew a deep breath.

"Care to talk about it? I would really like to hear it. Maybe…maybe I can help you in some way. The way you've helped me."

She exhaled hard. "Well, okay, but it ain't pretty, man, let me tell you. You sure you want to hear it?"

Trying desperately to contain myself—my excitement as well as my anxiety—I tightened my fist and rose to my feet. I relaxed my voice, made it both soothing and comforting. "Of course, I would, baby, I'd like to know about any and everything that's been troubling you."

A pause. "You sure?"

"Tell me, baby, please…"

"Okay…"

Sitting back on my bed I was frozen stiff as Linda began painting a picture, but not the typical picture you might expect someone to paint. But I didn't give a shit. I needed to hear it all.

Everything!

She went on to tell me things about her uncle Leonard Hayes, her father's older brother, and as she did, it was as though a low cloud had sunken over my bedroom, like a tent sagging in the rain.

For starters, she said her uncle Leonard used to hang out at a seedy bar in Louisiana, located way off the police radar, deep in the swampy woods, where illegal habits were not only the norm but highly encouraged: making and drinking moonshine, prostitution, gambling, drugs, things of that nature. A three-time loser, ugly as sin—tall, lean and lanky, Leonard couldn't win, compete, or match wits with his constituents—always lagging way *behind* the pack. Because of his looks along with no swag or flair, plus always broke, he couldn't get next to any women. They wouldn't have him. It was rumored he turned to men from time to time. With nothing working in his favor, he turned to Black magic, voodoo, tarot cards, palm reading, Ouija boards, tea leaves, seeking out witches and priests—all kinds of people and props— gimmicks and methods—things to up his ante for the game he wanted to be in.

Eventually he found the right people, *dark individuals*, who promised him results. A deal was struck and Leonard ended up trading away his soul. But he was impatient, he crossed the lines as well as the wrong people before things could be put in place. As a result, he was killed. *Brutally.* He was beaten until he lost all consciousness and then strung from a tree, dangling from a limb for hours until his neck finally gave way and snapped. Even after his death his chest had been gutted like a catfish.

But the backwoods people say, while dangling from that tree, Leonard promised to return, to exact his revenge and desires on any and everyone. They say, his wishes finally came to him, even in death...

Fuck...

After hearing this my entire body went numb. I couldn't feel a damn thing. I looked blindly around the room. My senses returned when I realized that Linda was still on the line, when I heard her voice.

"You still there, Derrick?" she inquired, in a soft whisper.

"Yea, baby, I'm here," I said cheerfully. But it was a struggle. Linda's voice, that story, my reactions—all of it was hard to digest and swallow.

And it wasn't over.

Not by a long shot.

Though things were finally making sense, Linda said that there was more to the story. I held my breath and closed my eyes. Even tighter.

She went on to tell me that Leonard repeatedly molested her while her aunt was at work. Every chance he got. He vowed to kill her as well as her aunt if she ever spoke a word about it. Occasionally, he'd buy her girlie toys and miniature dolls to keep her from saying anything. To keep everything *'mellow'* as he'd put it. At night, she told me, when the coast was clear, he would enter her bedroom, ringing a tiny little bell to announce his unwanted entry.

Linda said it sounded like *Sleigh Bells...*

Hearing that, my brows shot up and my mouth fell open. *What the f—...* I knew then that it was

Leonard Hayes, not Linda, who was causing these hellish, horrific acts on me. Somehow, in some *demonic twist of fate*, I was pulled into this madman's curse. His deranged quest for revenge. And I knew the deal. The reason why I was pulled in.

He wanted Linda...

He didn't want anyone else to have her.

It all made sense.

His voice said it all: *"You will never be hers..."*

Everything made sense.

Everything!

Cemented in place!

And I was willing to bet—on everything I hold dear!—that Linda's former boyfriend had also been cursed. That's why he was abusive to her. He was being manipulated and controlled. He never actually understood what was happening to him. And he couldn't beat it. *So, he committed suicide. By jumping off a building for a reason no one else could comprehend. It was to end his madness.*

I could only shake my head.

Like I almost did... I was so close to ending things myself...

But I hadn't.

Now, at last, I could allow myself to breathe. To finally check all the empty boxes that needed checking. But there was one last thing I had to ask Linda. Drudging up the final ounce of strength remaining in me, I asked Linda what kind of car did her uncle Leonard Hayes drive, when he was still alive.

I held my breath as I waited for a response. I wasn't sure I was ready for it but it came at me, anyway.

"I believe it was a black Crown Victoria," she said. "It was old and had tinted windows all the way around. He loved that car, always kept it clean and shiny." Linda paused then inquired, kind of cutely, "Baby, why would you ask me such an odd question like that? About a dead man's car? It seems so strange, so out-of-the-blue."

I couldn't answer.

I just sat there. Wide-eyed. Seeing everything but not seeing a damn thing. Still suffering from shock. But I needed to snap out of it. I couldn't let this disturbing revelation contaminate my mind. Maybe there was more to come…

Fully amused and relaxed at this point, Linda asked me again about my curiosity, concerning the car.

The black Crown Victoria…

Leonard Hayes' car…

Once again I couldn't answer. I was too busy thinking about everything, about the *other* things Linda had mentioned. Things that haunted and brought terror into my life. How they were all connected. The swampy smells. The *Sleigh Bells*. The voices. The crows. Those unexplainable moments when I didn't feel like myself. The strange sensations.

The beatings I endured. That car. Everything leading up to one thing: *to a man named Leonard Hayes.*

A weak, feeble man who died with a curse, somehow resurrected with multi-layers of dark power at his disposal, which made him stronger, invincible, and terrifyingly dangerous.

A man named Leonard Hayes.

Who was no longer a man—now something that was just a step down from the devil. One small degree of separation.

My brows were heavily pitched over my eyes. Once more, Linda asked me about the car.

Leonard Hayes' car.

The Crown Victoria.

I looked at the phone and placed it back to my ear. *I don't know why I asked you that question, Linda…* I told her. The words were spoken through my mind. It was the best I could do. I couldn't open my mouth if I wanted to…

CHAPTER THIRTY-FOUR

PART FOUR

'Preparing For Battle'

Sweating, fully aware of my too-rapid heartbeat, wondering if Danial and Aphelia could hear it pounding through my chest, I found myself rocking back and forth in the kitchen chair. Aphelia sat close to her husband, asking questions that he didn't bother answering. Once again, he asked her to leave the kitchen. Politely, as always.

When he was sure it was safe to talk, he turned his full attention to me. "We do not have much time. I need to try something on you."

I swallowed a huge lump in my throat. "Like what?"

"I need to put you under."

I frowned. "What does that mean?"

"I need to sedate you with something. So, you, as well as myself, can dwell inside your subconsciousness."

Again, I frowned. "I don't understand."

Danial nodded. "It's hard to explain but you have to trust me. You must go under."

"For what, may I ask?" I was afraid.

"I need you to go into *Leonard Hayes'* world. I need you to look around, to find the flaw in this curse. There must be one. There always is. Again, I need you to seek it out, locate it, and let me know what it is. It's highly imperative that you do."

My chest rose and fell as I asked, "And what will you be doing while I'm 'under'?"

"I'll summon *Leonard Hayes* to me. It is not wise to have both of you in one world. The results could be catastrophic. I need to communicate with *him*, to stall *him*, while you're in *his* world, while there's still time. If what you said is true, the next time *he* returns to this world it may be final."

"What then?"

Danial hesitated. I knew it meant trouble. *Trouble for me!* "What happens then?" I asked again, more like demanded.

Danial, no longer hiding his emotions, said, "If this final time does come, then *Leonard Hayes* will remain in this world forever, and the gateway to this world will also be closed forever."

"And me?" I asked, already knowing the answer. I could feel my stomach turning over and over. I felt like throwing up and then taking a massive dump. A shit to top all shits!

Danial sighed regretfully. "As I stated before, because of the curse declared, there can only be one presence permitted in this world. And the only way *Leonard Hayes* can enter into this world is through a victim of the curse, which is you. Very soon, I'm afraid, the time will come when that 'one-presence-only' law goes into effect. Which means if *Leonard*

Hayes is allowed to remain here, in this world, then you, my son…you will no longer be allowed to exist. *He* will come after you, stronger than ever, to destroy you. If that happens then you, meaning your soul, will be locked away in *another* world…inside of *Leonard Hayes*…forever."

With those words Danial turned his head; still, I could see severe worry in his face.

"Can you make things a bit more clearer?" I asked. "I need to know what's to become of me. What is the process of this thing?" I could feel my face wilting.

Danial hesitated; probably thinking of a way to soften the blow. He hesitated a second longer, then said, "All of your past experiences have been leading up to this point. Slowly, as time advances, you and *Leonard Hayes* will become as one. Your thoughts and memories will become *his* thoughts and memories, and vice versa. Actually, the process has already begun."

"Meaning what?"

"Meaning, *Leonard Hayes* will soon learn everything about you—where you live, where you go, names, the people you come in contact with. Essentially, *he* will become *you*, and as *he* becomes stronger and more aware, you will become weaker. I can only speculate at this point that *he* already knows of me and Aphelia, and others will soon follow, as well. Eventually, *he* will locate and destroy everyone associated with you. Which sadly includes Linda, your sister Melody, as well as her two kids."

Unbelievable...I could hear myself saying.

But I couldn't allow myself to panic, to fall apart. I sat up in the chair, trying to get a grasp on this 'going under' thing. "What happens to me while you try to communicate with this *Leonard Hayes* fucker? Will I just be floating off in space somewhere?"

"No, not at all. You will be allowed to roam in *his* world, totally uninhibited, in your physical form. Just as *Leonard Hayes* has free range in this world, you'll have the same right in *his* world." Danial reached over and took me by the hand, squeezing it. "But be warned, my son, stay in the shadows as you move about, in *his* world. Do not approach or say anything to anybody. The world that *Leonard Hayes* lives in is not like our world. It's tainted—contaminated with pure evil. It may appear the same as this world but it's a far cry from it."

I wanted to scream. I dropped my head but quickly raised it as Danial said, "There's something else: know that during the exchange, while you're under, until I can summon *Leonard Hayes* into this world, there's a chance that you may even see *him*— but by all means—stay far from *him!* If *he* even thinks you're in *his* world, *he* will immediately seek you out and kill you without reason or hesitation. *He* needs your soul to complete *his* final transformation."

All of this was too much. *Way fuckin' too much!* Like I was still a kid in grade school, I raised my hand. "Hold up, are you saying that there's a chance I could run into the man that's been tormenting me? Face to face? In real fuckin' time?"

Nodding his head, Danial said, "Exactly."

I slumped in my seat. *Maybe killing myself wasn't such a bad idea...*

Danial reached out to me, squeezing my hand once more. "I know all of this is rough on you, my son, trust me, I've been there. But you must go under and find the solution to end this curse. And once again, I must stress to you: when you arrive to this *other* world, you must be careful to stay in the shadows."

I could only shake my head. *Damn, did I really want to know? I did.* Sighing heavily, I asked, "Why?"

"Because you will be a stranger to *this* world, an outsider, an intruder. Which means you will be treated as such and considered extremely dangerous. There are 'secrets' in *this* world. Well-kept secrets. Things and people will conspire and try to destroy you to keep these secrets hidden."

Fuck...

Thinking this was some sort of a nightmare, I just sat there. *It was a nightmare!* I told myself. *All of it! I just knew it was! Dammit, it was!* And just like any nightmare, it would soon be over, and any second now I'd wake up and be a little kid all over again. Free from worry. Looking forward to Christmas. Opening my presents then gorging myself on Mama's sweet potato pie afterwards.

But I wasn't a kid.

Not anymore.

I was all grown up and faced with something that was simply unbelievable—mind-blowing!

I sighed and stared at Danial. *Going under,* I thought. *What would it be like? Most likely it would be dark, and scary, with all kinds of creepy things around! I'd be scared, that's for damn sure. Who wouldn't be!*

Still staring at Danial, I had to ask, "Have you done this before?"

He turned and stared back, not blinking an eye. "No. But I believe I understand the process. It was taught to me after my experience."

I wet my lips with a quick tongue. "So, I take it you have 'gone under', as you put it?"

"Yes."

It was hard to believe but I was actually fascinated to learn this. There was a thread of hope. I wasn't by myself anymore! If that made any sense. Wetting my lips once more, I uttered, "What was it like, Danial? Please, tell me the truth. Don't bullshit me, please. Tell it to me man-to-man."

Once again it was something I had to ask.

In response, Danial drew a deep breath and as always, steepled his hands; he then gave me a look that said he wasn't about to pull any punches, as I'd requested.

"I was safe in the beginning," he started slowly, "as long as I stayed deep in the shadows. I saw things while I was under, heard things—experienced things that were way beyond my imagination and comprehension. How could I put this…," seemingly grasping for words, glancing at the ceiling, "…I saw things. Things that were overly…'exaggerated'."

Suddenly stiff, I asked, "Exaggerated? What do you mean by that?"

Danial held his head down, looked up at the ceiling once more, then over to me. "There will be things that you may or may not see or encounter. Everyday things: people, objects, buildings, houses, cars and buses, animals, again, everyday things that you would see in this world. But some of these things will appear grossly 'exaggerated', as I stated before. Highly disturbing at times. But you can't let it sway you from your purpose. I...I just hope and pray that you don't run into any of these things."

After hearing this I watched Danial closely, his expression, his mannerisms; he was hiding something. "So, I take it, this *other* world will be dangerous?"

His face became somewhat relaxed. "It wasn't too bad until I slipped up and *they* spotted me. I'd been discovered, and then, from that point on, it was pure hell. It became something that I wouldn't wish on my worst enemy."

My heart hammered. "Can you elaborate again, please?" I really wanted to know. *Though I really didn't.*

"Things from out of nowhere pursued me—*viciously!*—all type of animals—even the trees and bushes seemed to reach out at me. I couldn't hide anywhere. People were after me, too—men, women, children, young and old, with one purpose in mind: to kill me. To see that I wouldn't return to my world. So no one could tell of *their* ways...*their* secrets."

I immediately dropped my head. I didn't *want* or *need* to hear this shit! I just wanted to scream—*why me, dammit! Huh? Why the fuck me!*

But I didn't. It wouldn't do me any good. Besides, I knew *why*, anyway. That had been made painfully, soul-destroyingly clear.

The questions that stood before me now were: *How and when do I go under? What would 'I' actually encounter once 'I' got there? Where would I find this miracle solution?* And lastly, *would I be able to return to my world?*

CHAPTER THIRTY-FIVE
'GOD Be with Me'

In the murky atmosphere of a swamp, I looked around, then up. Judging by the position of the sun it appeared to be around late afternoon, a couple of hours before sunset. It would be dark soon. And that meant my eyes couldn't be counted on. I desperately needed to find some type of weapon—not to hold at bay some creature that may be lurking in the dark, not even to defend myself against an attack, but to feel secure. To feel *something* in my hand.

Or whatever my mind needed to cling to.

As my legs trudged through thick, suction-gripping mud as well as thigh-high swamp foliage, I wondered if I had lost my mind. Then I wondered why I was even wondering. *Of course I had lost my mind! What else could it be?* I was way past the perimeters of sanity, and was now on a runaway freight train about to slam into the wall of total lunacy.

Already being fitted for a straight-jacket!

Had I 'gone under' yet?

All I could recall was swallowing some nasty purple shit that Danial had given me to drink, then being forced to lay back in the bed, in my bedroom.

Maybe it hadn't worked. Maybe it had backfired, and I was having a stroke as a result. Yep, I smiled. *That was it, all right. I was suffering from a stroke.*

That was the only credible explanation. It had to be. I almost prayed that was the reason. Then I—

I shook my head, said *'no, stay focused'*, and pushed forward, looking around and behind me every few seconds or so. The syrupy-black swamp I was trudging through was silent, without even the croak of a bullfrog, or the steady *creep-creep* of a cricket. No wind in the trees above.

Trembling, and soaking wet from the humid air, I paused, not having a clue as to where I was, where I was going, nevertheless forever cautious of my surroundings as well as every step I took. Though I had on clothing that was somewhat light, as recommended by Danial: sweats, a hoodie with Timberland boots on my feet, because of the humidity, everything felt like insulated artic gear, enormously heavy, like I was on some winter expedition in the Andes. Especially my hoodie.

I suddenly froze—remembering something. I dug in my hoodie pocket and pulled out my phone, knowing damn well it would be useless. I was right. The display face read: 'No network available'.

I tucked the phone back into my pocket and headed on. I came upon a tree with low-lying branches, lined with slimy moss and fuzzy-black fungus. The tree appeared to be dead, at best dying. I reached up and broke off a branch the size of a baseball bat. I used my right hand to scale off the remaining twigs, leaves, and some icky, snot-looking shit. I felt a little better now; I had a weapon. It wasn't the greatest but the way I planned to use it, it could do some serious damage.

I suppose I should be thankful for that.

Trust me, I was.

I headed on. After resting here and there, areas where I could sit or brace myself against something, I soon reached a clearing and spotted in the dim lighting, some kind of shack, made out of wood and nothing else. It was in pretty rough shape, almost deteriorating. Very faintly, I could see remnants of yellow lights slithering between the rotting cracks. I could also hear music. Juke-joint music: Blues. Rhythm & Blues, backwoods rockabilly—foot-stomping-hip-swiveling music. Somebody was having a 'funky good time'.

I started to head over there but naturally, I did not. I wasn't dumb. *Remain in the shadows,* I could hear Danial telling me just before 'going under'. I decided to stay put. *Besides, what was I to gain even if I went over there? Nothing.*

I crouched down and started to scrape the mud from my boots. Suddenly I felt a drop. Then another. Another and another. It was starting to rain. It soon became a light drizzle then turned into an all-out monsoon. The rumbling of thunder followed, with lightning ripping the skies, giving glimpses of the landscape below. I looked around and spotted a cluster of trees sporting wide, oversized leaves, resembling a canopy.

It wasn't exactly a roof over my head but it would shield me from the brunt of the rain.

As lightning struck overhead, I turned and headed for cover, pulling my hood over my head. I nestled into place and stared at the shack. Overhead, lightning struck again, this time viciously; the electric brilliance hit brightly—lighting up everything below for nearly five seconds.

That's when I saw it.

Or thought I did.

I had to wipe the rain from my eyes to be sure. I peered harder as the lightning struck once more, and my breath caught as if I were being choked.

It was a car.

A black Crown Victoria.

Leonard Hayes' car.

My head as well as my heart instantly felt as if they were about to explode. Simultaneously. I knew then I couldn't blame it on a stroke or a seizure, or resolving it to insanity, or even applying the nightmare theory. What I saw was *real!*

The man who'd brought so much extreme terror into my life was inside that shack. That make-shift juke-joint. *No, this was no dream. No trick mirrors.*

He was in there.

I knew I had to be careful.

In every step I made.

I was now on *his* playing field…

CHAPTER THIRTY-SIX

'Ante Up Time, 'Mookie'

Only twenty or thirty feet of rain-slicked tables stood between me and a black fucker named Dwayne Combs, aka, 'Mookie'. I had a personal vendetta to settle with him. *A serious one.*

On top of being one of the men who had beat the living shit out of me and then strung my black ass up from an old willow tree, leaving me to die, the prick still had the nerve to owe me five hundred dollars.

Five hundred dollars! That was a serious piece of change to leave on the table! The guy had some nerve! Even though I was dead and buried six feet deep somewhere in the swamp, he still could have given the money to Rachel, my old lady!

But he didn't.

I never did like the guy. He was a shady, lowdown fucker—crooked as they came. The kind of guy who could eat straight nails and shit out corkscrews! And now this nickel-slick, horse-looking, chunky-gut muthafucka was about to die.

I had some waitress bitch to keep him occupied, to keep him talking, until it got a little darker outside. Then, the moment he lost interest in the conversation, and went outside to take a piss, smoke, or to leave, I'd be right there behind him. Then I'd use my bare hands to twist his head from his fuckin' body. Afterwards

I'd go through his pockets to see if I could recoup my losses.

Better late than never, baby! I told myself.

Honestly, at this point, money didn't mean a damn thing to me. Where I was going it was useless. So essentially it was like wrinkly, light-green strips of *nothing!*—with a bunch of numbers and letters written all over it—useless faces of dead presidents printed on the front—*I could wipe my ass with it! Blow my fuckin' nose with it!*

Power was the answer.

The *only* answer. Obtain the ultimate power and you had it all. From the heels of your gator shoes to the very tip of your one-of-a-kind, signature-gray Fedora hat, you'd be the one calling the shots. *All* the shots. People would not only fear you but they would do just about anything you asked to stay in your good graces.

I know this.

Because I had this power.

And I was getting stronger every day. Nearly every second! About to go 'full throttle' on their asses! I could feel it!

And soon I'd ditch this world, to rule in another world. My world. *Leonard Hayes' world!* Where my power and strength could go unchecked! Unchallenged! I could have anything and anybody I wanted!

Starting with that *Linda* bitch…

Her name had finally come to me. It took a while but now I know. And when I get to this *new* world—

my world!—she'd be the first person to seek out. I plan on opening up her sweet body like a can of sardines! Peel back everything on her body to get to the tasty insides!

*...just a little more time...*I smiled, as I drummed my fingers on the tabletop. *...just a little bit more...*

The rain was pouring in pretty good from the roof I now noticed. The place was a dump, no bigger than a few shacks pushed together, with holes everywhere, with tables and chairs that needed serious repair, creaking floors and rat turds in every corner. But it did have one good thing working in its favor: an old jukebox that still billowed out the old school legends: Bobby Blue Bland! B.B. King! Little Milton! Bobby Womack! Otis Redding! Johnnie-*muthafuckin'*-Taylor! And Lord knows you couldn't leave out my favorite—the best: Tyrone Davis!

Tyrone Davis!

My man!

'Baby, can I change your mind'...I hummed. I loved that fuckin' song!

As more and more rain poured in, I looked around, smoking a Newport cigarette, thinking since the entire place could use a total re-do, from the roofing to the flooring and everything in between, I'd give the owner the money that I plan on getting from 'Mookie'. That is, of course, after separating 'Mookie's' head from his body. It would be my last 'goodwill' gesture, you know, before I leave.

More like a 'unplanned donation' on 'Mookie's' part, I grinned.

A few minutes went by and the waitress bitch finally walked away. I gave her a wink as 'Mookie' lit a cigarette and walked to the front door. The only door. The fucker was dressed to the gill, he always was, I'll give him that. The fat-gut bastard had on a red three-piece suit with red gators on his feet— sporting his trademark, wide-brimmed red hat. Looking like a true gangsta—playa of the year!—the pimp of all pimps!

Watch out there now! I chuckled.

With a cigarette dangling at one side of his mouth, between his dry, black lips, he made his way to the door and then stepped through it. Because it was raining, he pulled the collar of his suit jacket to his neck and did a walk-jog to his car.

Stubbing out my cigarette, I was right there behind him.

When he made to his car, a 1973 Chrysler New Yorker, deep blue with a white vinyl top, I hollered out, *"Yo, 'Mookie'! Lemme hollah at you for a second, Brutha man!"*

Squinting harshly against the falling rain battering his tipped, wide-brimmed hat and also his eyelids, he turned to face me. "Do I know you, nigga?"

"You should," I said, walking up to him.

"Well, I don't, so now what, nigga?" He turned away and took several drags from his cigarette, puffing away without a worry in the world, all the while digging in his pants trying to fish out his car keys. I couldn't believe what I was seeing. The fool had the nerve, the gall, to turn his back to me.

Didn't he know he was about to die?

I made a fist and began cracking my knuckles, each one, and calmly stepped closer toward him—as he gave his cigarette a final pull then thumped it away.

"Litterbug, litterbug, shame on you," I said, wagging a finger at him.

Impatient as always, 'Mookie' turned around and snapped, "You still here? Go on somewhere, fool, I got places to be, you hear me? Go on now, with your scraggly, bent-over-lookin' ass, before you catch a cold as well as a serious beatdown." Finally fishing out his keys, he opened the door and angled himself to get inside the car.

I made my move.

Before he knew it, I was on him like stank on an unwashed ass! I grabbed him and put his head in a solid chokehold. I tightened my arm around his neck and began wrenching his head back and forth. Clean, hard wrenches. Left, right, left, right, again and again. Quick, fierce jerks. No stopping. No hesitation or pausing. I did this until 'Mookie's' head popped off and fell to the ground.

No ripping or tearing.

No screwing.

No long, drawn-out pulling.

The fucker's head just came off.

POP!

All that was left was the headless body, which crumbled to the ground, into the mud. I looked at my hands to see if there were any signs of blood on me. Because, *boy-oh-boy*—there was a shitload on the ground! From the opening, just below where 'Mookie's' head *used* to be, the ground was saturated with blood—gallons of it—spreading into a sizeable puddle. It looked as if somebody had accidentally spilled a barrel of oil on the ground.

I guess the old heart was still pumping away!

I couldn't help but snicker as I peered down on the ground; try as I may, I couldn't hold it in, and shouted out loudly, *"Call the Hazmat Team, somebody! We got a severe blood spill over here!"*

After rummaging through 'Mookie's' pockets, finding only fifty-two dollars—*the cheap bastard!*—I turned and stared at the juke-joint. Fuck the owner, let him fix up his own damn place. I wasn't his brother's keeper! I took the money and shredded it into tiny pieces. Laughing. I threw the pieces into the air—I was making it rain *with* the rain!

I looked around.

The fun was over.

Fuck it, it was time to go.

I bent down and picked up 'Mookie's' head then tossed it into the brush. Afterwards I dragged his headless body over to the edges of the swamp and then, with all my might, I heaved the damn thing deep into the brush—extra far! I heard a loud *twoosh* sound in the distance, about a hundred yards away. I smiled, *What a toss! I should have been in the Olympics!*

I scanned the area one last time then walked over to my Crown Vic. Before sliding inside, I took a few steps back and just stood there, shaking my head, somewhat mystified. It was funny. Sort of crazy—as I peered into the sky, I noticed something. Something odd. It was the falling rain; more so the rain coming down on my clothing; I stood there dry as a bone.

I grinned, and my chest began to swell with pride. Not only was I powerful, but I was also *special.*

A chosen one.

The chosen one!

To prove it, I raised my arms into the air, in ceremonial fashion, turning my palms outward and spreading my fingers, wiggling them. Soon after a slew of bats came from out of nowhere, gathering in clusters, flying around me, hundreds of them, swooping down with their leathery wings fluttering.

Worshipping me…

Praising me…

I found myself grinning harder, *First the crows, now the bats.*

I could only tighten my grin; I was becoming invincible, this I already knew, more of becoming something bigger and badder on the horizon, no longer human. I knew my time for departure was nearing.

Soon I would have my own world to rule in.

I waved my right hand and almost immediately the bats swarmed together swiftly, tightly, obediently, into a dark mass. I nodded with deep appreciation. I waved my left hand, and then the bats all took off into the falling rain, disappearing into the darkening skies.

Still holding a grin, thinking I was the shit—*Fuck that, knowing I was!*—I turned to leave. I grabbed the door handle to my Crown Vic.

That's when something strange came over me. It felt strange. *I* felt strange. I tilted my head, concentrating. I could hear a faint voice calling out to me.

"Leonard Hayes…are you there? Answer me, Leonard Hayes, are you there?"

Instinctively, I balled my fists; I was more than ready to end another life. Easily. Shit, it's what I do. What I was made for!

The voice came again, sort of demanding this time around. Disrespectful. *"Leonard Hayes, answer me now, you hear me? I'm waiting for you…"*

Frustrated, more than pissed, my eyes shifted everywhere. *"Well, here I am, muthafucka!"* I shouted out defiantly. I spun my body slowly around, sneering. *"I'm right chere, dammit! Show yourself, fool! I'm ready for you! Make a move, baby!"*

With that, I felt something jab me; almost instantly my body began drifting into nothingness. Extremely fast and violently…

The smell of the swamp wasn't as bad now since the rain had let up. Though the sun was quickly fading, I could still make out a few things around me.

I noticed that the car belonging to *Leonard Hayes* was gone. With the rain coming down so hard, I must have missed *him.* Not seeing *him* or *his* car leave.

The weather and everything else around me appeared to be settling down, so I decided to head over to the shack, the juke-joint, thinking maybe what I needed could be found in there. But something came over me and I quickly changed my mind. I caught myself staring at the shack.

That juke-joint.

"*...don't go in there...*" a voice warned me.

For nearly thirty-two years I had lived my life daringly, always pushing things to the edge, which only led me to trouble. This time, however, I understood the severity of things. "Fools rush in where angels fear to tread", that was today's motto.

I knew I wasn't an angel but I knew enough to fear *something...*

I turned and headed back into the swampy marsh and disappeared as far as I could. I was suddenly bone-tired. Finding an old rotted-out tree stump to sit on, I looked around, tense, frowning, my eyes narrowing. *Now what was I supposed to do? Nothing, I guess. Just stay put, stay safe, and sweat it out.*

The sun was nearly gone; the shadows were already creeping in quickly; this was not the time or the place to be wandering around. I couldn't help but think of snakes, leeches and eels, centipedes and beetles, all kinds of *creepy* crawlers. Biting flies and mosquitoes buzzing around me, seeking tiny sips of my blood. I started brushing my sleeves rigorously. *Get the fuck off me!* I felt myself losing it so I worked hard to control my ragged breathing—gritting my teeth and mentally groping for pleasant thoughts.

Being with Linda.... Chilling with Melody and her two beautiful kids: Jayden and Marie. I even thought of their dog Saber, my new furry friend.

But no matter what, my mind always drifted back to Linda. I found myself smiling. But even as I smiled, despair filled me. *Would I ever be happy with her again? Or worse yet, could I? Even if things did turn out okay... Would I be forever haunted by the past simply by looking at her face? Every night when I'd be alone in bed with her, would I suffer a replay of each attack? Would my dreams always be haunted—*

I heard something.

A shriek split the darkness close to me, just over my head.

I held my breath as I clutched the tree branch, my weapon, tightly in my hand. I thought it would help. It didn't. Instead of being assured, it just made me more nervous, making me wonder if I would have to use it—as if it *were* something out there lurking in the shadows with me, wanting me to hear it—ready to pounce.

The noise came again and once more, I held my breath.

Several seconds passed before I realized that what I was hearing was the croak of a bullfrog. I expelled my breath in a whistling sigh. "Shit..."

I decided to head away from the area, in case it wasn't just a bullfrog. I weighed my options and then did the 'eeny-meeny-miney-mo' thing and chose to head southward, deeper into the swamp—away from the croaking sound. I could only hope I was heading in the right direction.

With my luck, you just never knew…

Because of the recent downpour, the footing was slippery and treacherous, with every step I took, especially wearing Timberland boots. The humidity was also thicker, almost tangible; it was almost as if the ground itself was sweating. Slowly, gradually, as small branches and twigs whipped and scratched my face and hands, I forged on. It wasn't long before the sounds of the swamp began to emerge, all around me.

Crickets. Bullfrogs. Swarming insects. Even the constant *'hoot'* of an owl, off in the distance. All of this shit made me jittery. Goosebumps crept over my skin. I kept glancing nervously around, and every crack of a twig or unexpected sound made me jump. I didn't think I'd make it through another second. Let alone the night.

It was more than eerie being here among the low-lying trees, in the foggy-gray thrones of darkness, as I headed deeper. Especially knowing as well as I did that I was in *somebody else's* world. That *something*—man, creature or otherwise, could come from out of nowhere at any time, to get me—from behind any given tree—or hiding within any shadowy clump of grass, it could be waiting…

…to end my life…

My journey continued, and soon I heard a creek running off in the distance. I decided to head in that direction. It was nearly dark under the trees, more of a thick gray than a pitch black, when the air became fresher, less rancid with dampness.

I suddenly came to an abrupt stop. For no reason. It was so unexpected that I nearly slipped in the mud. My heart pounded as I peered through a clearing.

That's when I saw it.

A *huge* log cabin, as big as a castle, standing on a slight rise in front of me. The shingled roof rising above the mist. The trees had been cleared around it, and a wide, patchy road led up past it to a covered shelter, some kind of barn. It was also *huge*.

Why? I wondered.

Looking over my shoulder, both to my left and right, then behind me, I crept further up the road. Just down the road from the barn, off to the side, I spotted a couple of animals: a large, black Great Dane and what appeared to be a very small, white Siamese cat. It was sort of strange seeing them in a place like this.

Both seemed to be engaged in some type of playful game, chasing each other, tails wagging, with the Great Dane at times looking like a small horse, towering over the cat, nearly stepping on it. After a few seconds the dog stopped and began sniffing a patch of grass while the cat sat off to the side, nonchalantly grooming itself, combing its face fur, scratching behind its ears.

For some reason the sight of this was pleasing to the eyes, to my soul; it brought a tiny smile to my face. A dog and a cat frolicking about, both joyful and uninhibited, nuzzling noses, seemingly buddies, probably raised together since birth.

It made everything seem pleasant; almost *normal...*

I watched as the dog hiked its leg and began peeing in the grass. That's when I saw the cat's eyes glitter as it raised up. Like an opening had been made. In a split second the cat dropped to all fours, lowering its body with its hind fur prickled, as it turned to face the dog, regarding it as a threat. With protruding red eyes and a mewling snarl—the cat lunged and began attacking the dog viciously, pinning it down by the neck with its teeth. The small paws clawed wildly at the dog as the cat's tail swished back and forth furiously.

Moments later, with its mouth and fur stained with blood, the cat backed off from its killer stance. It calmly cleaned and pruned itself and simply walked away with its tail curling and uncurling, leaving the large Great Dane twitching convulsively on the ground, sides heaving as it struggled to breathe. After a few attempts to rise, the dog lay still. Silent.

Dead.

Instant shock went off in my mind. *Don't think about it!* I said to myself—*dammit, don't even fuckin' think about it!*—knowing I was in a *strange* world. I had to block it out. Remain calm. I had to stay focused.

But still... Damn...

Somehow I shook it off and then once more, I took in my surroundings, focusing on the log cabin, still wondering—*why was it so damn huge!* The front door alone must have been wide enough for a herd of elephants to pass through! Who or what could possibly live there? And then there was the barn. What was in it?

I looked at the log cabin, then the barn. Both appeared empty. Vacant. My heart experienced a great, hopeful leap. *Maybe I could hide out here. In the barn. I could finally close my eyes for an hour or two, possibly stay there until the morning. By then, hopefully, I'd wake up back in my townhouse. In my own bed. In my own world.*

I could feel my hoping building but then my mind began to race in another direction. *What if somebody walked in on me? Somebody huge! Especially while I was sleeping. What would I do, then?*

I couldn't help but think of Goldilocks and The Three Bears. When the bears returned home and found Goldilocks sleeping in their home. In one of their beds. This time it wouldn't be Goldilocks.

It would be me!

I chewed my bottom lip as I stared back at the swamp. Then back at the huge log cabin. Over to the barn. *What should I do?* It was at that moment when a sharp *craaak!* came—piercing the darkness around me. And then something smacked hard into a solid object barely a hundred feet from where I was standing, behind me. Afterwards it sounded like a tree had fallen. I knew then that the chance of me surviving through the night was looking like somewhere between slim and none.

Five would get you ten, I'd never make it. I turned back toward the only place I knew to go.

That barn.

Saying a heartfelt prayer for myself—I decided to throw caution as well as my fears into the wind and take my chances in the barn. Slowly, gradually, dead tired but still on full alert, I emerged from the misty swamp and headed over to the barn, jogging as my sodden boots squished with each step. I never once looked back; I wanted to but I was too afraid.

I had good reason.

I'd heard another *craaak!*—even louder, as I made my way toward the barn. Followed by the sound of yet another tree toppling over.

Nothing I knew of could cause such a sound like that. Make trees fall like that.

At least nothing in *my* world…

CHAPTER THIRTY-SEVEN

'Tread On Me Very Softly'

The room was dark.

I was lying in a bed. In somebody's bed. In somebody else's house. Who's I hadn't the slightest idea. I tried to move but I was trapped. My limbs were locked in place. All of them. I couldn't get up from the bed. I was surprised. As strong as I was.

Once again, I tried moving my legs. Tried wiggling my toes. Nothing moved. I closed my eyes and summoned every muscle in my body, all my strength, to react.

Nothing.

Something held me at bay.

What the fuck was it?

I could make out something laying on my chest, just below the left side of my chin; it was a wooden stick of some kind, with a pointed tip, shaped like a knife or a dagger. For a minute I studied my situation, and as I did, I heard a man's voice.

"Hello, Mr. Leonard Hayes."

Since I couldn't raise my head from the bed, I shifted my eyes, straining to see who it was, trying to *feel* who it was. Just out the corner of my left eye I could make out the figure of a man. He was sitting in a chair beside me, wearing some kind of military outfit. Beige fatigues.

Somehow, I *knew* this man; his voice was familiar.

Almost immediately I wanted to bash his face in. Lucky for him I couldn't do it.

"Who are you?" I asked.

A pause. "Why don't you take a guess, Mr. Hayes. I encourage you to humor me."

My eyes began to narrow—filled with unbridled hatred. *"Yeah, I know who you are. I know exactly who you are."*

"Who am I, Mr. Hayes?"

"You're that black fucker named Danial. And you got a short, fat ass wife named Aphelia, who always wears that shit-smelling cocoa butter. Y'all the two fuckers that escaped from that house. Am I correct, Mr. Danial? Have I hit the nail on the head?"

"You have, Mr. Hayes."

Something *odd* struck me. Very *odd*. I raised a brow. *"You're not from around these parts, are you, Mr. Danial? Neither is your wife. You two are from some place quite far away. Far, far away."*

"You're correct in your deduction, Mr. Hayes."

"I thought so." His words brought an inner smile to me. I was growing forever stronger. I cleared my throat. *"So, tell me, Mr. Danial, were you the one calling me?"*

"Yes, it was me. In fact, I brought you here."

"Why?"

"Because we need to talk, Mr. Hayes."

"*About what?*"

"About you."

"*What about me?*"

"I need to know if there's any way to reason with you."

I immediately frowned. *Reason? What's this crazy bastard talking about?* I had to ask. "Reason?"

"Yes, Mr. Hayes, exactly what I said: Reason."

"*Okay,*" I smiled, "*that sounds doable. Why don't you free me so we can really talk?*"

"You know I can't do that, Mr. Hayes."

"*Why not, Mr. Danial?*"

"Because if I did, you'd kill me."

I chuckled. "*You ain't never lied, Mr. Danial. Best believe, I'd pull your fuckin' heart from your chest the first chance I got.*" I chuckled again, even louder.

"I know you would, Mr. Hayes. Now, can we talk like two civilized men?"

I couldn't help but laugh out loud. "*Civilized men? You bullshittin' me, right?*" If I could slap my knee in laughter, I would. "*Please, Mr. Danial, tell me you're bullshittin'.*"

"Not at all."

I tried to shift one of my legs. I was still unable to move. I couldn't comprehend what was holding me.

"Okay, Mr. Danial," I smiled smugly, *"you seem to have me at a slight disadvantage. For now. So, what did you want to talk about?"*

"I was hoping to reason with you."

"About what?"

"I was hoping that you would leave certain individuals alone. Allow them peace. That you would move on to somebody else. Or maybe simply go away for good. Stay in your *own* world."

A tremor of anger passed through me. The hot surges made me sweat. This prick of a man thought I was soft, vulnerable—that I could be reasoned with. It was obvious that this man did *not* know me. What I was capable of! But then I thought, *He needed something*...I decided to play along. Get him to relax, to place trust in me. Drop his guard. *Then*—the first chance I got—I'd crack this fucker's skull!

"What's in it for me?" I asked calmly, managing to once again raise an eyebrow.

A pause. "Let's call it: an act of kindness, one you have the power to provide. A goodwill gesture on your behalf."

My insides immediately clutched. *"Kiss my ass, Mr. Danial. Why would I want to do anything 'good'? Being 'good' is no longer what I do. I'm here to do 'bad'. Extreme 'bad'. Simply unspeakable, malevolent things. Perfectly pure, unchecked, evil shit. Mutha-fuck being good."*

"I'd wish you'd consider my offer, Mr. Hayes. I implore you to use good judgement. As you know, good judgement is forced upon us by age and experience."

"Huh?" I said chuckling, like I actually knew what the hell he was talking about. I tried to figure how to respond so I could get this darker-than-dark fucker to release me. *"Okay, I'll consider your request,"* I said. *"So, tell me, Mr. Danial, who is it that you want me to back off from?"*

"A young man, and a woman named Linda…Linda Hayes. Your niece…"

Suddenly my stomach felt tied up in knots. He was talking about *Linda;* I felt this ache of bewilderment, of deep curiosity. I'd been exposed, as if I'd been run through an x-ray machine. This man saw right through me. Or did he? How much *did* he see? How much did he really *know* about me? Is this how he summoned me and was now keeping me at bay?

I needed to learn more.

"I don't know a Linda or this young man," I stated with a mock frown of confusion. *"I'm telling you, you must have me mixed up with somebody else. Which means you're holding me against my will. And that shit ain't legal—in your world or mine! I wanna see my lawyer, you hear me! Bring his ass in here!"* I couldn't help but chuckle at my own words.

"Don't bullshit me, Mr. Hayes. You know *damn* well who they are. Now, do we have a deal? Will you allow these two people their freedom? So they can live their lives peacefully?"

Somehow I managed to shift my head about half an inch, maybe an inch. I then gave this man my complete attention. My complete and final answer. *"Go fuck yourself real good, Mr. Danial. I don't bargain or reason or make deals with anyone. I call all the shots—I make all the decisions—and believe me when I say, not only do I plan on inflicting some serious havoc in this world, I plan on doing this Linda bitch until her body disintegrates."*

A quick response followed. "I'm curious, Mr. Hayes, why do want your niece so bad?"

"Because I do, that's why."

"Are you afraid to tell me?"

"I ain't afraid of shit, you hear me!"

"Then tell me, Mr. Hayes. Prove to me that you are not afraid."

I could feel a tingling sensation in my toes. Gradually, at a snail's pace, one fiber at a time, my nerve endings started to vibrate. *Just a little more...* I smiled as the blood appeared to flow freer through my body. I closed my eyes, becoming in tuned with every awakening sensation.

In the meantime, this asshole kept probing me harder, more demanding—I mean, this prick-bastard wouldn't let up!—"Why do you want your niece so bad, Mr. Hayes? Why? Why?"—he kept on!

I decided not to tell him a damn thing. Besides, it wouldn't change anything, anyway. My brother's daughter was destined to be mine's forever, regardless. I wanted her! For myself! She was so beautiful! Damn my brother! That's why I ran him and his whore-bitch wife off the road with my Crown

Victoria—causing his car to crash into a solid wall—into a fiery *Boom!* *And just like that—both of them were dead! Gone! Out of my life and out of the way! Bye, bye, Bro! Bye, bye, Bro's whore-bitch wife!*

And then their precious daughter, Linda, my niece, was all mine...

No, I smiled, *thinking about it. I wouldn't tell this man a damn thing...* In fact, telling him why might even hurt my chances. And not only that, me giving in to this man would make me appear weak—like he had the constant upper hand on me. A solid foot pressed against my chest—and that was not going to happen!

The thought of this seriously enraged my insides. *"If I were you, Mr. Danial,"* I whispered in a seething voice, *"I would run back to wherever faraway place that I came from and never look back. You and that pint-size, bitch-wife of yours. Because when I do become free—and trust me, I will!—I'm going hunt you down and make you my personal project. Simply put: I'm going to destroy you, Mr. Danial, piece by piece, limb by limb. But first I'm going to gut you, by reaching deep inside your mouth, from your throat down to your asshole, and pull everything in between from out of your mouth. This, Mr. Danial, you can count on."*

That's when I heard this man chuckle. "I'm afraid that's not possible, Mr. Hayes. You can't even rise from the bed. You see, you can't enter into this world without going through me now. So, as it stands, you have to remain in *your* own world."

I was quick to respond. *"Your advantage over me is only temporarily, Mr. Danial, trust me. I'm going to figure out how to rise from this bed, how to reenter into this world, and when I do, you better hope and pray to whatever god you pray to, because I plan on ripping your body apart, slowly, until your torso resembles a fuckin' tree stump."*

He appeared unfazed by my threats. "That's highly unlikely, Mr. Hayes. I got you where I want you: like a dog with a tight collar around its neck, and I'm the man holding the leash."

"Fuck you!" I'd listened to this man long enough. I was determined not to give him the satisfaction that he had me by the nuts. *For now!*

Slowly, I could feel one of my hands, the right one, tightening into a fist. I knew then he couldn't hold me forever...

"*I'll see you soon, Mr. Danial...just you wait and see...and I'm going to enjoy destroying you...you and your foul, cocoa butter-smelling wife..."*

With those words I closed my eyes, totally reassured that this fucker had been jolted by my warning, by my promise, and was pretending not to be afraid. He was probably squirming as he sat there. Pissing and shitting his pants.

He was. *I could feel it!*

I took immense personal pleasure in knowing this. Even though I couldn't see it.

It was time to go.

The man couldn't stop me from leaving...

With my eyes shut tightly I let myself go, and soon felt my body dissolving and rising, away from the bed, away from this world, in the form of a mist, floating, as an opening presented itself; I gazed straight forward as I drifted toward it. I could feel a grayness enveloping what was left of my body, as it grew thinner, thinner, thinner still, until I felt like oily smoke. My body remained whispery-black, almost useless, but my mind stayed sharp as a tack.

I knew where I was heading. *Back to my world.*

The fucker could summon me from out of *my* world, and perhaps keep me from reentering into *his* world, but that was only temporarily. Little did he know I wasn't as subdued as tightly as I pretended to be.

I'd keep this little ruse going for just a bit longer.

I was getting stronger. And he didn't know that. He hadn't a clue. I'd catch him off guard. When he thought he had me at a disadvantage.

Like before.

I'd wait until just the right moment and then I would seize him—grab that black fucker—twist his body into a human pretzel—snapping every bone and ligament in the process.

This man would pay the ultimate price for mocking me.

Laughing at me.

Calling me a dog on a leash.

I plan on making him my best kill yet!

CHAPTER THIRTY-EIGHT

'A Subtle Light Begins to Shine'

Something nudged me!

Awakening me.

Then a voice came, *"Get up, Derrick! Get up and run! They're coming! Get up and run, boy!"*

It was Mama.

"Run!" she repeated.

"Shit!" I gasped, leaping from the ground. I looked around and suddenly smelled the pungent odor of formaldehyde, which made it hard to breathe and triggered a gag reflex.

"Run, Derrick!"

I didn't need Mama to tell me anymore. I bolted from the barn like a deer from hunters, head low, feet slipping and sliding on the mud and grass underfoot. Head spinning, heart pounding, I didn't know what I was running from or even to. But I was sure I'd be dead by now if I'd remained in that barn another second.

I ran harder, as though monsters were hot on my heels.

No doubt, it probably was…

"There he goes! Get him! Kill him!" I heard somebody yell. *"Don't let him get away! Get him!"*

I headed straight for cover, into the darkness of the swamp. I must have ran for nearly thirty minutes straight and finally, with my lungs giving out, I had to stop and rest. Thank God for the gym. I leaned against a large tree, hunched over with my hands on my knees, still breathing deeply.

Craaak!

It was that sound again. Something had been struck nearby. It was close. Probably another tree. I was sure it was; I could actually *feel* the blowback of splinters in the air. I almost screamed, but choked it back not to give away my location. I took off running, and as I dodged and weaved among the trees and thick brush, I realized I'd left my stick weapon back in the barn. But I couldn't worry about that now.

I needed to keep running!

It was still dark, but traces of sunlight were on the horizon. Which was bittersweet. I could see where I was going but *they* could see me! I soon heard running water. It was that stream I'd heard earlier. I ran toward it, still slipping and sliding to keep my footing. Above me, crows were beginning to follow my every move, some gathering in the trees, forming in clusters as they began calling to one another. Most likely to announce my whereabouts.

But to who?

To what?

I looked down at the ground hoping to find some type of weapon. Something long and sharp, a solid stick or maybe some sort of palm-size rock, so I'd have a chance at defending myself. I looked hard as I ran, stopping every now and then hoping to spot *something. Anything.*

But finding nothing.

I gave up looking and pressed on. I headed deeper, and that's when I heard a rumbling going on in my stomach, near the bottom. I knew what it was. It was that damn contaminant mixture that Danial always made for me. And it was doing its job. Again. I had to go to the bathroom, and not just to pee. But there was no time! *Hold it,* I told myself. *Find the strength and hold it!*

After running, walking, then jogging for what seemed like miles, I finally had to stop and rest again, and do what I needed to do. What needed to be done. I handled my bathroom business behind a large tree. I didn't like what I had to wipe my ass with but I did manage to wipe it clean.

Afterwards I found a large, moss-covered rock and took a seat; I glanced around; everything appeared to look the same. Same trees. Same *creepy* foliage. Same wet, rancid-smelling swamp. And I wondered if I was walking in circles. I pulled myself up by using a vine and when I got to my feet, I felt hideously tired; it hit me hard, like an endless dose of Melatonin was running through my veins.

Somehow I shook it off and headed on, feeling as if I had been walking around in circles, but then, just as despair began to grip me, I came to a creek; oddly, despite the *ugliness* of this place, the water appeared to be pure, clean, without a speck of debris flowing through it. The water tinkled merrily alongside the shallow bank. It sounded *happy* and I flashed a weak, pathetic smile.

Just like the trickle of water I felt a trickle of hope.

But then I heard the loud cawing of the crows—*"Over here! Over here!"*—they seemed to be saying—giving my location away, and all hope instantly faded away.

I almost felt like saying, *okay, fuck it, you win, dammit,* and giving up…

But there was no time for a pity-party—I had to keep moving!

I started to cross the creek but I didn't see anything on the other side. Nothing but an open field. No trees. No tall foliage or bushes. Nothing but beautiful green, lush grass, precision-cut at just the right height, as if regularly maintained.

Should I cross the creek?

Where to go afterwards?

Where to hide?

I decided to take my chances and sprint across the creek until I got to the other side—then run like hell over the open field of grass. But before I could take a step, in just that moment—in what could have been five minutes or even five seconds—I found that my body had seized up; I couldn't move a single limb. I stood there shivering, hot and sweaty, in a state of suspended animation; my feet were going numb because of the swampy water, which at this point, had soaked through my boots.

It was strange, unexplainable.

But I could actually hear Danial speaking…to 'someone'. Something about working out a deal with 'them'. Something to do with 'me' and Linda…about letting 'us' go…I don't know why but I could feel myself getting angry…wanting to lash out at Danial…wanting to rip his heart out, but I couldn't. I was being held by something. After expressing rage toward Danial and Aphelia, promising to return…I could feel 'myself' fading away…returning 'here'…

Coming out of whatever it was that had me, I stood there staring blankly. I shook myself and realized the danger that I was still in. I looked back at the swamp. I heard the caws of the crows, even louder, more frantic. But I also heard something else.

Something was coming…

I turned and started to cross the creek. That's when a bat suddenly darted from out of the brush, swooping down and nipping at my face and hands. Crouching down, I yanked the hood of my hoodie over my head. Soon another bat came.

Another. Then another. Then a multitude.

All demonic-looking, with red, bulging eyes, razor-sharp teeth, armed with long, spiked tentacles.

They started attacking me in waves. Pushing me away from the creek. Each nip of their razor-sharp teeth and slicing tentacles caused a burst of new pain to explode over my body. I scrambled and ran along the bank of the creek, dipping forward, slipping backwards, legs spreading and sliding sideways, almost falling flat on my back. The bats pursued me relentlessly, nipping, biting, cutting and slicing me with their tentacles, nonstop, driving me further from the creek.

And then they backed off.

Suddenly.

As if told to do so.

More like: commanded.

Heaving and sucking in air, giving my lungs a serious workout, I stopped and turned around. I searched the entire area for the bats, everywhere, especially the skies. They were gone. I didn't really believe they were gone. I just couldn't see them.

I finally caught my breath and that's when I noticed that I was bleeding everywhere. The bats had done a serious number on me. A vicious hit-and-run. There were at least a million remnants of the assault—tiny bite and slit-marks everywhere on my body, all through my clothing, from the top of my head down to my boots. All had signs of blood. The pain stung horrendously, like multiple syringes being jabbed into my skin—in, out—every place you could think of.

But I had survived. At this point, all I could do was be more than grateful that I was still alive. I glanced up to give God a well-deserved 'thank you', but wasn't sure if even He acknowledged this place. I looked around and noticed that the entire area had gone quiet.

Still as can be.

More than just...*quiet*...

Even the noises of the swamp had been seemingly sucked away.

It was scary to think that I was even here, that I would be stumbling around in such a place, through some wooded swamp, vulnerable to detection by things that never would have crossed my mind before.

Never. Not in a million years.

I could only shake my head, still wondering how in the hell did my life end up here…

As I looked around the silence began closing in.

I couldn't help but think some type of stage was being set. That there was some hideous, even more frightening disturbance that was about to happen… something mind-blowing and heart-bursting…lurking in the shadows, waiting to reveal its self.

I was right.

Just behind me, I heard another loud *craaak!*— coming from the swamp. It was close, whatever it was, and coming closer.

I didn't have to wait long.

Hammering thuds emerged, pounding the earth violently, as trees, bushes, and swamp grass began to sway, as if by the vibration. Even as I stood at the edges on the creek, about fifty yards away, I could feel the ground shaking beneath me.

Something was coming for me…

Something big…

Once again, I was right.

Clambering over the fallen tree it had knocked over, shrieking in triumph, a huge, serpent-like creature emerged. Its body, the size and width of an armored tank, resembled some kind of black, scaly reptile—an oversized Komodo Dragon. Defiantly, it loomed over the outer edges of the swamp. It started moving slowly, swishing its thick, leathery body from side to side in one sinuous motion, with each limb anchoring one over the other; its large, hooked claws dug into the ground as it eased further from the swamp, still surrounded by several trees.

Then it stopped, and its reptilian head raised up and scanned the area with yellow, demented eyes, which protruded like cue balls in the sockets.

A glossy-black forked-tongue as thin as a bullwhip, perhaps twelve feet long, soon emerged from its mouth, flicking and *tasting* the air every five seconds or so—most likely tasting the air for me—smelling the blood that the bats had caused.

...the perfect one-two punch...

I remained as quiet and as still as I could.

It didn't work.

The reptilian creature spotted me almost instantly. It shrieked again, louder, spilling mucus-spit from its mouth—revealing a row of jagged, clashing teeth. It then gave me a look that said it was here to kill me. That my death would not be an easy one.

All I could do was stare back at the creature, watching as it stared back at me with an inky-yellowish sheen in its eyes. I tried with everything in me to cling to my sanity which was slipping away quickly, perilously close to madness.

I watched as the creature moved each of its limbs, as it inched closer. I could see the tail; thirty feet long, as thick as a man's body—bristled with spiny thorns—writhing, dancing, twitching with obscene gestures. Without warning the creature whipped its tail, making a loud *craaak!* sound as the tail slammed against a nearby tree, causing the tree to snap in two.

I could only stare with an opened mouth as it inched closer.

The forked-tongue flickered furiously, every second now, *tasting the air—me!*—seemingly ready to strike at a moment's notice.

Not waiting for things to get any worse, I turned and ran—*hard!*—along the bank of the creek. I soon heard what I knew I'd hear: the creature in hot pursuit after me. With each step that I took I could hear the ground shaking under me; the creature was powerful enough to stir up its own earthquake in this twilight world.

Every few seconds or so, I'd turn my head back only to see that my time was nearing. The creature was closing in fast, and there was no place to run to. Nowhere to hide. I had only one choice.

The creek.

My only chance. A chance I'd have to take.

My heart thumped like a beating drum when I made a maddening leap into the creek. The water slapped me hard, engulfing me quickly as I thrashed about, as I heaved, hoisted, and lunged my body further and further into the middle of the creek. I lost my footing and went under. When I came up, I anxiously looked around. Nothing.

Where was the creature?

Where was it, dammit!

Frantically peering around, I spotted the creature over my left shoulder as it came to an abrupt stop. It looked at me strangely, turning its head sideways, both ways, as if studying me, sizing me up. It took a gradual step toward me then hesitated; it growled and hissed, seemingly calling me every name in the book, and then began backing away with its yellow eyes glaring harshly. I could see the tail rebelliously shuddering as it turned away and headed back into the swamp, plunging quickly into the darkness.

Seconds later it had vanished. Gone.

Just like that.

My heart somewhat beating normally now, I took a deep breath as I stared at the swamp, focusing on the area where the creature had slipped into. I thought it odd. *The creature was reptilian. Surely it could have gotten to me? Easily...*

I looked around. I couldn't believe that it was truly gone. *Maybe it wasn't...* I scanned the water, somehow waiting for the creature to surface. However, the way the water flowed, clear, clean, pure and nearly translucent, I would've seen it surfacing or coming at me. I exhaled a long, deep breath through my nose. Though things appeared to be somewhat safe, at least for now, I crept over to the other side of the creek, wading in the chest-high water until I reached the outer edges. Droplets of water dripped from my soaked body as I just stood there.

...again, I felt blessed...

...more than grateful...

Once more I exhaled hard and then knelt down on my knees like a little boy in church. I began splashing water all over me, my face, my neck, arms and legs. The cool water felt so good on my poor, battered body, as if soothing nerve endings. I closed my eyes and let the water rinse over me, *through* me, for several minutes.

That's when I noticed something.

The bat bites, the nips and slices, they were no longer plaguing me. I felt nothing but, I don't know, if I had to give it a name, I would call it...*relief*...

I slowly eased from the creek—not too far, mind you, and took a seat at the water's edge, just at the grass line. I took a deep breath and looked up at the sky. I couldn't explain it but, somehow, I could feel my body tightening up everywhere, deep inside, on the outside. There was a pause in which I stared at the creek and contemplated that.

This odd feeling...

I found myself leaning back on my elbows, one knee bent. I must have stayed that way for at least fifteen minutes, still staring at the creek, at the clean, crystal-clear water running swiftly past me.

That's when I noticed it.

Something staring directly at me.

Dead in the face.

It was the creek.

Not the creek itself but the water flowing through it. Though the ground was pitched downward, angled in a sloping position, the rush of the water was flowing in the *opposite* direction.

Upward.

As if defying the laws of gravity.

How could this be? I found myself scowling, deep and hard in thought, trying to decipher the logic behind this weird phenomenon. *A ground that slumps downward but water that flows upward...* I must have sat there for another fifteen minutes. Maybe even thirty.

Still scowling.

As daylight gradually approached, the sky far to the east a faded orange, a light shade of blue to the west, I found myself still gazing at the creek. The idea of water flowing against nature seemed more and more inexplicable by the second. I took several deep breaths, purging my lungs with fresh, pure air. I did this until I suddenly stopped.

...that's when a gradual smile emerged...

CHAPTER THIRTY-NINE
'Tidying Things Up'

The man's blows hadn't fazed me one bit. I shook it off without effect. It felt no different than a tap from a fly swapper. *A gentle tap at that.* The man repeated the process of retaliation by striking me in the face again, several times, but once more, the blows were ineffectual.

Becoming comical.

Something to laugh at.

I stared at the man; though his eyes had the look of a real badass, he knew all that bullshit ended with *me!* The man was once a great fighter, a real scrapper, who could handle himself well in a street brawl—simply knocking out those medium and lightweight contenders—all day long! But now he was facing a 'sho-nuff' heavyweight.

The ultimate *real* deal.

And I wasn't about to take a dive for nobody!

I watched as his chest continued to rise and fall, tight with apprehension. The poor bastard had tired himself out. He must have realized something as he gazed at me with frightened eyes: he knew he was about to die. In fact, I was willing to bet my Crown Vic that he was about to beg for his life.

...any second now...

...hold it...

...hold it...

"Please, man," he pleaded, "I don't want to die."

And ding, ding, ding!—there you have it, folks! I was right! Somebody please give me a cigar before I kill this man, dammit!

I looked at this shivering man as my dark, piercing eyes drilled through him. *"It's time to pay for all the pain you cost me!"* I sneered.

With lightning speed I grabbed him by his green-and-white uniform and lifted him nearly four feet from off the ground; his feet dangled wildly trying to reach the floor, trying to make contact with something—instead knocking over boxes of nails, washers, screws and bolts, and other shit which lined the shelves.

I gave this man one final look, so he could see *exactly* who I was—*exactly* who he was dealing with—*Leonard Hayes, dammit!*—and then I plunged my hand inside the chest of his little manlike figure, directly under his rib, where something twitched, throbbed, and throbbed again. I snatched my hand back and held the man's heart in my hand. It felt like a squishy balloon, half-filled with water, flaccid, and I squeezed it in my hand. The dark black tissue and oily blood threaded through my fingers. The man's body toppled backward into the shelves and then fell to the floor.

I smiled pleasingly at the lifeless body, the one with a big hole gouged in the chest area, spilling blood everywhere.

"*Clean up on aisle two!*" I shouted out, chuckling heartily. I stared down at the slumped body.

Douglas Young.

One of the three men remaining that I had to settle a score with. Men who had strung me up in an old willow tree, leaving me to die.

I soon left the hardware store, the one belonging to Douglas Young. He owned it. Or *once* owned it. Now the poor bastard didn't have a store, a life, or even a fuckin' heart. Before leaving, I flipped the front door sign around so it went from "Open" to "Closed".

I smiled, *the sign should have said: "Out of Business".*

Because I had just handled *mine*, leaving this man with absolutely none!

The tires of my Crown Victoria slowly rolled to a stop. In front of a clothing store that I used to frequent. Shutting down the engine, I stared at the small glass-and-brick building.

Hatefully.

The man I wanted worked here: Terrance Caldwell, a smooth-talking dude who had a velvety voice to aid him. He had a beautifully-built model's body, chiseled, washboard abs and all. On top of that, he was tall and good-looking—high-yellow, with wavy black hair, and deep, child-like dimples—dazzling green eyes—pretty as they come!

Damn!—plus the nigga could sing and dance his ass off, too! The women loved him!

...so did I...

When all the women rejected me, I thought he would want me—he said he did! I gave that bastard all the money I had at one time. *Nearly two thousand dollars!* Just to feel his sweet lips pressing against mine. But I never did. Instead, he took my money, kicked my ass like nobody's business, and then laughed at me as I dangled by the neck from that old willow tree.

But I wasn't dangling anymore.

The fuck if I was...

And now this man wasn't half the man that I used to be; he's a complete nobody, dammit! *And now it was time to make him realize how much he'd hurt me. Both physically and emotionally. He was the only 'man' that I truly loved...*

I stepped from my Crown Vic and then boldly walked inside the clothing store. As always, a tiny little chime: *'ding-dong'*, announced a customer's arrival. I looked around. There was nobody in the store. It didn't matter anyway. If they got in the way—*oh, well, too bad-so sad!*—they'd end up dead in some pleasurable way I could think of.

I really liked killing people! I thought with a sudden smile. *It was kind of fun—that certain way, that certain expression people made when they realized they were drawing their last breath—the way their eyes bulged in shock—just before they saw what was coming at them—or didn't!*

It was the best feeling in the world!

The absolute best!

As I searched for Terrance, my mind began searching for new ways to end his life. I decided it was time to be a bit more creative. Something totally different. Other than pulling heads from bodies. Or ripping hearts from chests. Or that one time when I kicked a man so hard through his stomach that my shoe nearly came off when I tried to pull my foot back out. Admittedly, those were all good, some greater than others, but I needed something special.

That one memorable moment…

Who knows, maybe this was it?

It wasn't long before I found Terrance in the stockroom, boxing up shoes and putting price tags on the new line of clothing coming in. I made my way closer. Taking one slow step at a time.

"Hello, Terrance," I announced, standing over him as he looked up from a stool he was seated on.

"Hey, man, you ain't supposed to be back here," he said indignantly. "Get your dusty, homeless-looking ass from back here before I call the cops."

Instead of taking offense, I could only stare. *Shit, the man was still fine as fuck! Prettier than the prettiest woman!* I could feel myself wetting my lips. At just that moment, I wanted to kiss him.

Desperately.

Deep and hard.

I wanted to feel his lips pressing against mine. Then maybe…just maybe, mind you…we'd start caressing each other, touching each other, as we kissed, the start of a slow grind.

Maybe he'd let me suck—

I was broken from my amorous wishes as the rude, uncaring bastard barked harshly at me, "Look, man, I ain't gonna tell you no more—get the fuck from back here before I throw you from back here!"

I peered down on him, totally indifferent to his threats. *"You don't remember me, do you, Terrance?"*

Brushing his sleeves as well as his pants, he stood up from his stool. "Nope, should I?"

"Look closer, Terrance," I said; I leaned in and coaxed him with smile, still wanting to kiss him, sort of hoping he'd kiss me first.

He didn't. Instead, he raised both hands and shoved me hard; I barely moved. "Man, I ain't got no time for this shit! Leave! Now! Find yourself a job! Can't you *see* that I'm busy!"

That's when it hit me!

Oh, hell yea! my mind shouted. Without a moment's hesitation, as though I would somehow forget, I reached out and clutched Terrance Caldwell by the head, *tightly*, palms on the sides, thumbs at his temples; with both hands locked in place, I shifted my thumbs until they found their way over to Terrance's pretty green eyes. I covered his eyes with my thumbs. Then, ever-so-gingerly, I dug my thumbs into his eyes, into the sockets, until I heard loud screams filling the stockroom.

I watched as Terrance's face went through a rapid-fire series of expressions: frowns, pouts, wincing; he even smiled—*and lo, and behold!*—there were those gorgeous deep dimples again! Funny, I thought, until I met this man, I never would have believed that I could be such a sucker for dimples.

But damn, here I am! Still a sucker!

Ignoring the screams as well as the body jostling, the fanatic squirming, my thumbs dug deeper until I heard faint squishy sounds. Those gorgeous green eyes got lost in a red-pinkish mush as I wiggled my thumbs, pressing harder. I suddenly became fascinated—like a kid playing with *play-doh* for the very first time—mashing, kneading, trying to make something out of nothing.

As a result, Terrance Caldwell hollered even louder, and started to twitch furiously—arms and legs flailing everywhere, while I treated the eye mush as if it were *play-doh*.

At first, I tried making different things: a dog, a cat, *a mouse, maybe?* But nothing seemed to work. Nothing wanted to take shape for me.

Darn it!

Then, as my thumbs sunk deeper, I treated the mush as something else, something totally different, like insects trying to get away: a bloated, black tarantula spider, carrying its babies on its back, that fly you finally cornered, or a scurrying cockroach running from a bright light that had been suddenly turned on.

The fun finally came to an end when I heard a *squish-pop!*—followed by what looked like strands of spaghetti oozing from the sockets.

Good old Terrance was still hanging in there, though—still shaking and flailing his body everywhere, either in pain, terror, or shock.

...like he was suffering from a terrible nightmare...with nobody there to wake him up...

I felt sorry for him. So, as a kind gesture, because I still loved this man, *well, kind of-sort-of*, I decided to show mercy. With wilting eyebrows as well as a loving expression locked on my face, I tightened my grip around his head, at the same time hooking and anchoring my thumbs deep into the eye sockets, as I gradually began to spread my hands apart, further, further, until I heard a *snap-crack*—the discreet tearing of a skull finally being ripped open, like a stubborn coconut.

I knew then that it was over.

Though this 'killing' was a bit gruesome, it needed to be done. *The bastard had fucked me so I had to fuck him back. Case closed.*

Nevertheless, I couldn't help but feel a little sad. I stared down at this beautiful man's body, with its split-opened head and punched-out eye sockets, and nearly shed a tear, fully aware of the internal turmoil going on inside of me.

But then, oh well—*just like that*—*it was gone*—*and it was off to the next one!*

—like it never happened!

Somehow though, I still experienced a shred of sympathy. Crossing myself, I squatted down and took Terrance by the hand, his left hand, squeezing it lightly. *"So long, pretty boy,"* I whispered tenderly, *"I'm so sorry it turned out this way, but as you know, bad shit happens from time to time. It's called karma, baby."* I squeezed his hand once more, but not *too* tightly—I'd crush it. *"Well, anyway, man, I gotta split. You take care now, you hear me, pretty boy. I..."*

I couldn't help myself; I felt a tear escaping and streaking my cheek. The left side.

That's the way it was with me, when it came to killing someone. Especially when you had the strength and power like I had. You were never quite sure how you would feel sometimes. Where your emotions would end up.

With that last one...

Nevertheless, I was *'feelin' good now'!*—like Mr. James Brown himself! I left the clothing store with a broad smile and no regrets, walking in a soulful stride—humming another one on my favorite Tyrone Davis songs: *'If I could turn back the hands of time'*.

Tyrone Davis!

My man!

Gone with your bad self, T.D.!

I hear you, baby!

I cranked up my black Crown Vic, still humming that Tyrone Davis song. In fact, it stayed in my head until I arrived at my next destination, on the south side of town, at some dude's crib that I knew, Norman Dixon, one of the men who had beat the shit out of me and then strung me up.

It was crazy!

The song was still bopping in my head, as I nonchalantly smoked a Newport cigarette. The song became addictive. Addictive as the Newports that I loved to smoke. The song *so* fit the occasion: *'If I could turn back the hands of time…'*

I even got Norman Dixon to sing along with me, when he came to every now and then, as I calmly pulled each one of his limbs, one at a time, from his torso…

CHAPTER FORTY

PART FIVE

'Once Again, No Rest for The Weary'

When I came to, my bedroom was well-lit. That might seem like a small thing, but it was enough to be more than grateful for. Considering where I'd just been. It also reminded me how messed up and distorted my life had become.

Bouncing in and out of different worlds.

What kind of life is this to live?

I stirred in my bed and looked around. My entire body ached, my head throbbed, and I needed caffeine like a burning itch needed scratching. I tried to rise up but I was so exhausted that I fell back on the bed.

"Welcome back, Mr. Archer," Danial whispered. "It's great to see you finally coming around."

Danial?

I turned my head and smiled. It *was* Danial. Sitting in a chair beside the bed. The man was a sight for sore eyes. My insides couldn't help but do a little dance. Huffing a big sigh of relief, I sat up in the bed. "Hello, sir," I nodded. I turned and saw Aphelia sitting off in a corner, nearly in tears.

"Welcome back, Mr. Derrick Archer," she sniffed, wiping her eyes with a balled-up napkin. I could see wads of napkins in the small waste basket next to her feet. Apparently she'd been sitting there a while, anxiously waiting for my return.

"Hello, Aphelia," I smiled, giving her a small wave. Smiling brightly, she returned my wave with one of her own. I nodded then looked down at myself, at my clothing, then back over to Aphelia; I couldn't explain it but I didn't want her to see me like this: exhausted, disheveled, unshaven, probably appearing gaunt and somewhat haggard, not to mention the zillion prick-holes in my clothing, with tiny blood stains at every hole. I pulled the covers over me, knowing I looked bad.

But as my gaze slid over to Aphelia, as much as my fuzzy vision would allow, my heart did a little double-skip. I knew I was thinking foolish; Aphelia was like a second mother to me; she could care less how I looked.

I couldn't help myself; I waved to her again. And true to her nature, she waved back.

"What happened while you were there, Mr. Archer?" Danial asked with a sense of urgency in his voice. No doubt, he was *not* impressed with the little wave thing we had going on. He wanted answers.

I sat up even further in the bed, and that's when my mind seemed to stall. I shook it off and sighed heavily. I then told Danial about my experience, how when I came to, I found myself in some kind of swamp, a dark everglade, which included strange sounds and noises as I wandered about in this *other* world. I told Danial about the small juke-joint, with *Leonard Hayes'* car parked just outside. *His* black Crown Victoria. I went on to explain about the barn that I'd come across, how I sought refuge inside to rest. I told him about how my mother had come to me and told me to run, that people were coming to get me, to kill me, people that I never did see.

After pausing to gather my thoughts, I told Danial about the bats, how they attacked me, leading to the blood-stained holes in my clothing, and about the huge, lizard-like creature that pursued me, until I managed to escape by jumping into a creek.

Once more, my mind stalled.

"Then what happened, Mr. Archer?" Danial urged, grabbing me by the shoulder and giving me a fierce nudge.

I rebooted my brain, scrubbed a hand over my face, then said, "After jumping in the creek, I noticed that the lizard creature seemed afraid to go in after me. It hesitated then turned and disappeared back into the swamp."

Rising to his feet, Danial steepled his hands and began pacing the room. "What did this creek look like, Mr. Archer? Describe it, please, if you will."

"It was clean, clear, almost pure," I told him.

"What else?"

I thought on it. "The water felt strange. It was like something was…"

"Was what, Mr. Archer?"

"Like something was repairing me. Rejuvenating me. I felt…renewed. Like—" I immediately threw back the covers and swung my legs from the bed. In a fury I began rolling up my sweat pants. There was nothing there. Breathing hard, I bent over and tore away my hoodie, sending my cell phone flying across the room. I examined my arms, my chest; I peered at both of my shoulders—as much as I could see—rubbing my hands over them, feeling nothing—even looking at my hands afterwards.

There was nothing!

Not a single bite mark on my body!

I looked over at Danial. Everything was coming back to me—in a rush! I told him about the creek water—how it flowed *upward* instead of downward on a slope. Danial smiled back knowingly. *It was the creek water!* he seemed to be saying. I nodded back, thinking the same exact thing—mentally giving him a high-five, a solid fist-pump!

We both knew then what was needed. With everything in me, I dreaded even *thinking* about it. But yet, I knew what needed to be done.

I had to go 'back under'.

I had to once more find this creek, and bring back a sample of the water which flowed freely through it. As much of the water that Danial deemed necessary.

All of it, if possible.

It was the only way to stop the oncoming terror that was certain to come. Because if we didn't, then a man—*Leonard Hayes!*—*who was no longer a man!*—would emerge unchallenged, nearly unstoppable, and overtake this world. And left unchecked, unchallenged and nearly unstoppable, this world would never be the same.

The signs were all there: *Leonard Hayes* was steadily growing stronger, with each passing hour—becoming more confident—possessing total dominion over anything and everything *he* desired. Which would soon include *this* entire world as we know it.

Slowly but surely, like a black, menacing plague, *he* would emerge, and the world be overwhelmed and then be fully engulfed, and everyone from that point on would be at the mercy of *something* totally consumed and driven by pure *evil*...

My eyes blinked open.

I didn't know how long I was out, where I was, where I was headed to, or how long I would be here. I was still unsure on how this 'going under' business worked. I just hoped and prayed that I could find what I came here for, and that Danial could bring me back before anything *bad* happened to me.

With groggy, fuzzy vision still plaguing my eyes, I looked around, focusing the brunt of my vision back and forth between a huge log cabin, an old barn, and a swamp.

I remember being here.

At this very same spot...

If my memory served me right the creek shouldn't be too far from here. I looked around trying to get my bearings, still trying to familiarize myself in this *other* world. Although I remembered this area, nothing looked the same—as though the entire landscape had been somehow shifted. I spotted a vacant field that was about a hundred yards away, just to the right of me. I didn't recall seeing this, either. The field was barren, dry-looking and treeless. Ahead of that, in the far distance, I could see a rise stubbled with scraggly vegetation.

Did I go that way? I wondered.

I wasn't sure but I decided to take the chance that I had. Under the cloak of semidarkness, I had on a pair of fresh, dark-blue sweats with a long black overcoat lined with an array of kitchen knives, just in case. I also had on a pair of thick boots, and strapped to my shoulders was a small backpack. I crouched low and headed over to the open field, in the direction of the rise. The ground was covered with velvety moss, and whatever was beneath the moss was as thick as a mattress, spongy soft. I soon came to the rise, which was more like a ridge once you got up on it. I got down on my hands and knees and peered over the edge.

My breath left me instantly…

Below me I could see the busy part of a city. Just ahead of that I spotted the tops of vehicles caught in stop-and-go traffic. I saw buildings, bridges, high-rises, traffic lights, shops and businesses. With my eyes leading me, I peered into the sky. My mouth hung open. There was a plane, more like a jet aircraft, extremely high in the sky, with thin plumes of exhaust that looked like chalk marks coming from the engine.

With my mind racing and my mouth still hanging open, I could only stare in disbelief. It was like it wasn't real. An illusion of some kind.

There truly was another world here…

Probably filled with restaurants, gas stations, shopping malls—everything one could find in a 'normal' world...

I took a quick glance behind me.

Nothing there.

I cast another glance over the city below me. With its *other* cars, and buildings, and people—I wondered how everything was governed. *Who ran things here? Were there laws and rules to abide by? Or was it every man for themselves?* A thought hit me. *Maybe 'this' world was actually 'my' world. And the swamp, the people, the animals and creatures, as well everything else in it and surrounding it, was a world in itself. By itself...*

I couldn't worry about this. Besides, I had to ask myself: *did I really want to know?*

I didn't.

I peered at the city below me for a final time, and then I turned and headed back over the vacant field, back to the dark covers of the swamp, hoping I was headed in the right direction. I trudged through the thick, soggy mud, the tall, wet grass and hanging tree limbs, praying I wouldn't run into anything. Especially anything resembling a giant lizard. After a mile or so, I soon heard a familiar sound.

It was the creek.

I shifted the backpack tightly over my shoulders and headed toward the sound, where I soon spotted the creek—with its clear, unblemished waters running through it—still running *backwards* on a slope.

Upstream.

My hastily conceived plan was to rocket over to the creek, snatch off my backpack, retrieve the five empty plastic bottles inside, fill each one with water, place them back inside my backpack and then hightail it out of there. But as I looked closer, *this* world had other ideas.

Something was perched at the edge of the creek.

It was a figure of a man—*massive!*—like a statue—standing tall as a three-story building, probably weighing ten tons, as wide as a small bus, and built like something carved from stone, marble, and steel. The massive figure resembled some kind of a lumberjack man, that *Paul Bunyan* character, wearing something that a lumberjack man would wear: dark brown coveralls with straps over the shoulders, a red-and-black checkered shirt underneath, buttoned loosely at the neck—thick, brown boots and wearing a dark blue wool cap.

In its oversized, calloused hands I could see the makings of a mammoth chainsaw, yellow in color. Instead of the large ax that lumberjack men usually carried. The imposing figure looked downright menacing as it scanned the creek and everything surrounding it.

Apparently the word was out that I'd been here.

Getting water from the creek wasn't going to be a simple walk in the park, this I knew. Still, I had to make a move. Before Danial unknowingly brought me back too soon.

Slowly, crouching flat to the ground, shrinking my body as tightly as I possibly could, I made my way over to the creek, crawling belly to mud, crab-like, limb over limb. I soon made it to the edge of the creek, about fifty yards from the massive lumberjack man—who looked as if he'd grown another fifty feet in height! Another ten tons in weight!

I could make out his face now; he was a white guy, burly and heavily-bearded—crimson red—with thick brown hair, bushy and tussled in curls on his head, protruding from underneath his wool cap—the entire body from the wool cap down the boots, appeared to be dipped in polyurethane, ceramic-coated and shiny—as solid as a rhino!

The mere sight of this thing was unnerving!

It dawned on me; there was no doubt remaining on who lived in that huge log cabin…

I shook off my fear and quickly went to work. I shrugged off my backpack, reached inside and one by one, keeping a piercing eye on the lumberjack man, I filled each of the sixteen-ounce plastic bottles, all five of them, with the creek water; then, after making sure each bottle was properly sealed, I tucked the bottles back into my backpack. Afterwards, I leveled my body with the ground and began scooting away, inch by inch, until, slowly but surely, I saw the distance widening. I started to feel a wave of relief. That the dreaded moment had come and gone and was finally over with.

That's when it happened.

I soon heard the roar of a chainsaw coming to life—*eeerraaahhhh!*—the sound was deafening! I looked up only to see another one of my nightmares coming to life, staring directly at me.

Wearing a severe scowl, the lumberjack man stood there looking like a stone monument, menacing; he placed the chainsaw on the ground and then started unbuttoning the cuffs to his checkered shirt, rolling up the sleeves—revealing the undersides of his muscular forearms, the veins looking like twisted binds of steel.

Run! I heard my insides screaming. *Run like you've never run before!* But I didn't. I couldn't. I was stricken with fear, from head to toe. After a moment of stiffness I rose from the ground, staring face to face—eye to eye, with the lumberjack man. I watched as he slowly bent down to retrieve his oversized chainsaw; he gave it a couple of revs—still staring at me.

I could see a smile breaking across his face as he headed toward me. I gradually began backing away, then forward at bit, finally sideways, towards the creek. The lumberjack man hesitated. His smile, though stiff, remained on my face until I gradually entered the creek. Not taking any chances I plunged further into the creek, so rapidly that I lost my footing and went under. When I came up, I immediately glanced over to the lumberjack man perched at the outer edges of the creek.

That's when things changed in an instant. He glanced down at the creek then raised his gaze and met my eyes. He wasn't smiling anymore, and it didn't appear as if he were coming any closer.

He wanted to kill me, I could tell; there was no doubt he wanted to sever my head clean from my body. But he couldn't. There was *something* about this strange, opposite-flowing water that held everything in *this* world at bay.

What it was, I hadn't a clue. Actually, I could care less. The water had saved my life—twice! And that's all I needed to know.

I stared at the lumberjack man, knowing I had him at a *huge* disadvantage. I suspected that he knew this, too. He gave me an evil glare, revved his chainsaw several times in frustration, then, after a moment of stiffness, he turned and slowly walked away, back into the swamp. In the distance, I could hear the clatter-noise of the chainsaw falling silent.

It was over…

I drew in an extra hard breath and exhaled strongly through my mouth, nearly emptying my lungs. I soon felt a somber expression brightening on my face; it was the long-anticipated glow of knowing that maybe—*just maybe*—I'd finally found the answer to my prayers.

CHAPTER FORTY-ONE

'No Turning Back Now'

The stage had been set.

I can only hope and pray that it would work. I found myself gritting my teeth and balling my hands into tight fists. *It would!* I told myself. *It had to! This was it—do or die!* And I did not want to die.

Aphelia gave my arm a fond squeeze, then moved away from the rental vehicle. I gazed into her face, her eyes, reminded of how fortunate I was to have her and Danial in my life. By my side. I grimaced a smile at Aphelia and then looked over to Danial, sitting in the passenger seat.

"Think we can do this?" I asked him.

"We have to," he nodded firmly. He saw that my hands were shaking and placed his hand on my shoulder. "I understand your nervousness, my son, but from this point on, we cannot have any doubts circulating in your mind, or in your heart. You must be strong and extremely sure about what we are about to undertake. Otherwise, your doubts and nervousness could breed hesitation, which could cost you your life, along with the lives of the entire world."

Tightening my posture as I sat behind the steering wheel, I nodded strongly. Danial was right. So much depended on this thing working.

So damn much…

I couldn't help but think of Melody as well as my niece and nephew, Marie and Jayden. And then of course, Linda. It was at that moment when everything inside me seemed to lock in place; as though I was strapping myself in for the ultimate rollercoaster ride.

With my confidence brimming, my hands no longer shaking, I looked over at Danial. "Let's go kill us something evil," I grinned.

Danial responded with a grin of his own. He glanced up at the sky then leaned back in his seat, strapping on his seatbelt. "Better hurry," he said, "Both the rain as well as *Leonard Hayes* will be arriving soon, and we need to be ready."

Before stepping onto the pavement of a desolate, seemingly forgotten area located about fifty miles from the city, Danial hesitated, and then began emitting a low, barely perceptible chant, seemingly to himself. The rain was a steady drizzle and after finishing his chant, Danial opened the umbrella I had given him, then he pulled up the collars of his beige shirt as he stepped away from the vehicle.

A rental vehicle: a burgundy Buick GMC truck.

It was nearly dark and there were no signs of any life, no vagrants, bums, or homeless people. Except for the thick bushes lining the area, the place looked like an old construction site, with a vacant parking lot, although cars with busted-out windows and missing panels, some torched, could be seen off to the side, in the not-too-far distance.

I watched as Danial found a spot he was satisfied with, a little ways from the truck, and then he knelt to his knees still holding the umbrella. I could see him reaching for the dagger that he always kept strapped at his side. He glanced down at the dagger in his hand, his right one, and began once more, from what I could determine, was a low, deep chant. I stared, puzzled.

Approximately fifteen minutes had past when Danial returned to the truck. After closing the door, he looked over at me; though he tried to remain calm I could see that he was nervous. I saw wetness building up on his forehead and sliding down his face. I knew it wasn't from the rain.

"There's no turning back at this point," he said, exhaling forcefully through his nostrils. He looked directly into my eyes. "Prepare yourself, my son," he warned. "*Leonard Hayes* will be soon be here."

Hearing those words I immediately felt my stomach churning, feeling as if I could take a massive shit. I could almost see myself opening up the truck door and running away from this nightmare. But of course, I wouldn't. All I could do was close my eyes and pray to God, for safety, for a positive outcome, for everyone involved. Other than that, what else could I do? *'The man' was coming. Like it or not, 'he' was on 'his' way. Like Danial said: "There was no turning back at this point."*

Both Danial and I just sat there. Waiting. In total silence. Alone with our own private thoughts.

I sighed deeply as I found myself staring out the driver window, as the rain continued to streak all the windows in the truck, painting a sad, morbid image from nearly every angle.

I closed my eyes and shook my head, thinking, *what a hideous night to die on…*

It was midafternoon when I drove away from the juke-joint. An hour before that, I had just finished tying up the last remaining ends of the people who had wronged me. People who had disrespected me. In this case, her name was Sandra Shane, a beautiful woman—a stallion—chocolate and bowlegged, with a body that could make *any* man think about fornicating. All tits and ass—with a snatched waist and killer legs—a complete, toe-curling, dick-throbbing, turn-on. Her face was smoking hot, too, with full, juicy lips, deep, brown eyes, and hiked cheekbones.

A face you couldn't turn away from.

But not now.

Your stomach couldn't take it.

I made sure of that.

With my foot planted firmly on her chest, after pleasuring myself—pounding relentlessly inside her body till I got my rocks off—*real good!*—I took a vial of hot acid and slowly poured it over her face, making zigzagging designs all over her pretty features, while she screamed out in agony.

I didn't kill her, however. That would be letting her off the hook. Like giving her a pass. No, she would have to endure far worse. I had something far better in mind. More satisfying. She'd have to walk around with that fucked-up face. A face she'd have to wake up to every morning. No one else *but* a loser would want her now.

I couldn't help but laugh. *The uppity bitch got exactly what she deserved! How dare she turn down my early advances—laughing at me, calling me ugly, skinny, a scarecrow, a fuckin' loser not worthy of licking her boots! Now look at you! Your face lookin' as if it's been through a blender—still wearing lipstick! Ha, ha, ha! Deal with it, bitch!*

But I wasn't done seeking my revenge.

Not hardly.

It wasn't long before I found myself pulling up to my old job. Textile Industries, to be exact. Where I worked as a janitor. Another place where I was disrespected, in my former days. Where the guys used to tease me and call me ugly—*"Hook-nose-Hayes"*—they'd say—*"the only man who can open up a can of beer with his nose!"*

Then it was my foreman, Joe Mitchel, who said I wouldn't amount to anything in life, nothing more than a useless toilet bowl cleaner, armed with bleach, a Brillo pad, and rubber gloves, bending over on my hands and knees wiping and scraping up other people's shit and piss, slopping and mopping up floors, emptying trash cans, cleaning mirrors, and disinfecting urinals. That really hurt me.

In fact, so many people had done me wrong...

My co-workers, the white-collar supervisors, the entire stuck-up staff, even the ladies who worked there, who never *once* gave me a kind word or an encouraging smile, or offer me that extra piece of homemade cake or pie they would often bring in, like they did the other guys.

They would all pay.

All of them had been real mean to me.

And now it was my turn.

It was time to wreak some serious havoc here.

Probably snap a few dozen necks as I worked my way up and down the aisles, when I barged into the breakroom, once I kicked open the door to the supervisor's office, after I paid a personal visit to the headman-in-charge, Mr. Charles, and last but not least, when I finally met up with Joe Mitchel, my foreman.

The man who had me fired.

The man who was always in my face, clowning on me—talking foul, embarrassing shit to me. Belittling me. In front of everybody.

Now it was my turn to confront *him.*

Face to face.

To see and hear just how much foul shit he had to say and dump on me *this* time!

When I finished up with him, there wouldn't be much left to scrape from the walls. I'd tear a new asshole for him to shit out of.

Then make him clean it up!

"Get on your hands and knees, Mr. Mitchel," I'd say, laughing, standing over him, *"you get down there and clean up all of your black-and-brown shit! Every drop, chunk, and splatter! You hear me, Mr. Mitchel—now!"*

I'd probably place my foot to the back of his head and then mash his face in his own shit, keeping my foot there, applying steady pressure, more, more, until his skull finally caved in.

Sneering evilly, I parked my Crown Vic and made my way to the factory entrance. There was always some kind of guard stationed at the front entrance, checking work badges and other ID's, and today was no different. He was a big, black, buffed-looking guy, solid, wearing a tight-ass dark uniform, probably pumped some serious iron when not working as a rent-a-cop. I guess he thought he was intimidating.

As I stepped up to him, he looked at me strangely, disrespectfully, giving me the once-over, the side-eye, trying to appear all tough and shit.

I could only shake my head, chuckling.

"Can I help you, sir?" he asked as he stepped up to me, his right hand near a heavy flashlight holstered at his side.

I just smiled. *"Actually, I'm afraid you can't. In fact, you won't be able to help anyone else...not anymore..."*

I made my move, still smiling, but before I could snap my first neck, I heard a voice. Somebody was calling me. Summoning me. Like I was some damn snot-nosed kid.

I knew exactly who the fuck it was.

Danial!

A bitter anger, the urge for revenge—a severe loathing—all of it swelled in my heart—*my fists!*—screaming for release!

Why this black mutha—!

In my rage, I drew back a fist and punched a hole in the guard's throat. He instantly dropped to his knees. Wide-eyed. Gasping and grappling at the gaping hole in his throat, gushing blood every damn place. I raised my foot and shoved his sorry ass to the ground.

Boiling and seething with a manic need for redemption, I turned from my former place of work and walked away. I felt my teeth grinding and my fists balling tighter as I headed to my Crown Vic.

It was time to answer a call!

CHAPTER FORTY-TWO

'A Time to Fear'

"I am here!" announced *Leonard Hayes* defiantly, as *he* emerged from *his* Crown Victoria, parked in the shadows. A sort of artificial light blurred around *him*, then burst into fragments of color which lit up the entire area as *he* approached closer.

The call had been made, *he'd* answered, and *his* entrance into our world was undeniable. Spectacular! Leaving *him s*tanding center stage, on showcase—making it clear that *he* was here to kill me!

And it was also clear that *the man* was here for another purpose—a more sinister and permanent one—to destroy any and everything which stood in *his* way. To rule, to conquer—to dominate.

I grew faint.

It was more than terrifying finally seeing my tormentor in *real* time, nearly face to face, menacing and terrorizing. But oddly, as I watched in total shock and horror, chewing my bottom lip and wringing my hands together, I noticed a change in *his* appearance.

Something was definitely different.

An upgrade had taken place.

A very dramatic one.

He was no longer garbed in simple, throwaway rags. *He* stood there on a whole new level—clean, well-groomed, refined—dressed as if *he* were about to attend some ritzy affair: a black two-piece suit, neatly pressed, a white starched shirt underneath with a narrow, black tie knotted at *his* throat.

From the signature-gray Fedora hat tipped just so above *his* eyebrows, down to the black-laced alligator shoes on *his* feet, even smelling of lilac, *he* was actually a very good-looking man. However, behind *his* distinguished features and well put-together outfit, I could not allow myself to become swayed, blindsided or distracted, not even for a second.

All of this was a ruse.

A rather clever one.

This man was here to kill me—and anyone else who stood in his way!

His menacing posture left no doubt.

I slid down in the driver seat, ready to put the plan in place, as *Leonard Hayes* approached closer to the truck. As instructed by Danial, I opened one of the plastic bottles and gulped down all of the creek water it held, careful not to waste a single, precious drop. Danial, crouched down behind me in the backseat, did the same. We waited anxiously, ready, as *Leonard Hayes* slowly advanced closer to the truck.

The sound of *his* gator shoes echoing in the darkness, against the flat pavement, became more prominent with each step.

The footsteps came to a stop. That's when I heard a whistling tune as I saw *Leonard Hayes* peering into the lightly-tinted passenger window, tapping on the glass, scraping and etching it with a fingernail. The sight alone almost stopped my heart from beating.

"I know you're hiding in there, little piggies," he taunted with a chuckle. *He* cupped *his* hands and brought *his* face to the window, peeking in, looking from side to side. *"Come on, guys, really? Is this the best you can do? With all the shit I've done, do you really think hiding in a fuckin' truck is really going to save your ass?"* The chuckling became louder.

Seconds later, *he* no longer tried to conceal *his* motives. A single fist came crashing through the window. Right after that the passenger door came flying off the hinges. Both Danial and I escaped through the opposite side, going in separate directions.

As I expected *Leonard Hayes* came after me. It was simple: killing me—absorbing me—would be the final task left to end this thing. The last checkmark on *his* 'to-do' list. And *he* knew this!

Without looking over my shoulder, I ran as hard as my feet and legs could carry me. I made it to the edge of the vacant lot where a few bushes lined the area—hoping to melt into the shadows where *he* couldn't see me. Once here, I was hoping that Danial could somehow creep up on *him* from the rear. If I had to, I'd move away from the shadows rather than hide out in it, then circle and maneuver, in sort of a 'keep-away' game—until one of us could douse *him* with the creek water. Then hopefully we could finish *him* off with the dagger that Danial always carried.

It was a longshot, I knew, *but hey...*

I sunk deeper into the shadows, waiting on Danial to give me the cue. I could hear *Leonard Hayes* coming after me, ripping up bushes and tossing them to the pavement. I could also hear *his* frustration as *he* sought me out. *He* came closer, picking up my whereabouts like a bloodhound, and I slipped deeper into the darkness, careful not to make a sound; my mind kept pace with each and every step *he* took.

Don't panic, I told myself. *Keep it together.*

I shifted further into the darkness then glanced behind me. That's when the wind was slammed out of my chest. I went flying nearly forty feet into the air and landed roughly on the pavement. I could feel everything inside me shattering. Somehow, by some miracle, I managed to gather myself and immediately looked around.

There was nobody there.

Hit and thrown like that, I knew it had to be *Leonard Hayes*, but I had no idea where *he* had disappeared to. I crawled over to the truck and shrank back against the driver door.

I heard a faint sound.

Too late.

I felt my body being seized then hauled violently from the ground. I soon saw a large fist materializing from out of the darkness and slamming into my face—several times—so hard that my teeth came down on my lower lip and I tasted blood. Then an arm came over my neck while a hand clamped tightly over my mouth, cutting off my breath. I was yanked backward against something solid and hard, unyielding. Like a brick wall.

It was *Leonard Hayes'* body.

I was being choked to death.

The shock, the frustration and fear, it all brought bile into my throat. I could feel myself becoming lightheaded as I struggled for oxygen.

I'd been a damn fool, I thought on the verge on passing out. *There was no way to beat this thing. This man. I should have simply given myself up in the very beginning—submitted to the inevitable—not trying to defeat or outsmart something that so obviously knew what the final outcome would be. I—*

"Fight back, Derrick!"

In my last waning breath, I heard Danial calling out to me. "Fight back! *This man* cannot kill you! Can't you see? Fight back with everything you have inside you! You can do this!"

The words were music to my ears! It was the nudge that I needed. I began struggling against the plier-grip that held me—realizing I had the creek water in my system—I should have been dead by now! It was my mind that was giving up and shutting down—*not the fury of Leonard Hayes!*

I'd become my worst enemy!

Nevertheless, the pain was undeniable. My neck hurt like a son-of-a-bitch, but it was obvious that *this man* hadn't yet discovered that it was just severe pain *he* was putting me through.

Not the pathway to death.

His fury around my neck became even more intense, but try as *he* may, as I felt my neck being squeezed in a maddening grip, my mouth and nose sealed off from any kind of precious oxygen, it became clear—as clear as the creek water flowing through my system: *Leonard Hayes* could *not* kill me...

Naturally, because of this, I became renewed with hope and to some degree, maybe even a little stronger. I managed to pry my mouth free and I bit down on *Leonard Hayes'* hand, the meatiest part of *his* palm, just below the thumb, drawing black blood. As a result, I was smacked so viciously that I went careening through the air, landing roughly on my shoulder. The pain was excruciating. Everywhere on my body. There was no way I would make it to my feet.

But something odd happened.

The pain suddenly went away; me being struck hard across the face, landing even harder, every bone in my body should have been broken; but I felt no after effects. None whatsoever.

The creek water...

I slowly rose to my feet. That's when I saw Danial streaking across the vacant lot holding one of the plastic bottles in his hand. With a manic lunge, he dumped the creek water over *Leonard Hayes'* body— then retreated quickly over to me. Huddled together all we could do was hope, hope, and hope even more—*pray!*—that the water had some kind of damaging effect.

Looking around stunned, *his* body tensing and shaking, *Leonard Hayes* brought *his* hands to *his* face.

Apparently, *something* was going on.

Terrified stiff, I watched as *his* entire body began to seize up, then it started contorting into positions I didn't think was humanly possible, as mystic smoke, as thin as a white veil, rose into the air. *He* yelled out violently as *his* body continued to spasm.

After a minute or so it *he* stopped moving and went silent, with *his* head hanging low. Seconds passed and then *he* slowly stirred and eased *his* head up and began looking around—spotting me and Danial—staring hatefully at both of us with *his* teeth flashing viciously. Then, as if suffering from an unexpected gut punch, *he* doubled over and clenched *his* teeth until *his* jaw muscles bunched.

He went silent.

Everything seemed to.

That's when it happened.

Slowly, humming lightly, *Leonard Hayes* gradually straightened *his* body until it became rigid as a steel beam.

"Enough of this bullshit!" he proclaimed loudly.

It became clear that the effects of the creek water were only short-lived against *him*. Somehow, I knew exactly what was needed. But I would have to wait for the right opportunity. That perfect moment. I could only pray that I would get the chance.

Now, having seemingly reached *his* limit, giving me and Danial an evil, devilish grin—as if for a final time, *Leonard Hayes* raised *his* arms into the air, and began a low, whispering chant. A chorus of *evil* mantras, a spiritual calling. The tempo began to build as *he* exhaled *his* pent-up rage into the air.

That's when I smelled it.

The horrid stench of a swamp. Of everything *unholy.* Rancid and throat-clogging in every way.

It took everything in me to keep from vomiting.

"It is time!" proclaimed *Leonard Hayes* once more, proudly. *"Come forth, my dark, obedient allies, come forth and partake of this world! Under my rule, everything you see is yours for the taking!"*

That's when I knew the shit was about to hit the fan.

Like never before.

From out of nowhere, above and below, a deep rumbling could be heard, coming in from every direction. A bone-shattering turbulence. The air suddenly whipped violently, becoming hostile, rebellious, and the temperature around us suddenly plummeted to near freezing levels.

Yet, the chill that gripped me wasn't from the frigid air; it was from something else; something beyond words, beyond comprehension, as the skies above me suddenly became more and more chaotic—swirling—intertwining—resembling an oily-water mixture, something distorted, and ugly.

Off in the distance, I could hear the sounds of rolling thunder approaching, then came the undeniable feeling that the entire universe itself, was about to weaken, crack, and split open. Armageddon was close at hand; this I knew.

I felt Danial gripping my arm, tightly, which surprised me. Shocking me, actually. He'd never once showed signs of being afraid. Not a one. But now, to my dismay, he appeared deeply uneasy—on the borderline of being scared shitless.

Soon the blackness of the sky was pierced by the unnatural glow of a lightning strike being frozen in time. Held in place. The sky then flickered and fluttered, like an exhausted bright light giving it all it had before finally going out. Suddenly, the atmosphere seemed to burst with a brilliance like I've never seen before—lighting up everything like an exploding sun.

I knew then something big was coming.

Something no creek water could go up against...

The air around us became even more turbulent, chattering, disturbing the area, kicking up dust and debris and nearly blinding us. Nevertheless, I could still see *Leonard Hayes* standing there defiantly in the middle of this traumatic chaos, *his* arms still raised. I could see *his* eyes, which glowed fiercely.

I zeroed in on *his* face.

He was smiling.

At me...

"Run to the truck, Derrick!" shouted Danial above the rustling wind. He jammed something into the pocket of my hoodie then pushed me away and headed off in another direction, away from the truck.

"Where are you going?" I yelled.

With dust and debris battering his face and eyes, turning his face nearly white, he yelled back, "I'll try to distract *Leonard Hayes*—or whatever it is that's coming—away from you!"

It was hard for me to comprehend what I'd just heard. Frowning, a bit confused, I shook my head. I couldn't believe that a man would do such a thing, to risk own his life to save another, meaning mine.

But then again, Danial wasn't just a man. He was like a father to me.

"Run now!" he screamed as he turned back, both surprised and pissed off that I was still standing there. Looking stupid. "Run now! Drive away—go, dammit! Go hide somewhere! *Leonard Hayes*—or something unholy—will be coming for you!"

I nodded and ran to the truck where I slid behind the steering wheel and started it up. I turned and saw where the passenger door had been ripped from the hinges. My heart dropped and my breath shivered as I peered out the window ahead of me. I found myself unable to move—shocked, paralyzed, disoriented, undecided on which way to go, where to drive to.

That's when I saw it…

The sky.

The one directly above me.

An extreme force was mounting, building, as if *something* was ready to burst through at any moment. I put the truck in gear but didn't drive away. The sky held me in shock. In total disbelief.

There was a powerful pressure of gravity happening—*from this world*—permeating in the air, as a group of dark, purplish-gray clouds worked in unison into antigravity—*the other world*—coming together—pulling apart—creating an opening. The sound of an electrical grid being activated soon appeared.

Pressure waves battled the sky as *something* was struggling to break loose of confinement, and burst full-blown into this world. Throbbing and sizzled crackling began matching the mounting pressure waves.

That's when I heard it.

The sound of an apocalyptic roar.

It was the heinous announcement of doomsday.

Something truly evil had broken through…

Wiping the sweat from my eyes, I began to drive away. Slowly. There was no need to drive like a maniac, bolting away on screeching tires.

Not at all.

Besides, I hadn't a single clue as to where I was headed to. It didn't matter anyway. There was no way to outrun this thing. There wasn't a single, safe place to hide.

One simple glance at the skies said it all.

An opening had been torn between two worlds. And now an unfathomable *evilness*, with monstrous thick-reaching tentacles—*something* from a parallel universe—was being allowed entry into this current world.

My world.

I took another glance into the sky.

It was truly over.

The world was finally coming to an end. It was just a matter of time.

Heaven help us all…

CHAPTER FORTY-THREE

'Narrowing the Gap'

As my hands gripped the steering wheel, I found myself grinding my teeth. I was more than pissed. Fucked up in the head. Big-time. That was the only way to describe how I felt as I maneuvered my Crown Vic through the dark streets.

The way that inferior, bastard-of-a-man—*Danial!*—had outwitted me *again!*—seemingly at every turn! The way he could trick me back into his world. Hold me at bay after doing so. The thought of him knowing my inner thoughts and secrets.

Then it was that other fucker. His trusty sidekick. The *'Robin'* to his *'Batman'*. 'Derrick' he called him.

What was up with him, anyway?

Try as I may, I couldn't pull that fucker's head off to save my life! But somehow, I knew I needed to get to him. I needed to get to his inner soul! To complete things. To at last release that final chunk of *evil* into this world. But it would take a little extra time.

Apparently, somehow, some sneaky fuckin' way, they found out about the creek water, the powers it contained.

The prospect of this made me angry.

I would have to alter my plans, devise another way of getting to them. Especially to this 'Derrick' asshole, the one I was looking for now. I'd snatch whatever scraps I needed from him and then find the old geezer Danial and make him pay too.

I had a personal score to settle with him anyway!

And, boy-oh-boy, did I have some shit lined up for his ass! Next time *I'd* be the one holding *him* down. I'd look into his eyes and then I would pull strips of skin fragments from his body, some the size of licorice sticks, others like saltwater taffy, and then I would jam them into his mouth!

Make him chew on it!

All of it!

Afterwards I'd wrench his head around permanently, so he could never witness the things to come—the finer things—a rearview of life would be all that he could see! *Would ever see!* I'd—

I felt myself losing it.

Again.

But I couldn't control myself!

Reaching down into my gut, I came up screaming, *"I'll kill you, Danial, you hear me, dammit!"* I gripped the steering wheel harder, screaming even louder, *"Kill, kill, kill—kill them both—both him and Derrick—then kill everybody else, you understand me! Kill everyone who wronged me. Kill—"*

Suddenly I stopped. A curious moment crossed my mind.

Kill everyone who wronged me…?

I knew why I was losing it.

It made perfect sense...

Until this moment, I'd forgotten all about my former job, and what I was about to do: *kill everyone in that damn place.* But I never got the chance to carry it out. That *Danial* bastard had lured me into this world before I could step inside and snap my first neck. And there's no way in hell I was going to miss having a crack at his ass! I *had* to answer the call! And he knew this!

Still...

All those mean workers.

Even the innocent ones.

So many lives left untaken...

I had to let it go.

From this point on my former job, my former world, no longer existed. Both were gone. Everything was gone. Crashed and burned in my mind. I couldn't go back now even if I wanted to. The portal between the two worlds had come to an end. That revolving door was now permanently closed.

These were the facts.

And I would just have to deal with it.

For now, I had a couple of marauding morons to deal with. Two troublesome loose ends to tie up.

To bend, twist, and snap, more like it!

With deep focus, I scanned the roads ahead of me. That bastard Derrick was somewhere. He could run, but the son-of-a-bitch definitely couldn't hide. I had too many things working in my favor. So many eyes.

Allies.

The entire dark universe was on my side now, more than eager, more than pleased to aid me in every way. In this case it was the crows and the bats, the hawks and the eagles, the sparrows and the owls, which circled high above me. With razor-sharp eyes that twinkled and glittered like diamonds across the blackened skies, scanning the ground below—I would know at a moment's notice when the bastard was spotted.

Until then, I'd just keep on cruising, keep on keeping on, centering my vigilance on the streets below.

I had a few more things working for me: the moon itself, now nothing more than a cutout circle, shined dimly with a faint, acrid, milky-white yellowish-glow—which was all I needed. I could manage easily in this kind of darkness, but those two fuckers couldn't. And the sun wouldn't be rising anytime soon.

Not until *I* said so.

As the minutes turned into hours, I checked the backroads, the alleys and all the side streets, all the while keeping an eye on the skies above, waiting for a sign, a signal, from my winged associates.

...it was just a matter of time when I got the call...

I pulled the GMC truck under a highway underpass. I shut down the engine and looked around.

Hopefully I'd be safe here. At least for a while. At least until sunrise. So I could gather my thoughts. My bearings. I couldn't help but think about the skies above me. Everything looked chaotic and heinous—like some warped painting created by a demented madman slinging a paint brush everywhere on a canvas—using every kind of color.

If hell did exist, I was sure it was making its way through that gaping hole in the sky.

Once again, as I'd done at least a dozen times, I glanced over to the passenger seat and saw where the door had been ripped away by this madman. My mind then drifted to the large A/C unit that had been torn from the wall and then heaved at me through a third-floor motel window. I could only close my eyes and shake my head.

Un-fuckin'-believable...

I looked down and saw Danial's trusty dagger, wedged between the passenger seat and the console where I had placed it. I prayed that he was okay. I picked up the dagger and stared at it. I recalled what Danial had said about the dagger: that it would take the dagger as well as my Mama to defeat this thing.

Sighing, nodding and shaking my head at the same time, I placed the dagger back inside my hoodie pocket. I stared blankly at the dark recesses of the underpass.

It was odd.

There wasn't a single rumbling of a car crossing overhead—where there should have been plenty—

hundreds. Thousands. In fact, as I thought about it, there was no sight or sound of anything at all. No people. No honking cars. No soaring planes above. No ambulances or fire trucks. No birds or insects. There was nothing.

It was happening.

The signs were all there…

The strange, purplish color of the skies. The skies itself constantly shifting and reforming in chaotic patterns and designs. The crushing boom and then the unknown entity slowly entering into this world as if ripping through cheap fabric.

It could only mean one thing.

…the world was already shutting down…

CHAPTER FORTY-FOUR
'The Deadline was Dawn'

The roaring Crown Victoria rammed me from behind, hard, and then fell back. It was apparent I'd been discovered. Snitched on, more like it, from the eyes in the skies, above.

I punched the GMC truck and the vehicle surged forward. The Crown Vic was in hot pursuit. It caught up to me and rammed me again, harder than before, and the tailgate went flying off. I was rammed again, over and over, and the truck shook and shuddered as though it would fly apart like a deck of playing cards.

Looking into the rearview mirror, I spotted the harsh glow of headlights barreling down on me again. I could also see *Leonard Hayes* behind the wheel.

He was grinning.

I came to an intersection and hit the brakes hard, simultaneously turning left which caused the Crown Vic to overshoot through the intersection. I instantly heard the squeal of brakes and knew the Crown Vic was making a rough U-turn. Like a fuckin' rocket, the Crown Vic made up for lost ground and I was struck again on the passenger side. Over and over. Each impact jarred every bone in my body. I could see a huge grin on the face of *Leonard Hayes* as *he* continuously rammed me from nearly every angle— making the truck wobble and rock from side to side.

He was enjoying himself, this I knew.

There was something about *this man's* demeanor which horrified me to the point that I was faintly nauseated. *To be the focal point of this man's inner thoughts and drive, his soul intention only to kill me...*

As I was rammed over and over, then rammed again, I could only shake my head weakly, thinking, *this nightmare will all end soon, and then somebody will wake me and tell me there will be no more...*

But then I shook my head. Strongly! I had come too far to give up! I forced a smile—telling myself to face my fears! With every muscle tensing inside me, I whirled my head to face my tormentor, who was right beside me, still banging the shit out of the vehicle.

I pounded on the accelerator demanding everything from the engine, but it was no use. Every assault on the GMC truck was crippling; I knew I wouldn't be able to coax anymore speed out the vehicle. Nevertheless I still tried. The truck responded sadly as it chugged forward, loudly rattling and spewing steam from underneath the hood.

I rounded a corner and the truck was struck violently this time then clipped on the rear quarter, which sent the vehicle flying on its side, spinning in several full revolutions until it came out of the roll landing on all four wheels. One of the front tires exploded on impact sending rubber shrapnel into the air. The engine soon sputtered and stalled, hemorrhaging fluids all over the ground.

Not wasting a single second, knowing the Crown Vic would be closing in, I unhooked my seatbelt, opened the driver door, and fell to the ground. I jumped to my feet then reached into the backseat and grabbed the last two bottles of creek water from my backpack; I jammed both into the pockets of my sweats.

I looked around; the street was wide, dusty, and completely deserted. Not a single sign of life anywhere. I then saw one of my worst nightmares heading toward me. It was *Leonard Hayes* and *his* Crown Vic! The sight of the headlights and the sound of the horn blaring at me was deafening.

He was coming in fast!

The sight held me. I was frozen stiff—like a wandering deer caught in oncoming headlights—*literally!*

Nearly hypnotized, I continued to stare as the bright lights and the loud horn declared my fate. I closed my eyes and grimaced. Waiting for the inevitable. Suddenly I was snatched out of harm's way by a pair of hands and thrown roughly to the ground. Just in time! Another second and there wouldn't have been another second! I would have been dead for sure.

Somehow I knew this.

I *felt* it...

I immediately knew what had happened.

...*Mama*...

Telling myself I'd thank her later I made it to my feet. This was not over. *Leonard Hayes* would soon be making a second pass at me. Already I could hear the sound of brakes piercing the night, and the Crown Vic being thrown in reverse. Then in drive.

He was coming!

I looked around and spotted a grocery store with large glass windows. There were no lights on inside; it appeared abandoned. As did everything else around me. It was that 'world shutting down' thing, I knew. In a rush I ran over to the store. I checked the glass doors by pulling on them and found both sides locked. *Fuck!* However, I wasn't dissuaded. Hopefully the creek water inside me still had my back. I reared back, shut my eyes tightly, then threw my body into the door and smashed my way inside. I dropped like a cinder block to the floor and laid there on my back motionless for a few seconds. Staring up at the ceiling.

Waiting…

Nothing broken.

A small amount of pain.

No blood.

I was okay…

Brushing a few glass chips from my body, feeling more than grateful, I leaped to my feet hoping I hadn't made too much noise.

To my dismay, I spotted *Leonard Hayes* pulling up seconds later in *his* Crown Vic. Which didn't have a single fuckin' scratch on it!

Sneering evilly, not wasting a second, I watched as *he* stepped away from the car. A certain light still shined around *him*, from nearly every angle; I was able to see *him* clearly. I hated to look—the terrible familiarity of *his* profile was enough to make me break out in a cold sweat—but I couldn't help myself.

There was a morbid fascination seeing this face out of my nightmare and then in the flesh again.

And then it was the fact that even though there was nothing outright intimidating about *this man*, there was the mysteriousness of just that. That a man who appeared as literally nothing to fear was indeed—*something to fear!*

I watched as *his* eyes scanned the area. Within seconds *he* peered over in my direction, at the grocery store, where I remained crouched and hidden in one of the aisles, well out of sight. Still, *he* knew I was in here. Maybe it was the broken glass door, with glass scattered on the ground. Maybe it was the noise that I had unknowingly made when smashing through the door.

Perhaps it was something else. Something coming from me. A gasping breath. A subtle swallowing of the throat that only *he* could detect. Maybe it was the pounding of my heart which gave me away.

It didn't matter.

My biggest fears had become realized.

Leonard Hayes was headed directly toward the grocery store—peering through the glass windows—sending me a piercing look that made the hairs prickle on the back of my neck…

Tonight was different, no doubt about it.

I could *feel* it! My throne was waiting for me! As soon as I disposed of this 'hide-and-seek', 'tag-you-it', little twerp, it was time to shake things up around here! In my *new* world! But first things first. I had a job to do.

I knew the scary little prick was in here. He thought he could elude me by hiding in some fuckin' grocery store. *Fat chance!* I took my time and scanned the layout of the store, every aisle, unsure of which one to take. There were quite a few. I crept down the first aisle, the one nearest to the door, then slowly, carefully, thoroughly, I would take my time and work my way down each one.

Remaining vigilant.

Always checking behind me. Around me.

Step after step, occasionally stopping and hesitating, concentrating, listening, I made my way down a few of the aisles—shoving shit to the floor in case the prick-bastard was hiding—trying to flush his scary ass out. I made my way to the can goods section. I strolled calmly down the aisleway, my gator shoes gliding silently over the white and green-speckled tile. One by one, like a roll of dominoes, I began knocking cans to the floor.

"Come out, come out, wherever you are, my little piggie," I taunted merrily, cheerfully. *"I know you're hiding in here, and I'm gonna huff, and I'm gonna puff, and then I'm gonna cave your little fuckin' skull in. So, come out, come out, wherever you are..."*

I made my way through each aisle until I came to a bakery section. There was a small display case, with a sign which read: "fresh donuts daily". I peered inside the case and saw several shelves lined with flavored donuts. A shitload of them: Glazed, Jelly-filled, Apple fritter, Chocolate frosted, Boston crème, Bear Claw.

Thinking they all looked rather tasty, I smashed the glass case and took out a glazed one, biting it— *what the f—!* I immediately spit it out—the shit tasted horrible! I mean, don't get me wrong: the glazed icing was on point—but the donut itself tasted like packed sawdust! *Yuck!* In my disgusted anger, still spitting the donut residue from my mouth, I reached out and ripped the case from the wall, then sent it flying across the floor, causing donuts to glide over the tile like hockey pucks on ice.

That's when I heard it.

A noise near the back of the store.

Tightening both fists, I rushed toward the coolers, where I figured the noise had come from. Something caught my eye. A dark silhouette darting into the stockroom. A door quickly closing and locking. I was right there when it locked. I twisted the doorknob in my hand and tore it away—then I kicked the door in, shattering it, only to find the stockroom empty.

No one was here.

To my left I spotted a small bathroom. The door was closed. Probably locked. I rushed over to the bathroom and tore the door from the hinges, sending the door flying somewhere behind me. There was no one in here, either. I looked up and spotted a small window. It was open. The fucker snuck out through there!

Breathing like a bull I rushed from the stockroom area, then the store. I hit the deserted street looking around wildly. Then I smiled. More than pleased. It was my elusive prey, standing next to my precious Crown Vic. Which was strange.

The dumb fuck didn't even try to run.

He just stood there.

Holding a plastic bottle in one hand with the other hand tucked inside the pocket of his hoodie.

I saw there was an empty plastic bottle on the ground. I also noticed something else.

The idiot was smiling at me, looking even dumber than before. I couldn't help but stomp my foot and do a little twirl. *"Fool,"* I chuckled, coming out of my spin, *"you done lost your rabbit-ass mind, ain't you? Don't you know I'm here to end your worthless-ass life? You's an ignorant son-bitch, you know that?"*

I could only shake my head as I brushed the sleeves to my suit jacket, as I prepared myself. To finally end this bullshit. In the middle of my actions, I caught myself. *Damn,* I had to admit as I took inventory of my newly-acquired attire: *I am clean to the muthafuckin' bone! Cleaner than a broke-dick-dog!*

After giving my gators a once-over, I looked up at this moron, still trying to be brave and shit. I tightened both my fists, ready to finish this. I stepped closer.

"Let's do this, *Mr. Hayes,*" he said, tauntingly. "Let's end this thing right here and now. Before dawn arrives."

I couldn't help but find this 'stand-and-fight-finale' bullshit entertaining. I stifled a laugh then chuckled again, *"Look around you, asshole. It's already a done deal. I win. Game over, baby. There won't be another dawn. Not ever again. Not as long as I have a say in it."*

"Then there *will be* another dawn," he smiled; he raised a fist in the air. Refuting my declaration.

I folded my arms across my chest, feeling my rage building. *"You really think some toilet water from a fuckin' stream is going to save your ass this time around, don't you? Man, if that's what you're banking on then you might as well turn around now and get ready to take it good, deep, and hard, with no Vaseline."*

He sneered. "I don't think so."

I sneered back. *"I know so."*

"Then make a move, *Mr. Hayes*," he glared at me, stepping closer. "I'm ready whenever you are, *baby*..."

Instead of rushing over there and tearing his scalp off, then killing him, I found myself hesitating.

Something wasn't right...

I watched this man closely, his mannerisms—training my eyes on his hands as he readied himself, as he reached into the pocket of his hoodie. *Something was in there. But what? And why had he become so defiant all of a sudden? What could have happened in just that short time? One second running like a little bitch with his panties twisted, the next stepping up to me like he'd grown himself a pair of bull nuts! It...it* didn't make sense. It...it made no sense at all. None... None, dammit! You hear me—none! None!

Shrugging my shoulders beneath my black suit jacket, I fought back my rage and revulsion, instead letting my wits surface, as I smiled, *"You must have hooked up with that whore-bitch Dorothy, and all those other parading idiots and visited the wonderful Land of Oz, huh, little man? Tell me, is that it, baby? Did you pick up a heart along with a new set of balls while you were there?"*

He returned my smile. "Maybe."

My nerves were getting the best of me as I watched his brown eyes darting this way and that way, confirming what I already knew: *I was being baited. Somebody else was here. But who?*

I was obviously curious. Slowly, I looked around. No one was here. But yet, there was.

I could feel them...

Time to face the truth.

The thought was horrifying.

I was gambling on something that I was uncertain of. *No!* That was a bad sign. I had to remain positive, as Danial had stated: *"Remove all doubts from your mind as well your heart..."*

He was right! I had to believe in myself. That this idea would work. *And, dammit, it would!* It had to!

Nevertheless, as I glanced around seeing nothing but an eerie, dim-yellow bleakness, as I saw buildings and skyscrapers that were once tightly knitted and straight, now crooked and spaced like uneven teeth, as I peered into a sky that I no longer recognized, I could once again feel despair challenging my courage.

The ultimate test was facing me. The battle between success and failure. Good versus *evil*. Right against wrong. And the scales were *not* tipped in my favor.

I slowly brought my gaze back to the face of my tormentor: *Leonard Hayes*. That's when I saw it. *'His' expression seemed frozen, as if 'he' wasn't sure on what to do. How to react...*

I was momentarily frozen myself as I witnessed this rather strange event—coming from a *man* with such arrogance, confidence—unbridled rage!

I watched as *he* glanced around, slowly turning *his* body with *his* head and eyes leading the way. All of a sudden *he* frowned and then bellowed out in a full-throttled roar, *"Where the fuck are you! Show yourself! I know you're here!"* With olive-black eyes which shined menacingly, *he* glared at me with a look that could have split a wooden log in half.

"It ends now," he seeped indignantly. *His* brows quivered, and *he* appeared to be inhaling deeply as *he* began to approach me. *He* smiled, and brought *his* hands to *his* mouth and began licking *his* fingers, as if there had been something sweet and sticky on them. Afterwards, *his* hands balled into steel fists.

Then—in a maddening rush—*he* slammed me back against *his* car—knocking the wind out of me. *He* grabbed me by the neck—clutching it tightly, and began lifting me off the ground. I felt my neck being crushed and began slamming my fists and knees into *his* body. *He* didn't move a muscle. Not an inch. A glance at *him* told me that *he* was once again enjoying *himself*, immersed in extreme pleasure, and was having trouble keeping *his* excitement in check.

His jaws were clenched, *his* eyes fiery red, and *he* was grinning from ear to ear.

"You, my rather good-looking, elusive prey, are about to die," he chuckled. *"So, tell me,"* he added softly, tightening *his* grip in the process, grinning menacingly, *"did you like that sweet kiss we shared in the bathroom some time ago? That was me, in case you didn't know."*

Though I clearly remembered, I wasn't about to acknowledge that heinous, unforgettable moment.

Struggling against *his* grip, the grip that was now threatening to crush my windpipe, I managed to utter, "You…you can't kill me, you son-of-a-bitch."

"You're right…" he nodded, searching fiercely around *him*, then at the empty plastic bottle laying on the ground. *He* turned *his* gaze back to me. *"…I can't kill you, not with my bare hands I can't. But what I can do, and most likely will do, is simply choke you out, then flop your limp body in the middle of the street. After that, I'll start up my car and then back it up over your head, forward and backward, side to side, probably do a few burnouts, until your brain scraps become wedged in the threads of my tires. Then, after you're dead and rotting in the street, I'll drop in on Melody, you know, see how things are going with her and the kids."* His grip tightened—

"*How does that sound, 'Mr. Derrick-fuckin'-Archer'!*"

Still struggling and kicking, pulling roughly at the hand around my neck, I grunted, "That's not going to happen, *Mr. Leonard Hayes*—best believe this!" With everything left in me about to slip away, I reached into the pocket of my hoodie and grabbed the dagger. I drew my hand back, angled the dagger, and sent it flying into *Leonard Hayes'* chest.

Hard as I could!

Almost immediately, *Leonard Hayes* looked down from a cornered eye, and I watched as *his* face glowered in surprise and shock. Pain soon set in and *he* screamed harshly into the air, throwing *his* head back and thrashing it from side to side. Without wasting a second I unscrewed the top from the plastic bottle. I waited until I saw my moment.

The right moment.

With *his* head still thrashing wildly, it didn't look like it was going to happen.

That's when Mama stepped in. I could see the head of *Leonard Hayes* being held, solidly—presenting me with the perfect opportunity to act.

I did.

I raised the plastic bottle and began pouring the creek water into *Leonard Hayes'* mouth. As a result, almost immediately, *he* began fighting and lashing out like a cornered wildcat—cringing, convulsing, coughing and spitting, trying to turn *his* head away—but Mama held on tightly as I continued to pour the creek water into *his* mouth, all of it, until the bottle was empty.

That's when I felt the grip on my neck finally loosening up as *he* staggered away from me. *He* doubled over gripping and clutching *his* stomach. Then *he* fell to *his* knees. In the space of a couple of heartbeats, *he* looked up at me, with an expression that said: *'this can't be real...'*

But it was.

Mr. Leonard Hayes had met his match...

Finally!

Seizing the opportunity to be certain, I walked over to *him*, knelt down, grunted something crazy, and then plunged the dagger, to the very handle, further into *his* chest. Yelling loudly, *he* fell to the ground and began frantically trying to pull the dagger from *his* chest, but it was useless. Yet *he* tried over and over to no avail. Realizing it was useless *he* rolled over on *his* side and tried to rise up.

He couldn't.

He was dying.

But somehow, surprisingly, *he* made it to *his* feet. Turning back and looking at the ground, staggering, *he* appeared thankful for that simple achievement. That one, small victory. I watched as *he* glanced around, dazed, lightheaded. It was at that moment when I saw the frosty-glowing aura which always seemed to surround *him* starting to fade.

The impeccable-looking outfit *he* had on was next, gradually turning into dust and tattered rags. With holes nearly everywhere. The hat that was once tipped so 'sugary-sweet' over *his* brow, was no longer there. Even the slick black gators on *his* feet were gone.

It was like witnessing *Cinderella* after the clock struck midnight...

I could only watch *Leonard Hayes* as he no longer appeared as 'Leonard Hayes', as his entire demeanor resembled nothing more than a common street bum searching for pennies on the streets. Broke and homeless. And then another event happened; the handsome face he once sported had been quickly pulled and stripped away, leaving him with a face that was as ugly and as wrinkled as a baboon's ass. Still seriously lightheaded he moaned and brought a hand to his face, not believing that his sculptured features had been stripped away...

Desperate, steadily declining, seemingly melting away, he whimpered, and began patting himself—frantically—everywhere—dazed and fretting—not giving in to the transformation. Still not believing. Still not wanting to believe. That's when a small, tarnished handbell slipped from his tattered overcoat and fell to the ground.

In a pathetic gesture, he reached out for it and grabbed the tiny handle. Managing a sneer, he looked at me and tried to ring it. But the hinged clapper inside failed to make a single sound.

The strained expression on his face said it all.

There would be no more ringing of the bell.

It was game over, baby...

Staggering to his car, swaying like a drunk from a week-long binge, Leonard Hayes turned and looked at me. Frowning and saying something that I couldn't quite make out. Yet, I could feel his eyes boring into me.

As for me, I just smiled and waved.

That was nothing left to be said or do.

The nightmare was finally coming to an end...

Whirling his head around, I watched as Leonard Hayes gasped, stumbled, and slid into his car.

His ride.

His whip.

His *precious, beloved, shiny, blacker-than-midnight: Crown Victoria.* He started it up and the engine roared to life, rumbling fiercely as always. He gave it a few taps on the accelerator to make it rumble even louder. I could feel Mama grasping at my hand as we both watched as the car slowly drove away.

When it got about a quarter mile down the street, I braced myself.

That's when I heard a thunderous *Boom!*—followed by a huge fireball which lit up the sky. I'd expected this to happen. Either sooner or later.

After escaping from the grocery store, I took one of the last two remaining bottles of creek water and poured it into the gas tank of the Crown Victoria.

If all else had failed it was my last line of defense against 'Leonard Hayes'.

And hopefully saving the world...

I swallowed hard as I saw the fireball still reaching high into the sky. That's when I saw the makings of a sunrise appearing over the horizon.

A dawn was coming…

I also heard something else.

Signs of life.

Or normalcy.

Streetlights suddenly appeared. Traffic lights came on. I could hear cars once more. Horns honking. People's voices. Planes overhead. Ambulances and fire trucks. Birds chirping. Dogs barking. It was like everything and everybody was checking in!

Like rollcall!

It became too much for me to handle.

Overwhelming.

I started choking up and soon felt tears streaking my cheeks. "It's over, Mama!" I cried out, looking around with my arms stretched as I twirled about in the middle of the deserted street—my voice echoing off everything around me. "It's finally over, you understand!" I became so overwhelmed that I fell to my knees; my voice fell to a whisper as I cried into my palms, "It's finally over, Mama. And I…I couldn't have done it without you. I couldn't… Thank you so very much, Mama. Thank you for never *ever* leaving your baby boy…"

As tears streaked my cheeks, I looked up and then looked around.

Smiling.

Everything was *alive* again.

Up and running again.

More tears streaked my cheeks as I looked around.

Needless to say, I was more than grateful…

CHAPTER FORTY-FIVE

'This Side of Heaven'

Two weeks had passed when I finally decided to go see Linda. It was on a Tuesday, late in the evening, and I knew my visit would be unexpected. But I didn't care. I needed to see her. Badly. As I pulled up to her place I saw her car, a light blue Acura, parked in the driveway, so I knew she would be home.

I could only pray she wasn't seeing somebody else. My heart couldn't take it.

I would simply die...

Driving yet *another* rental vehicle, a silver Kia Sportage this time, I pulled into the driveway behind Linda's car and shut down the engine. I drew a deep breath and then stepped from the car and walked up to the front door. Instead of ringing the doorbell, I knocked on the door. In a series of gentle taps.

About thirty seconds had passed and then I heard, "Who is it?"

It was Linda.

"It's me, Linda," I whispered strongly, "it's...it's me...Derrick."

After a brief hesitation, the door gradually opened. Linda stood before me wearing nothing but her traditional sweats and tee shirt. No socks. Her hair was pulled back into a ponytail with a set of reading glasses perched on the top of her head.

The both of us just stood there, staring at each other, emotionally reconnecting…the best we could…

Okay, reality check: she didn't exactly appear overjoyed by seeing me standing here; there was definitely a hint of frustration and anxiety on her face. She even grimaced as she fiddled with her hands, wringing her fingers. Which all led up to one thing: she was afraid of getting hurt.

Of ever letting me back in.

The thought of this made my heart stammer. *There it was, the one thing I didn't want to face: that Linda would never again trust me with her heart. That I would somehow crush it again…*

It would never happen!

Baby, I've missed you so much! I wanted to cry out, but, remembering how delicate the situation was, I swallowed the impulse, standing rigid instead so I wouldn't blow the moment. I could tell by the look on Linda's face that she, too, was hoping that the right words would be spoken.

"Hello, Linda," I smiled as she invited me inside. When she closed the door, I handed her a bouquet of yellow roses and she accepted them with a challenging expression. I could see tears welling up in her eyes as she glanced over the flowers. My smile faded as I reached out and wiped the tears from the corners of her eyes, regarding her in a truly loving way.

"Thank you for the roses, Derrick," she sniffed. "They're so beautiful."

"Just like you, baby," I whispered. *Shit,* I thought sighing, *I should have brought a ring instead of flowers. Flowers didn't say: "I love you, baby...will you marry me?"*

But the moment wasn't lost as I slowly pulled Linda toward me, simultaneously enveloping her in my arms, pressing my face against hers. At first she held back. But as she felt me holding her, *clutching her*, she relented. She wrapped her arms around me and, giving a soft gasp, began squeezing me tightly. I didn't want to let her go, ever.

"I love you, Derrick," she whispered. Her lips were brushing my ear. "I love you so much, baby."

My insides melted. Hearing those words was like having a great weight lifted from my shoulders. With my face still pressed up against hers, I said, "Then prove it to me, Linda. Say...say you'll marry me. Say you'll be my wife. Forever. Say it, baby, say it..."

Slowly, gradually, Linda pulled back from me with a serious expression scrawled on her face. With piercing brown eyes, she studied *my* face, *my* eyes, seeking honesty and sincerity, and most of all...clarity.

I guess after about a minute or so I must have passed the test. Gently, tenderly, she cradled my face with her hands. Tears streaked her cheeks as she whispered, "Yes, Derrick Archer, I will marry you."

With those words I exhaled deeply, smiling. "Whew, damn, okay, *that's* good to hear. Actually, that's great to hear." I felt my eyebrows wilting as I caressed her cheeks, as I peered into her eyes. "Linda, baby, I promise to make you the happiest woman—"

Linda threw her arms around me, nearly knocking me over and slamming me into a wall. She pried my lips open with her tongue and the two of us hugged and kissed fiercely without any further words.

Without any further doubts.

Or worries.

We would make it! I knew we would! Even Mama knew it! That's what she'd been telling me all along: "You will be hers…"

Because of this—Mama's stamp—I was sure of it!

In fact, in a short while, in just a few months, I could already see us married, and then we'd settle down and buy a house in the 'burbs, raise a family, with cats and dogs, rabbits and fish—*whatever!*—live happily ever after. All that good shit!

Too simple for you to believe? A little too pat? Sound a bit too 'fairy-tale-ish'? Maybe…

But you know what—so what! It was going to happen!

After all I'd been through, this commitment stuff was going to be a 'duck walk'! A simple stroll through the park! I was finally living—*thank you!*—not just existing!

And when you *really* look at things, the way I do now, you realize there's a few things that you might have overlooked or forgotten about during your travels. The main one being: you only get *one* life down here, and there's no guarantees that you will be blessed with a long one. So, you'd better make the very best of it!

And by all means: do the *right* things along the way! Because karma is a bitch!

And from this point on, that's exactly what I plan on doing! To live, do the *right* thing, and enjoy life with the most beautiful woman that GOD could have ever created for me: Linda, my wife, right by my side…

For this, as well as for everything in the past, including everything that's ahead of me, I will forever remain, and will always be, more than grateful…

CHAPTER FORTY-SIX

EPILOGUE

'A Parting Miracle'

"Hey, lil Bruh!"

Melody sounded delighted. We hugged and then I threw a smile back at her, clearly enjoying the fact that *I* was there to see her smiling.

She peered over my shoulder, stooping and squinting and looking around the living room. "Hey, where's Aphelia and Danial, the two people that you've been talking about so much? I finally get the chance to meet them. I'd like to thank them for watching over my baby brother."

The thought of this made me sad, and I cast a quick, disheartening glance around the room. *They were truly gone,* I sighed. *Gone before anyone ever had a chance to meet them...not even Linda.*

My insides wilted like a flower starved without sun and water, and that's exactly what Aphelia and Danial meant to me. They were my sun and water. One to nourish me, the other to keep me strong. When I needed it most. It was funny, as I looked around my living room, I could still smell the sweet cocoa butter scent of Aphelia...

I turned to Melody and uttered, "Unfortunately, something came up, and they had to leave in a hurry. I just dropped both of them off at the airport, not too long ago."

"Awww, I hate I missed them," Melody sighed. "Sounds like really great people." Almost instantly she slipped off her gym shoes and padded in her socks toward the kitchen, drawn by the smell of coffee. She took a seat at the table while I poured her a cup. As I did, she placed a thick photo album on the table, filled with a ton of old family photos and mementos.

Old driver's licenses. Marriage licenses. Birth certificates, newspaper clippings, family recipes, and a slew of old, handwritten letters, many slightly yellowing with some dating back to the early 1920's.

I'd asked her to bring it over; at this point in my life I really wanted to trace my family roots, seeing I only had Melody, Jayden, and Marie to actually call 'family'.

A green-and-white Krispy Kreme box took up a small space on the table as Melody began opening up the family album. Pale morning sunlight streamed in through the window, over the table, while she showed me each picture, explaining in detail who the people were and how they were related to us. I found it all fascinating; I was overwhelmed and quite emotional to learn that we'd had such a large family tree, with branches that stretched back well over a century, nearly a hundred and fifty years.

After an hour or so, Melody finally came to the last page. I had just poured myself as well as Melody another cup of coffee, our third one, when I sat back down.

That's when she looked over at me with saddened eyes. Without warning, without any indications that there was anything wrong or had been wrong, she began to cry, at one point uncontrollably, nearly unconsolable. I rose from my seat and wrapped my arms around her. I asked her what was wrong. After nearly five more minutes of crying, she mentioned something about having cancer in her right breast, that things may turn seriously ugly. She asked me to take guardianship of her kids in case things didn't work out.

As I held her tightly, I looked up. *I knew something was wrong. The subtle signs had all been there. Nearly each time I had visited her…*

Naturally I assured Melody that things would be okay, and that I'd be there with her every step of the way—all of us: me, her kids, Linda, and Mama. I did this until she finally pulled herself together. She seemed okay as she wiped her eyes and blew her nose, nodding with a smile. I took a seat and held both her hands, reassuring her once more.

With a firm outlook on life accompanied by an even firmer smile on her face, Melody took a sip of coffee, swallowing and then sighing deeply. Afterwards, she turned the photo album right-side up and slid it over to me.

"See these two people here," she said sniffling and dabbing her nose with a napkin; she was pointing at an old black and white photo near the top of the page. "They were Mama's grandparents."

Calmly taking a sip of coffee, trying desperately to be strong for Melody, I peered down at the photo. A sudden chill came over me as I gazed over the photo, as much as I could make out: there was a man, sitting in a chair, and a woman seated next to him.

My heart did a little skip.

It was them!

Danial and Aphelia!

I wrenched my eyes from the photo and stared at Melody.

"What is it, Derrick?" she asked, placing a hand over mine, patting it gently, as much to settle the crisis she was going through.

Trying to remain calm, I swallowed hard. "That's them, Melody. That's the two people that I wanted you to meet. The two people that's been staying with me all this time." I glanced back at the photo.

Sure enough, it was them!

Aphelia—with glasses on—one brow raised with that certain, demanding look on her face. Then Danial—sitting stoically with his hands together—steepled as always!

The sudden realization of this—to say nothing of the way in which nobody had *actually* seen them—*nobody but me!*—made my breath catch.

I stared blankly at the walls. *It all made sense. That's why Melody hadn't seen them when I came to her house, while they sat in the car. That's why when I picked up Aphelia from the airport, she was just standing there waiting for me. Outside the terminal. Off to herself. The same thing when I dropped both of them back at the airport. They refused to let me accompany them inside. "We got it from here, my son," I remembered Danial saying with a smile...*

Then there were the other *small* things. Things that were now dawning on me as clear as day: though I'd talked with Aphelia over the phone, numerous times, mind you, I never did actually *see* her phone.

How was that possible?

Were we communicating spiritually?

Like me and Mama?

As I sat there stunned, I began recalling even more things. Very *delicate* things. My mind centering in on the conversation that I had when I'd first met Aphelia, in Las Vegas, how she arrived at my room at such an *odd* hour, how she spoke on *going where she was needed,* about *visiting* Chicago to see her *granddaughter*: which was actually *Mama!* Until Mama came to stay with *her.*

Her *other* family…

Then it was the bedroom.

The spare bedroom.

The one Danial and Aphelia slept in: from time to time, I would pop my head in, to see what was needed, fresh linen, pillow cases, cleaning, dusting, things of that nature. But the room was always neat and clean, always appearing the same, like nothing was ever moved, or disturbed, where it should have been. The television was never on. The remote always in the same place, never used. And the bed itself, uncreased, unruffled, looking always as if it had never been slept in.

My God…

Slowly, I brought my gaze back to Melody. I started to ask her about the two people in the photo,

Aphelia and Danial, starting with *"where did they live?"* But I already knew: somewhere in Lexington Kentucky, some place *way* off the grid. In an old, neatly-styled stucco home; a home that probably no longer existed.

Danial and Aphelia, I thought as emotions began welling up inside. *My great grandparents. What a loving pair. How blessed was I to have had the chance to interact with them...to talk, laugh and cry with them.*

Both had given me so much.

...so, so much...

As I sat there, I remembered something else. Something Danial had mentioned just as I dropped them off at the airport. *"I left you a little gift in the frig, my son, put it to good use,"* he'd said, giving me a warm pat on the back.

In a rush I leaped to my feet, grabbed the refrigerator by the door handle and pulled it open.

And discovered exactly what Danial had left me.

It was a plastic bottle, placed dead in my face. A bottle of creek water. *How could this be?* I wondered. *All the bottles were used. All five of them had been accounted for. Unless...yes, that's it: Danial hadn't used his bottle. He...he only pretended to. When we parted ways, he took the bottle with him. Actually, when you think about it, he never did really need the water...not at all...*

I stared blankly, still seeing his image.

Oh, my God…

"What is it, Derrick?" Melody asked, still sniffing lightly. She rose from the table and peered over my shoulder, leaning on me. "What is it?" she asked again.

I couldn't answer. I simply could not. Total silence was probably not such a good thing, especially concerning Melody, especially at this time, but my brain had gone numb; my heart fluttered and my stomach went all fluttery. I reached out with a shaky hand and picked up the plastic bottle. I saw a small label taped to the front of it.

Which read: *'For Melody'*.

Tears immediately flooded my eyes. I opened my mouth and gasped in total exhilaration.

"What's wrong, Derrick?" Melody asked, thinking I was finally breaking down because of her cancer prognosis. And in a way, I guess, I was…

I turned to her and whispered, "I have something for you, big Sis."

"What…what is it?" she asked as she stared me and then at the plastic bottle.

I handed the bottle over to her and simply smiled. "It's a gift. A gift from our great grandparents, Danial and Aphelia."

Naturally curious, Melody frowned. "I…I don't understand. I…"

"Just drink the water inside," I said, holding my smile. "Trust me, after you do, from this point on, you won't ever have to worry about the cancer that's inside you. Ever again."

Slowly, giving me a confused look, yet fully trusting in her baby brother, Melody unscrewed the top off the bottle, raised the bottle to her lips, and began to drink. All I could do was watch, knowing the results would be extremely good!

Great!

Tears streamed down my face at the thought. Because I *knew*—without a doubt—that Mama and our ancestors were still watching over us.

Especially Mama…

She saw her two kids in trouble and put the word out. It was just that simple.

Melody was right when she'd said to me: *"In spite of what you think, Mama's spirit is still with us."*

She was *so* right.

Spot on.

Actually, I had known this all along. Me still being here, alive, was living proof that Mama was steadily keeping an eye on me. Protecting me. The same went for Melody, her precious little daughter.

I sighed, thinking that maybe one day, in the far, far future, mind you, I'd tell Melody everything. About all the things I went through. Of course, leaving out all the *bad* parts. I caught myself smiling. She wouldn't believe me, anyway.

Would anyone believe me?

Nope!

I mean, how could you tell someone that you, your Mama, and your ancestors, were the reason that the world still existed.

How?

I mean, how could you?

You couldn't.

So...I wouldn't utter a single word about this to Melody. *Good or bad.* And if she did ask, I'd just tell her what I *believe* was best. Something she would *want* to hear. Until then, I'd just sit back, do the *right* thing, and enjoy life.

To the fullest.

Without a care in the world.

I stared at my big sister, as she continued to drink, and all I could do was smile.

Rather brightly.

And be more than grateful…

ABOUT THE AUTHOR

Ray Burton was born and raised in Detroit Michigan, and now resides with his family in Nashville Tennessee. *'The Past Comes Looking'* is *Ray's* first *'horror'* novel following the chilling thriller novel: *'The Entitled'*—winner of "THE 2024 REGIONAL NEW AUTHOR AWARD".

Both books are available on Amazon (both in Paperback and on Kindle), also at Bookshop.com, Barnes & Nobles, Books-a-million—anywhere books are sold. As always, if you would like an autographed copy(ies) of either *'The Past Comes Looking'* or *'The Entitled'*, or for book signings, as a guest speaker, and/or appearances, feel free to contact *Ray* at rayburton9313@gmail.com or hit him up on Facebook Messenger.

Lastly, if you enjoyed *'The Past Comes Looking'* and/or *'The Entitled'*, please tell your friends and family about both, either by word of mouth, on your social media page, or by leaving a favorable review on Amazon. I sincerely hope you enjoyed the ride!!!!

As always, thank you for your generous support and friendship, and GOD bless you and yours…